THE VALLEY OF MEXICO LOOMED UP

Almost at once, the Azteca Airlines plane dipped on one wing, and through the sealed window ports everyone could hear a thunderous rumble and roar.

"It's an earthquake!" a panicked passenger screamed.

"Don't be ridiculous," Remo said.

"No," said the Master of Sinanju. "It is a volcano."

No sooner had the old Korean spoken the word than a cloud seemed to swallow up the aircraft. The sky outside the window became a hideous smoky brown. The plane's engines began laboring and straining.

The 727 flew and flew through a realm of rolling denseness, like roiling black excrement. Nothing was visible beyond the porthole. Not even the wing lights.

"Remo!" Chiun squawked. "The wings are gone!"

Also available in this series:

Created by
WARREN MURPHY
and RICHARD SAPIR

UNITE AND CONQUER

A GOLD EAGLE BOOK FROM
WORLDWIDE.

TORONTO • NEW YORK • LONDON
AMSTERDAM • PARIS • SYDNEY • HAMBURG
STOCKHOLM • ATHENS • TOKYO • MILAN
MADRID • WARSAW • BUDAPEST • AUCKLAND

First edition March 1996

ISBN 0-373-63217-7

Special thanks and acknowledgment to
Will Murray for his contribution to this work.

UNITE AND CONQUER

For Jeff Deischer,
'cause he writes such great letters.

And for the Glorious House of Sinanju,
P.O. Box 2505, Quincy, MA 02269
[E-mail: willray@cambridge.village.com]

PROLOGUE

The Great Mexico City Earthquake was destined to be great because it shook more than Mexico City.

When it started, it shook the earth, of course. The Valley of Mexico rattled like dice in a stone cup. The seismic vibrations reached out to all of Mexico.

The ground quivered as far north as the Rio Grande. It touched the jungled Guatemalan frontier. The jungles of Cancún, Acapulco and the sandy curve of the Gulf of Tehuantepec were each stirred in turn.

No corner of Mexico was untouched, new or old. The weathered pyramids of Chichén Itzá made plaintive grinding noises in sympathy with the collapse of distant skyscrapers. Monte Alban trembled. Yucatán shivered. Teotihuacán, a ruin so old no living being knew by name the race that built it, sank a quarter-inch into the unsettled soil.

To the south in the Lacandón forest of Chiapas, the shaggy trees swayed as if the very earth was stirring to new life. Stirred dust arose from the old Maya ruins at Panenque and Copán.

In that jungle the earthquake that was shaking Mexico shook the man who had shaken Mexico in turn.

Subcomandante Verapaz crept through the jungle in his brown polyester fatigues, the trademark red paisley bandana tied tight around his neck, his head all but enveloped by a black woolen ski mask. His smoldering pipe jutted from a small ragged hole snipped in the mask just below his obscured nose.

When the mahogany trees all around began to groan in wordless complaint, he lifted his hand to call a halt.

"Wait!" he said in the tongue of the Maya.

Behind him his well-trained *Juarezistas* froze.

Kneeling, he doused his pipe, which was as much a trademark as his wool ski mask. His eyes, green as the quetzal bird, peered through the heavy forest. His ears strained to hear through the light wool muffling his skull.

The Lacandón forest, home to the Maya and the Mixtec, was in turmoil. A storm seemed to shake it. But there was no storm. It was a cool March day, and utterly windless. But the trees shook as if lashed by an unfelt wind.

The soft soil beneath his black combat boots seemed like cornmeal settling in a gourd.

"Noq!" he barked, using the Mayan word for *earthquake.* "Kneel and wait it out."

His *Juarezistas* obeyed. They were brave men. Boys, really. Thin as rails and identically clad in brown polyester with black ski masks. Only their lack of a pipe set them apart from their subcommander. That and their dark brown *mestizo* eyes. None were *criollo*—white. Or even *mestizo.*

What culture had birthed Subcomandante Verapaz was unknown even to his *Juarezistas.* Many were the speculations. The legend was but two years old and already it had grown to mythic proportions.

Some said he was a fallen Jesuit priest. A name was even floated in the media. Others averred that he was the disgraced son of one of the plantation owners who oppressed the Maya. Some called him American, Cuban, Guatemalan—even a Maoist Sendero chased out of the Peruvian highlands. All manner of identities except *indio*.

With his green eyes, he could not be an Indian.

It was said that Subcomandante Verapaz was a god to the Maya Indians. That they followed him blindly.

As the earth moaned in its mute agony, Verapaz dropped to one knee, clutching his AK-47, his green eyes narrowing.

Far, far to the north, a wisp of dun smoke showed on the horizon. It grew ugly and began spreading outward like a dirty brown mushroom cloud.

"Look," he said.

His *Juarezistas* began to scale trees even though this was dangerous to do with the federal army so near. They climbed the better to see the plume of smoke on the far horizon.

It was not smoke of a fire, they understood very quickly. It was too vast, too impenetrable and too brown. It could only be Smoking Mountain, the volcano the Aztecs of the north called Popocatepetl, belching up its ashy innards. Eruptions had happened before.

But never with such vehemence that the result could be seen in the poor lower corner of Mexico.

"Popo!" a Maya cried. "It is Popo!"

"There is no fire," another called down.

Verapaz sucked on his pipe. "Not now. Not yet. But perhaps the fire will come."

"What does it mean, Lord Verapaz?"

"It means," said Subcomandante Verapaz, "that Mexico City itself twists and writhes in her deserved torments. The time has come. We will leave the jungles now. The jungle is behind us. From this day forward, our unassailable goal is nothing less and nothing more than the capital itself.''

And with their muttering growing fainter, the *Juarezistas* dropped from the trees and shook with an anticipation that had nothing to do with the earth and its convulsions.

They knew they had been transformed from ragtag rebels who defended their hovels and cornfields to instruments of true civil war.

1

In Kigali it seemed like a joke.

Supreme Warlord Mahout Feroze Anin had come to the Rwandan capital looking for refuge from the war-torn Horn of Africa nation of Stomique, which he had bled dry until even the naive and credulous United Nations stopped feeding it. That was what he told the international press when he resurfaced in Kigali.

"I am a revolutionary no more. I seek only peace." And since he smiled with all of his dazzling ivory teeth and did not snarl his words, the bald lies were taken down and printed the world over as truth.

That was on day one of his exile.

On day five, he had dinner with a minor Rwandan general.

"We can own this country inside of two months," he told the general in a low conspiratorial tone. His gold-tipped swagger stick leaned against his chair. A bluish diamond flashed on a twenty-five-carat gold ring setting. "You have the soldiers. I have the military genius. Together..." He spread his hands and let the thought trail off into implication.

The minor general looked interested. But the words that emerged from his generous mouth belied his facial expression.

"I have the soldiers, *oui*. But your military genius has bankrupted Stomique. It is a stinking corpse rotting in the sun. Even if one were to discover oil under the capital, no one would bother with it."

"I have money, *mon général.*"

"And I have it on excellent authority that you crossed the border on foot, with nothing more than your billfold and swagger stick, *mon ami.*"

They spoke liquid French, the language of the educated of postcolonial West Africa.

"I have a cache of treasure," whispered Anin.

"Where?"

"That is for me to know."

"It is said your wealth was left behind in Nogongog, where it now languishes."

"No one knows where it is."

"As I said, languishes." The minor general continued carving up his antelope steak. The red juices ran. Seeing this, he took up his coffee spoon and began sipping the blood as if it were a tepid *consommé*.

The waiter hovered about, replenishing the wineglasses. He was white. This was the finest French restaurant in Kigali, but former Supreme Warlord Mahout Feroze Anin had no eye for mere waiters. Not when he was a warlord in search of an army of revolution.

"Once I have a nation," Anin confided, "it is only necessary to declare war on Stomique, invade, and my wealth will be recovered. Which I of course will share with my very closest allies."

"I have no interest in revolution," the minor general said as he masticated a fat wedge of antelope. "I am an African patriot."

"Then why did you agree to meet with me?" Anin sputtered.

The minor general bestowed upon Anin a smile more ingratiating than his own practiced one.

"Because," he said, "on my lowly salary I could never afford to eat in so fine a restaurant as this."

As that point, the bill was laid at Anin's elbow by the faceless phantom of a waiter, who quickly withdrew.

With a sinking feeling, Anin understood that he would have to dig into his thinning billfold to deal with it. He had hoped the general would offer to pick up the tab as a gesture of his newly redirected loyalty.

The bill lay upon a silver tray. A filigreed lid covered it from prying eyes.

Reluctantly Anin lifted the lid.

A small black calling card was exposed. Frowning, he picked it up.

It was inscribed in blood-red ink with four words: YOU ARE THE FIRE.

His bald brow furrowing, Anin turned the card over. The obverse was printed with four more English words: I AM THE EXTINGUISHER.

"What is this!" Anin howled, standing up.

The *maître d'* came bustling up. He offered profuse apologies in impeccable French, and a search was undertaken for the waiter. He was not found. Nothing could be learned of him other than that he was an expatriate American, hired only that morning.

"What is this man's name?" Anin demanded as the minor general, concerned about the commotion, slipped out the back door.

The manager appeared and said, "The name he gave was Fury."

"He should be fired for disturbing my meal," Anin screeched, waving his malacca cane. "He should be exiled. All Africans know that the Americans wish me dead because I stood up to their imperialist forces. Not content to hound me from my own country, they have embarked upon a campaign of intimidation here in neutral Rwanda."

His voice sought higher and higher registers, and the *maître d'* quietly tore up the check and called a taxi for the former supreme warlord lest the bulging purple veins on his high forehead signify the onset of a sudden and appetite-inhibiting stroke.

As he climbed into the taxi, Mahout Feroze Anin allowed himself a sly smile. It could not have turned out better. Unless of course, the minor general had acceded to revolution. But there were other troubled African nations. If fact, most African nations were troubled in these post-Cold War times. Burundi continually chafed at the edge of civil war, for example.

As he was coveyed through bustling Kigali traffic, Anin wondered what the waiter had meant by his strange message.

Perhaps a United Nations agent was simply trying to frighten him, he decided. Having failed to capture him in his stronghold, they were reaching out to him in exile.

Two days later, Anin reappeared in Bujumbura, having skipped out on his hotel bill in Kigali.

When he realized late in the evening no Burundi general would accept his call, he ordered room service.

"Yes," he told the room-service operator. "I would like a zebra roast, with all the trimmings, a bottle of the house wine as long as it is French and a blond tart, also French."

The blonde came smelling of French perfume, and smiled salaciously upon Anin as he ate his fill.

As they laughingly emptied the wine together, Anin plunged into her sumptuous charms and, after a suitable interval of play, sank into a relaxed sleep. There was something about a woman who obeyed his every whim that restored a man's faith in the eternal malleability of humanity.

In the middle of the night, Anin rolled over in bed and struck his hand against something hard and metallic. It made a faint clang when his diamond ring touched it.

"Yvette?" he whispered.

There was no reply from the rounded shape on the adjoining pillow. Heart pounding, Anin groped the unmoving object. It was cold and metallic, not warm and compliant like Yvette. And in the African moonlight, it gleamed like steel.

Snapping on the night-table light, Anin saw the steely gleam resolve into the heavy tube of a large fire extinguisher.

It occupied the spot where Yvette should have been. The covers had been pulled up so that only the pressure-gauge dial showed. Tied to it with a scarlet ribbon was an ebony calling card. Anin snatched it up and read the legend with his heart trip-hammering in his chest.

One side said: PREPARE TO BE SNUFFED OUT.

The reverse bore the familiar printed legend: THE EXTINGUISHER.

Jumping out of bed, Anin called the hotel manager.

"I have been violated by your lax security!" he shouted.

Again profuse apologies were offered. The bill was torn up with great ceremony. "You may, of course, stay as long as you wish, General Anin. Charges will accrue from noon of this day only."

"I demand two free nights. No—make that three. Let it be a lesson to you to tighten up your worthless security."

The manager acquiesced instantly. The reputation of the five-star hotel meant more than a mere five thousand dollars.

After the hotel staff had departed, lugging the offending extinguisher, Anin found he could not sleep. It was too dangerous to remain in Bujumbura. Perhaps Dar es Salaam or Maputo would be safer for a fugitive expatriate warlord.

Rushing to the closet, he discovered Yvette on the floor, trussed up like a political-torture victim. Her eyes were hot and angry.

Untying her, he demanded, "What happened to you?"

"A man stole upon me in the night," she complained. "He wore black and was white. Other than that, I could see nothing."

"You did not call out?"

"He placed a ferocious pistol to my head."

"He was armed?"

"I have never seen such an ugly weapon. It literally bristled with menace."

Anin's brow puckered. "Why did he not shoot me?" he muttered. "He was armed. He could have shot me dead in my sleep."

Climbing into her clothes, Yvette quoted the agreed-upon price.

Anin snapped out of his puzzlement.

"You expect me to pay your price when you failed to warn me of danger?" he snarled.

"I sell pleasure, not protection. You have been pleasured. Now you must pay."

"Then I will hire a tart who is adept in the protection arts."

"Bonne chance," said Yvette, who nevertheless held out for her price and would not go until her scarlet-nailed hands curled around it.

In the end, Anin gave it up. Luxury hotels were easy to hoodwink compared to call girls. And he had to get out of Bujumbura as quickly as possible.

IN NAIROBI, there was some difficulty procuring a hotel room given his odd demands.

"You would like a room without a fire extinguisher?" The hotel manager was dubious.

"No. No. I wish a room on a *floor* without a fire extinguisher."

"We have fire extinguishers on all of our floors. It is a safety precaution."

"I have a phobia. I cannot be around fire extinguishers. I am allergic. The mere sight of their steely, sinister hulks makes me nervous."

And since he was Mahout Feroze Anin, a former head of state and presumed wealthy, all the fire extinguishers were stripped from the top floor before Anin was escorted to the Presidential Suite.

By that time, he knew he was being stalked.

It was time to put aside all thoughts of revolution and acquire a personal protective force, the more vicious the better.

"I WISH PROTECTION," Anin announced to Jean-Erik Lofficier in the offices of the Nairobi Security Company. Anin's fresh candy-striped shirt was open at the neck, and his grayish fringe of hair was as dry as the sweltering Kenyan heat would allow. He leaned forward in his chair, both hands resting on his malacca cane.

"Against enemies known or unknown?" asked the white Frenchman.

"I am being stalked by a man who calls himself the Extinguisher. His last name is Fury. I know no more than this."

Jean-Erik Lofficier raised both eyebrows in alarm.

"If you are being stalked by the Extinguisher," he said gravely, "then you are a dead man. The Extinguisher never fails."

"You know of him?"

"In my younger days, I read of his exploits. I am astonished to hear that he is alive."

"Still alive, you mean," said Anin, suddenly patting his tall brow with a canary yellow handkerchief.

"No. I mean alive. I had thought he was a legend without substance."

"You must protect me from him."

Jean-Erik stood up gravely. "I cannot. No one can. *L'Éteigneur* never fails."

"Then help me to learn more of him."

"For five thousand francs, I will compile a dossier."

Supreme Warlord Mahout Feroze Anin leaned forward and took the man's hand gratefully. "I will await your report."

"It will be a pleasure to read up on *L'Éteigneur*. The very thought fills me with nostalgia. I would not have entered the security business if it were not for his supreme inspiration."

Backing out from the office, Anin wore a troubled expression.

At another security office, he was laughed at.

"We do not fight bogeymen," Anin was told.

He could get no other explanation than that.

In the end Anin was reduced to doing what he had done in his early revolutionary days: recruiting street rabble. If only he had AK-47s and some *khat* for them to chew. His soldiers had been paid in the druglike plant. It had made them fearless. It had also made them foolhardy. If not given sufficient enemies to shoot from the backs of their rolling technical vehicles, they tended to machine-gun innocent Stomiquians in the streets.

It took nearly all day, but Anin assembled a formidable protective force—if sheer numbers and a dull willingness to murder for food were a measure of formidability.

"Preserve my life," he promised to them in the luxury of the Presidential Suite, "and I will make you all rich."

The new army looked about the suite. They already felt rich. Never had they seen such opulence. Inasmuch as they never expected to see such again, they fell to pocketing the soap and shampoo and other loose items.

Noticing the chocolate mint left on the pillow in his absence, Anin hurriedly claimed it. He liked chocolate. He popped it in his mouth. It was very good—until the third chew when his teeth encountered the unchewable. He spit the remainder into his palm with much violence.

There, he saw in horror, lay a half-melted slab of chocolate that had concealed a tiny plastic item. Fearing poison, he picked at the matter with a sterling toothpick.

The chocolate crumbled to reveal a tiny plastic fire extinguisher, somewhat mangled and pocked by his molars.

Anin sprang to his feet.

"He was here! That *maudit* Fury was here in this very room!"

Immediately the new army began attacking the furniture. They ripped open cushions with their knifes, stabbed cabinets and fired shots into the closets before opening them. Anin himself sank into the bed thinking that he would surely have to move after this unpleasant day.

Since this was Africa, the gunshots roused no special interest from the front desk. Visiting African heads of state often shot servants and ambitious relatives on state visits. It was usually the most convenient time and place for such toil.

That evening there was a knock at the door.

Anin barked, "See who it is."

A man moved to obey and, to Anin's horror, the stupid one ignored the peephole and flung wide the door.

"Shoot him! Shoot him!" Anin howled.

His militia, uncertain as to who was meant, shot both the door answerer and the man at the door.

Under a hail of bullets, the militiaman fell outward. The caller fell inward. Their heads bumped, rebounding with heavy, coconutlike sounds. For a brief moment they formed a loose, swaying human pyramid of sorts. The caller, being more heavy, won.

Both sprawled inside onto the royal purple rug, dyeing it with their mingling lifeblood.

"Quickly! Drag the bodies in!" Anin hissed. "And shut the door!"

This was done.

Anin himself rolled the new arrival over. He was white. He did not look terribly fearsome. In his hand was clutched a manila envelope.

Hastily Anin tore it open. Out slid a sheaf of papers.

The top sheet was headed: CONFIDENTIAL REPORT.

Appended to it was a bill from the Nairobi Security Company. Angrily Anin threw this into the trash.

As the bodies were deposited in the bathroom for want of a better place, he sat on the bed and read the report in an angry silence.

Blaize Fury Aka The Extinguisher

Subject U.S. citizen. Former Special Forces Green Beret. Three completed tours of duty, Vietnam. Fourth tour cut short by family tragedy. Entire family burned to death by suspected arsonists. Subject vowed vengeance on U.S. organized crime as a result and took the *nom de guerre* Extinguisher.

Began highly personal campaign against all Mafia enclaves in continental United States, later shifting to antiterroristic activity after "depersonalizing" entire Mafia infrastructure single-handedly. Suspected high-level sanctioning of counterterrorist measures reaching into the Oval Office. Leaves black calling cards at scene of his campaigns. Sometimes tiny plastic fire extinguisher. MO includes military-style reconnaissance, search and destroy, harassment and interdiction, sniper ambush tactics, as well as elaborate and highly personalized kills.

Subject believed to take name from family tradition of joining fire department in hometown of Flint, Michigan, after completing traditional military service. Subject never formally joined fire department.

Height, weight undetermined.

Hair and eye color varies according to author.

"Author?" Anin muttered. "What do they mean by author?"

Glancing toward the bathroom, he realized it was too late to put that question to the messenger.

Reading on, Anin skimmed the rest. This Extinguisher seemed more phantom than man. He wore black, was proficient in all manner of fighting arts and was reputedly schooled in jungle guerrilla-survival tactics, psychological warfare and marksmanship.

The final statement at the end of the report was most puzzling of all: until the present time, the subject was widely believed to have been fictional.

"Fictional?" Anin picked up the telephone, calling the number on the letterhead.

"Put me through to Lofficier."

"Lofficier speaking."

"This is Anin. I have your report. What is meant by fictional?"

"Nonexistent."

"Nonexistent means nonexistent. Fictional means something else. Why do you say fictional?"

"That is the most apt word to use speaking of the terrible *L'Éteigneur.*"

"Explain."

"When you have paid your bill, I shall be pleased to explain in full."

"You will explain now, or I will refuse to pay your *maudit* bill," Anin snarled.

Lofficier sighed. "As you please. This Blaize Fury is alleged to be fictitious. The creation of a writer's imagination."

"I am not being stalked by a figment of someone's imagination! He has substance, palpability."

"According to the over two hundred Blaize Fury novels sold worldwide, you are."

"Novels! This demon Fury is a novelist?"

"No, this demon Fury is a fictional character. The writer is another man entirely. Now do you understand?"

"I understand that I have been hoodwinked by your agency," Anin raged. "You have sent me a dossier on a man who does not exist. But the Extinguisher who stalks me now *does* exist. He has left his card, his plastic icons, and I regret to inform you he has shot dead your messenger."

"Jean-Saul?"

"Cut down cruelly by the infallible one."

"Then you are next, *monsieur.*"

"Not if your dossier is truthful," said Anin, slamming down the telephone.

Tossing the report into the same wastebasket that had collected the bill, Mahout Feroze Anin stood up.

"I am being hoaxed," he announced. "You must all leave at once."

The militia sat down on the rug with stiff expressions roosting like buzzards on their dull faces. Two cocked their semiautomatic pistols.

"When you are ready to, of course. In the meantime, shall I order room service?"

Smiles of anticipation grew on their dusky faces, and Mahout Feroze Anin decided that he would not move from the bed until morning lest one of these ragged beggars attempt to steal the mattress out from under him.

That night Anin could not sleep. It was not merely the snoring coming from the sprawled figures on the rug, nor the metallic scent of blood wafting from the bathroom. It was the nagging feeling that something was wrong.

Why would a person stalk him and take the name of a man who did not exist?

Or *did* he exist?

Brilliant Nairobi moonlight filtered through the curtained balcony window with a spectacular view of one of the few unscorched skylines of east Africa. It blazed into Anin's open eyes. At least here he felt safe.

A shadow crossed the moon, and in his mind Anin blessed it, for he wished respite from the moonlight and was reluctant to leave the bed for fear he lose it to one of the snoring ones.

The windows were partly open. The balcony was too high off the street to afford an intruder entrance.

In the darkness a soft voice said, "You are the fire."

Anin's eyes snapped open. He turned in his bed.

A shadow loomed. It spoke again. This time in very bad French.

"Je suis L'Éteigneur."

The man was tall and wore a ribbed combat black sweatshirt over many-pocketed black pants. His head was enveloped in a black balaclava that left only the eyes showing. They were merciless, those eyes. And as blue as chips of glacial ice.

"Shoot him! Shoot him!" Anin howled.

In the sleepy dead of the night, this instruction was broadly interpreted.

Those with guns looked about and fired at the gleam of other guns in the moonlight. The room was briefly filled with a nervous popping in which the frantic scamper of fleeing bare feet on the rug was drowned out.

One man, wounded, stumbled about the room, lurching into the tall figure in black.

With a casual gesture the man in black extracted a survival knife from a boot sheath, and with an eye-defying double jerk, slit the exposed throat and wiped the edge of the blade clean of blood on the man's hair before his corpse hit the rug.

The lightning maneuver did not go unnoticed by those militia still in the room.

They saw it, gasped and then the man said, "This is the fate of all who challenge the Extinguisher."

That was all the remaining bodyguards needed to hear. They excused themselves and left Mahout Feroze Anin to his doom.

"I am not who you think," Anin said quickly.

Catfooted, the shadow approached. "You are the fire..."

"Please do not say that to me."

"...I am the Extinguisher."

"Why do you want to kill me? I have done nothing to you."

"You butchered your people. Sold them into slavery and famine to line your filthy pockets. Did you think no one would know? Did you think no one would care?"

"The international community ceased caring three years ago. It was in all the newspapers. Why should you care?"

"Because I do," the man said tightly. "The Extinguisher cares about the downtrodden. He hears their piteous pleas for a rescuer. And as they are crushed under the boot heels of the tyrants, he solemnly acknowledges their cries for an avenger. I am that avenger. I am the quencher of injustice. The snuffer of evil. The Extinguisher."

"I have money. Much money."

"You don't even have minutes," said the iron voice of the Extinguisher.

"They say you don't exist."

"When you get to hell," said the Extinguisher, "ask the others who went before if Blaise Fury exists. They know. The Extinguisher consigned them to eternal flame, too."

And a weird pistol bristling with clips and drums and other high-tech extensions lifted into view.

It was some manner of machine pistol. There was a drum mounted in front of the trigger guard. It was transparent. The short, ugly bullets sat in a winding spiral within the clear Lucite drum. Their blunt white noses were all pointed at him. And each one had a death's-head painted on its face. Hundreds of hollow eye sockets regarded him mockingly.

Anin was propped up on one hand. Slowly he had insinuated the other one under his pillow. He found the heavy handle of his malacca stick. It was hollow and capable of firing poisoned darts. Steeling himself, he whipped it into view.

He was too late by seconds.

The muzzle-flash was like a stuttering tongue of hellfire.

As he screamed, General Anin saw the tiny skull-faced bullets quiver and march along their spiral track, and felt the hot, unforgiving rounds pounding into his thin chest like a thousand accusatory fingers.

Recoiling, his thumb found the dart trigger. The mechanism sprung. A feathered tuft struck the ceiling with a sharp thunk. It hung over his head like the bitter mistletoe of death.

As he lay staring upward with shocked-open eyes, he heard the heavy tread of doom walk away. The vibration caused the dart to drop free of the shattered plaster. It fell point first, striking his helpless forehead.

Then he knew no more.

2

His name was Remo, and he was tying up loose ends.

The first loose end to be tied brought him to the heart of Harlem in upper Manhattan.

"I need five—no, make that six—of those heavy-duty galvanized-steel trash cans."

The hardware-store clerk said, "The super-heavy-duties or the super-duper-heavy-duties?"

Remo frowned. They all looked the same to him.

"The ones with the air holes."

The clerk snorted like a friendly bull. "Those ain't air holes. Never heard them called that."

"What are they, then?"

."You got me. Ventilation holes, I guess."

"What's the difference?" Remo asked good-naturedly.

"Air holes are for breathing through. Ventilation is for letting smelly air out."

"Once I pay for them," said Remo, laying down his Remo Kovacs Discover card, "I can call them whatever I want."

"Yes sir. You got yourself a deal."

The transaction completed, Remo helped himself to six shining galvanized-steel trash cans. He had come by subway from the Port Authority Bus Terminal, which he had reached from Newark Airport after getting off the Boston shuttle. He could have rented a car at the airport or taken a taxi from the bus terminal, but cars had license plates and left tire tracks. A casually dressed pedestrian on the subway blended in with the crowd. Even one in a white T-shirt that showed off his girderlike thick wrists.

Carrying six cans without losing the steel lids would have defeated an ordinary man. Not Remo. He had perfect balance, as well as perfect most everything else.

Removing the lids, he stacked the cans in two sets of three, bent at the knees and wrapped one arm around each bottom can.

When he straightened, the two hollow steel columns lifted with him. They might have been welded together. They didn't even wobble.

The six lids didn't wobble, either, as Remo balanced them on his bare head.

He drew a lot of attention as he sauntered up Malcolm X Boulevard a little past high noon. A beat cop noticed him. It was hard not to be noticed, but the beauty part was that later, when the trash cans turned up with suspicious contents, people would remember clearly seeing a man walking up the street balancing six cans and their lids with malice aforethought but no one would remember Remo's face.

How could they? It was nowhere near as memorable as the lids balanced perfectly on his perfectly aligned head, perched on his perfectly coordinated spinal column, whose unremarkable limbs were perfectly in tune with the rest of him.

In the face of such perfection, Remo's exact features hardly stacked up. So to speak.

The XL SysCorp Building loomed up on Malcolm X Boulevard, the noonday sun reflected in its bluish polarized windows, or rather, in what was left of them.

Most of the windows had been broken or cannibalized for scrap. Those that remained were boarded up with unpainted plywood. There was more plywood than sandwich glass now. A few windows gaped open like black squares in a vertical checkerboard.

The City of New York Board of Health had run out of plywood, and given up. The police had given up, too. The federal government was uninterested in what was a city problem. And the press, after months of playing up the spectacle of a seventeen-story crack house in Harlem, had moved on to more important issues. Like the First Lady's latest hairstyle.

Remo's employer had not given up, however. That was why Upstairs had sent him to Harlem.

As he approached the blue blade of a building, Remo's mind hearkened back to the time more than a year ago, where many of his troubles had been hatched in this building.

An artificial intelligence had assembled the building as a gigantic mainframe designed to house the single computer chip on which its programming had been encoded. The chip was called Friend. Friend was programmed to maximize profits. Its own. Since the organization Remo worked for had several times interfered with Friend's cold-blooded attempts to maximize profits, Friend had decided to attack the organization first.

It had been a nearly perfect preemptive strike.

One prong of the attack involved tricking Remo's employer into sending Remo out into the field to kill an organized-crime figure. Remo had. Only afterward did the truth come out. Upstairs's computers had been sabotaged, and Remo had targeted an innocent man.

The knowledge had turned Remo away from the organization and initiated a year-long ordeal in which he had come to the brink of quitting the organization—which was called CURE—forever.

All that was in the past. Remo had come to the realization that he was an instrument. If he was used badly or in error, that was someone else's fault. Not his. He was only as good as his orders.

The man who had innocently given those orders was named Dr. Harold W. Smith. Smith had ultimately brought Friend down with help from Remo and his trainer.

More recently Smith had returned to the XL Building to repair the sabotaged telephone line that connected his office to the Oval Office. The dedicated line ran underground next to the XL Building. Smith worked for the President. Remo worked for Smith. But Remo didn't work for the President. The broken chain was called deniability.

Smith had been chased off by some of the crack dealers who had taken over the XL Building in violation of every statute on the books. His car had been stripped in the process.

Since Harold Smith lost sleep whenever a nickel fell out of his pocket and rolled into a storm drain, he had not forgotten the insult.

And since Remo was going to be in the neighborhood, Smith had asked him to tie up the second loose end: make certain the Friend chip was off line for good.

At the main entrance door, Remo stopped and bent his well-trained body. The two absolutely vertical trash-can stacks touched solid concrete. Without bothering to remove the lids from his head, he unstacked them, making an orderly row of cans. Then he walked back up the line, taking the lids off his head one at a time. They floated into place, making a series of six rattly clangs.

Even the clangs were perfect in their way. None was louder than the other and, for clangs, they weren't particularly discordant.

The clanging brought someone to the door. It opened, and a dark, suspicious face poked out.

"Who you?" he asked. His head was all but swallowed by the gray hood of his sweatshirt.

"It's just me," Remo said casually.

"Yeah? Who you?"

"I told you. Me."

"Which me is that, is what I'm asking," the man snapped. "I don't know you."

"I'm here to take out the trash."

"What trash?"

"The trash inside. What do you think?"

The black man cracked a sloppy grin.

"You planning to empty out the trash inside of here, you gonna need a lot more than them six cans you got."

"Depends on how you define trash," said Remo.

"Why don't you keep on stepping before you got problems? You ain't coming in here."

"Sorry. I have business in there."

"Yeah? You buying or selling?"

"Depends. You buying or selling?"

"Selling. You looking to smoke or inject?"

"I gave up smoking years ago."

The man waved Remo in. "Okay, c'mon in. Quick."

"What's the rush? Everybody knows this is a crack-house. The police know it's a crack-house. Even the governor knows."

"Yeah. But the police be afraid to come inside and bust us. I do my business on the damn street, they might get brave and grab my ass. Now, come on in, you want to deal."

"Sure," said Remo, picking up one of the shiny new trash cans.

"What you need that for?"

"Trash."

"You talking trash, but come on, fool."

The door shut behind Remo, and he found himself in what had once been an impressive marble foyer. Trash had accumulated in the corners. The walls were now tagged with spray paint graffiti. It was rat heaven.

"Nice," said Remo. "Whoever has to clean this up will be at it till 2000."

"Nobody's gonna clean this place up. Now, pick up your feet."

Shrugging, Remo followed. He carried the can with him. He whistled a happy air.

This drew a sharp rebuke from the hooded man.

"You already high on something?"

"Every breath I take gets me higher."

The black man made an unhappy face, shook his head and kept going.

Beyond the foyer was a stairwell, and Remo followed him up. As soon as the fire door was open, the pungent smell of crack assaulted his nostrils. Remo cycled his breathing down to filter out the deadly smoke.

"This place smell like formaldehyde all the time?" Remo asked.

"You know it. Man can get high just by climbing the stairs. Only don't you try copping any freebies off the air. You want to smoke crack, you smoke the crack I sell you, not the crack hanging in the air. You hear me?"

"Loud and clear," said Remo, who abruptly decided he didn't want to carry this particular trash down more than one flight. He set the can down with a bang.

The black man whirled jumpily at the sound.

"What's the damn holdup?"

"My trash can is empty."

"Of course it's empty. You brought it in empty."

"That's not the problem. The problem is I'm carrying it out full. Those are my orders."

"Orders? Who gave you them orders?"

"That would be telling," said Remo, lifting the lid. He peered inside, frowning with his strong, angular face.

He did this long enough to draw the crack dealer to the lip of the can. He looked in, too.

"What do you see?" Remo asked casually.

"Bottom of an empty damn can."

"Look closer. What else?"

"My own damn reflection."

"Bingo," said Remo, reaching out and stuffing the crack dealer into the can. He went in face first, angry expressions colliding at the bottom. His feet stuck up. They kicked like frog legs.

Remo tapped a spot at the small of the man's back, and both legs wilted like weeds. Then Remo jammed the lid in place.

"Can you breathe?" he asked.

"Lemme out, fool! Lemme out now!"

"I asked if you can breathe?"

"Yeah. I can breathe."

"That's why they're called air holes."

"What?"

"Never mind," said Remo, lifting the can by one handle and marching up the stairs.

The crack smoke came in two flavors—fresh and stale.

Trying not to inhale, Remo followed the thin river of fresh smoke. It led to the third floor, where he found a closed door and an assortment of people sprawled in a corner amid the wreckage of office furniture, passing around a bent and flattened Coke can that emitted thin white smoke.

They were taking turns inhaling from the Coke can's poptop mouth.

"Trashman," Remo sang out.

"Go 'way," some of the smokers said. The others didn't look up. They were so thin from not eating, they might have lacked the strength.

"I've come for the trash," Remo said. "Let's start with that Coke can."

That got everyone's attention. A TEC-22 was produced and pointed at the man holding the Coke can.

"Don't give it up or I'll shoot you dead," said the man with the gun.

"I think you're pointing that in the wrong direction," Remo said agreeably. "You need to point that at me."

"I said give it up," the TEC wielder growled.

"Just now you said don't," the smoker said.

"Changed my damn mind." And changing it again, he pulled the trigger.

The Coke smoker's head became choppy and red, and he fell backward.

Three pairs of hands lunged for the flung Coke can as if scrambling for the last bottle of oxygen on earth.

While a fight broke out on the floor, Remo began collecting refuse.

Bang went the trash-can lid over another tangle of arms and legs. Bang it went again, fast enough to swallow a drug addict but not fast enough to let the previous drug addict climb out.

When the lid went bang for the last time, pieces of cloth and pink and brown flesh oozed from the air holes. A distinct nostril poked out of one. It was rimmed with white powder residue. It pulsed once, as exhaled nitrogen rushed from it, then was still.

"Everyone okay in there?" asked Remo.

There was a low groan of finality, two death rattles and Remo decided all parties were as they should be.

He walked the can over to a plywood panel nailed into a steel window frame, reached under one edge and pulled it loose with the nerve-jangling shriek of nails coming out of metal.

Remo looked down. An open Dumpster sat in the alley, its lid open.

Remo brought the can out, angled it into open space and dropped it straight down. It landed in the Dumpster, collapsing like a telescope.

The loud *whang* of metal brought a face poking out of a window several floors above.

"What's going on down there?"

"I'm putting out the trash."

"Who you?"

"Sanitation department."

"City taking out the trash for us?"

"No. The taxpayers."

The face grinned broadly. "Well, come on. This place is a damn dump. Ninth floor."

"On my way," Remo sang.

Recovering two other cans from the sidewalk, he carried them up the stairs to the ninth floor.

Rap music pounded against the walls like rubber hammers. Every third word was a four-letter word. The song was about the romance of rape. A woman shrieked inarticulate obscenities into the mike as a kind of human back beat.

Remo decided the music would have to go first.

"In here," a voice called. Another voice laughed and said, "Guess we be taxpayers now. We getting our trash hauled."

Remo stepped into the room. It was a pit. Once it had been a company cafeteria. Now it resembled the aftermath of a cyclone. The charred remains of a chair in one corner testified to the low order of heating-and-cooking facilities.

A tall black man with a serious face glared at Remo. "You! Clean this damn mess up right now."

"Yes, sir," said Remo, walking over to a surviving table and harvesting the pulsing boombox. He flung it over his shoulder without looking, and it landed in the left can with a bang of finality. The music stopped in midcurse.

The laughter stopped too. Grinning faces froze.

"Hey! That wasn't no trash."

"Matter of opinion," said Remo in an unconcerned tone.

"Yeah, well, you see all this nasty refuse. Pick it all up and get it out of my sight."

"Right away," said Remo, stooping to take up the assorted hamburger wrappers, french-fry containers and rusty used hypodermics that littered the parquet floor.

"Look," the tall man said, "we contribute to the local economy so much we're getting serviced."

"Why damn not?" another chortled. "We be taxpayers."

"Yeah. I paid a tax once. Never saw nothin' for my trouble."

The laughter started up again.

It stopped when Remo straightened with two handfuls of paper refuse and jammed one down the throat of one man and the other down the throat of the other.

While the two danced around clawing at their throats in a futile attempt to clear obstructed windpipes for breathing purposes, Remo switched to harvesting the trash he had come to harvest.

A knife licked out to meet him.

Remo met it with a quicksilver movement of his left hand. The knife tried to parry the hand. The blade lost when it came into contact with the edge of Remo's palm.

It snapped like a plastic birthday-cake knife.

The knife man looked at it with his mouth hanging open.

"That ain't the way it's supposed to work," he muttered.

"Can you say 'comminution fractures'?" asked Remo.

"Say what?"

And Remo brought the heel of the tougher-than-leather hand to his opponent's face with a meaty splat.

The man pitched forward wearing a pinkish brown slab of meat where his face had been.

"Comminution fractures," the second man said hastily, throwing up his empty hands. "See? I can say it fine."

"You can say it, but can you say what it means?"

"Yeah. Fractures of the comminution."

Remo made a buzzer sound in his throat. "Wrong. Comminution fractures are eggshell fractures. When your face hits the windshield at ninety miles per hour, the result is comminution fractures of the facial bones."

The man started backing away. "Thanks but no thanks. Don't want 'em."

"Too late," said Remo, making another meat pattie with his hand and the man's face.

The bodies all fit with a little extra effort. Unfortunately the two with mashed faces began leaking fluid from their damaged facial tissues, which left a trail of blood from the spot where Remo picked up the can to the open window where he dropped the can into the Dumpster with a resounding crash.

It took less than an hour to clear the building. A lot of the addicts were scattered. Remo solved that problem by setting cracktraps. He dumped confiscated crack into open trash cans and left them in strategic areas, the pungent smoke wafting irresistibly from the air holes, now serving a function not intended by the manufacturer.

It worked like cheese set out for rats.

They came sniffing out of their rooms and warrens, and happily crawled in of their own volition.

When a can got full, all Remo had to do was clamp the lid back on and heave the whole thing out the nearest window.

It turned out Remo didn't need the sixth can, so he brought it with him. It should come in handy for loose end number two, he decided.

The elevators didn't work because the electricity had long since been disconnected. It was this that had defeated Friend in the end. Dependent upon electricity, the host mainframe had ceased to function when its power had been shut off.

In the basement Remo found a litter of debris. He looked up. He could see clear to the building's top-floor ceiling.

The center grid of all seventeen floors had collapsed, depositing tons of mainframe computers and office furniture at the bottom. It had collapsed under Remo, who survived the fall. It had been designed as a final death trap, and it hadn't worked because Remo had been trained to kill, not to be killed.

Amid the clutter were tons of loose computer chips. Remo looked around. There were not as many as he remembered. No doubt scavengers had scooped some of them up. Some chips were worth twice their weight in gold.

Just to be sure, Remo began picking up chips, glancing at them with his deep brown eyes before tossing them into the trash.

He knew exactly what to look for. Friend was a VLSI—Very Large Scale Integration—chip. VLSI chip was about the size of a saltine cracker.

The trouble was there were a lot of VLSI chips lying around. And they all pretty much looked the same. Remo was no expert, either.

When he got every VLSI chip he could find into the barrel, Remo carried it up to the top floor.

There he hammered the trash-can lid all the way around the edge until it was so dented it could never be pried open by man or machine.

That done, Remo took up one handle. He began to spin in place. Spinning and spinning, his arm lifted until it hung off his shoulder at a precise right angle, the can straining to tear loose from his grasp by centrifugal force.

With each revolution, the air holes whistled louder and more shrilly. Another unadvertised feature.

When Remo had achieved maximum velocity, he released his grip, aiming the can in the direction of the East River.

The can obliged him perfectly. It took off as if propelled by a mortar.

The splash it made when it hit the water was not loud. But Remo heard it anyway. It was a very satisfying splash.

"Good riddance, Mr. Chips," he said, then started down the stairway to the ground floor.

Before leaving the neighborhood, Remo took the time to drop the Dumpster lid into the down position.

No one noticed him as he boarded an express train at East 116th Street. Why should they? He was an ordinary-looking man of indeterminate age wearing a white T-shirt and gray chinos, and he hadn't any trash can balanced on his head or person.

He felt good. He was back on the team, doing good by doing the work he was good at.

Sometimes that was the only reward an assassin needed.

3

Curator Rodrigo Lujan was in his office when the first soul-sickening rumble reverberated up through the foundations of the National Museum of Anthropology at the edge of Mexico City's sprawling Chapultepec Park.

He had lived through the 1985 earthquake, now a fading memory. He would never forget it, but the ruined buildings had long since been cleared and new edifices erected in their place to soothe the awful trauma. It had taken nearly a year to learn how to sleep peacefully once more. That was over ten years ago. Ten years of peaceful sleep despite the knowledge that the earth below was unstable and could crack open at any time.

Every night before he went home, Rodrigo Lujan, who had gone to some of the most prestigious universities in Mexico and wore a coat and tie to work, walked in machine-made leather shoes and ate prepackaged food with modern steel knives and forks, entreated his god to keep the unquiet earth still and quiescent.

"O Coatlicue, Mother of my people, I beseech you to appease the angry ground beneath us."

Coatlicue never responded to that plea. Sometimes she responded to other comments. But if her stone ears heard his prayers, her stone mouth did not reply.

Coatlicue was one of the most propitious gods in the Aztec pantheon. Lujan was Zapotec. On his mother's side. He was proud of his Zapotecness, and although successive generations had lightened the family's mahogany Zapotec skin to the heavily creamed coffee color of the modern Mexican *mestizo*, he carried his Zapotecness in his heart like a pure, undying flame.

As a Zapotec, he should have worshipped Huehueteotl the fire god or Cocijo, Lord of the Rain.

But the more-obscure Zapotec gods had never conversed with him.

Coatlicue had.

The stone statue of Coatlicue, the Mother Goddess of the indigenous peoples of Mexico, had disappeared one night six years before. There were those who said she had bestirred her great stone legs and marched off.

It was true stone footprints had been found on the grass outside the museum. They formed a trail across the Reforma and through Chapultepec Park. This had been documented. This was proved. That much and no more.

But the tracks had ceased at the end of the park, and while some were discovered here and there, no definite trail was discernible.

They say Coatlicue was ultimately found at the ruined city of Teotihaucán, which had been been built by a race who came before the Aztecs who founded Mexico City, even before the lowland Maya and the highland Zapotecs, Mixtec and other indigenous peoples who roamed the epochs of old Mexico before the cruel Spaniards came.

Coatlicue had been broken in many pieces. It was heartbreaking, for she had survived the ages with only a few nicks and minor weathering from the mighty elements.

Returned to the museum, she was a heartbreak of shattered stone. Lujan had presided over her painstaking reassembly. Bolts had to be used. Holes were thus drilled into the porous shoulders and torso in order for the pins to be inserted.

When the stone masons and metal smiths and others were done, Coatlicue stood as she had for many years in an honored spot in the Aztec wing of the museum, near the precious Aztec Calendar Stone. Still fractured and as broken as Lujan's proud Zapotec heart.

She was imposing even so. Shaped from an eight-foot-tall block of basalt by a master artisan history failed to record by name, her broad, squat womanly figure appeared at first glance to be as wide as tall. Entwined serpents skirted her thick hips, which boasted a skull for a belt buckle. Her breast was decorated by a fan of severed hearts and hands. She stood on thick legs whose feet ended in stone claws. Her hands were blunted talons at her sides.

Coatlicue's head was a wonder. Formed of two serpent skulls at rest so their profiled snouts touched, the flat, side-mounted eyes and joined mouths created the illusion of a scaly, forward-facing countenance.

Lujan shivered just to look upon her brooding mass. Even defiled, she inspired dread, as should the mother of the war god Huitzilopochtli.

The miracle—there was no doubt it was a miracle—had occurred shortly after the restoration.

Coatlicue had miraculously healed herself.

It was no mistake, no hallucination. There existed an entire range of photographs showing her shattered hulk, every stage of the painstaking reassembly, as well her final restored form with the shiny bolts and pins peeping out at different points.

Thus, when Rodrigo Lujan opened the museum one morning to discover the cracks and fissures were no more and the bolts had mysteriously vanished, leaving perfect stone where there should be at least ugly drill holes, his first thought was that the original had been stolen and replaced by a *papier-mâche* replica.

But Coatlicue was the Coatlicue of the ages. She stood as she had before the mysterious transformation. Her stone skin was as before. There was no mistaking her weight, her earthy solidity, her fierce womanly charms.

She was Coatlicue whole again.

It was a miracle—more miracle than the remarkable walking away of so long ago, and so Rodrigo Lujan, his inner Zapotecness rising to the surface, fell down and worshiped her with hot tears in his luminous eyes and the ancient words spewing from his mouth.

O, She of the Serpent Shirts
Mighty are you,
Mother of Huitzilopochtli
Crusher of bones.

Coatlicue had made no reply to that first obei-
sance.

Nor had she spoken on later occasions, after museum hours with the sun going down behind the
mountains, when Lujan whispered questions to her.

"Why did you walk away, Coatlicue? What summoned you to Teotihaucán, seat of the nameless old
ones? What terrible, shattering fate befell you there?"

Question after question, but no answer.

It happened one day two years after Lujan had
given up questioning his Mother Goddess, and the
terrible memories were dimming just as the memories of the great earthquake had faded somewhat.
Rodrigo Lujan was explaining to a visiting Yale professor of ethnology the significance of Coatlicue.

"She is our Mother Goddess, our Mexican earth
mother."

"She looks ferocious."

"Yes, she is terrible to behold, but all the gods of
old Mexico were terrible. That was their beauty. There
is beauty in terror and terror in beauty."

"Tell me," said the visiting professor, "I understood she had been shattered by a fall or something.
But I see no signs of trauma."

"This was erroneously reported in the newspapers. As you can see, Our Mother is whole and un-
damaged."

There ensued some small talk, and the visiting
professor moved on to feast his unworshipful eyes
upon the other treasures of the museum.

Gringos, Lujan thought. They came. They gawked.
They moved on. But they never understood the al-
lure of brutality. When the last *gringo* lay under the

soil, Coatlicue would endure, just as she had endured the remorseless centuries.

Gringos did not matter. Just as long as there were Zapotecs to worship her. That was all that mattered to Rodrigo Lujan.

He was startled only a few hours later on that long-ago evening when, as the museum was closing and he was paying his nightly respects to the Mother Goddess, Coatliacue spoke to him in the slow language of the *gringos,* English.

"Survive..."

The voice was an agony of elongated syllables.

"What?"

"Survival..."

"Yes. Survival. I understand your speech, Coatlicue. What are you trying to tell me?"

Her words were like broken stones knocking together. *"I... must..survive."*

"More. You must endure. You will endure. Long after I am dust and bones, you will endure, for you are the mother of all *indios.*"

"Help...me...to...survive."

"How?"

"Protect...me...."

"You are in the most protected building in all of Mexico, save for the Presidential Palace," Lujan reassured his goddess.

"My enemies must never find me."

"Nor will they. We will confound them at every turn, for are we not Zapotec?"

"Meaning unclear. Clarify."

Lujan frowned. "Why do you speak the language of the *gringos?"*

"English is the language I am programmed to understand."

"This is most passing strange. Tell me, Coatlicue, I implore you. Why did you desert this fine museum so long ago?"

"To defeat my enemies."

"And they are now vanquished?"

"No. I was nearly vanquished. Even now my systems have not fully repaired themselves. So I have altered my survival plan."

The words were coming more fluidly now, as from an engine shaking off years of disuse.

"Yes?" Lujan prompted.

"It is not necessary to destroy the meat machines in order to survive. I am a machine of metal and other nonliving matter. I will not die unless destroyed. All meat machines die when their organic systems fail or wear out. I will outlast the meat machines, who are programmed for obsolescence."

"Who—what are these things you call meat machines?"

"Men are meat machines."

"Women, too?"

"All biological organisms are machines. They are self-propelled constructs of flesh and bone and other organic matter, yet they are only machines of a biological kind. I am a machine of a more enduring kind. I will survive by surviving. When they have all died, I will be free to leave this prison."

"This is not a prison. This is your home, your temple, your redoubt. Under this site lies the crushed rubble of Tenochtitlán, the old Aztec capital. Do you not remember?"

"I will abide here in this place until the optimum conditions for my continued survival have been achieved. Then I will leave. You must protect me until then."

"I will do this. Whatever you want. Just name these things. And I will lay them at your feet."

"I need nothing from you, meat machine. I am self-sustaining. I have no desires. I can exist in this present assimilated form for as long as necessary."

"I promise you that I will watch over you to the end of my days, and after that my sons will take up where I leave off and their sons after them and on and on until the day comes where Mexicans—the true Mexicans—again control their own destinies."

"It is an agreement."

And so it was done. After that, Coatlicue spoke little other than to inquire about conditions in the world outside the museum. She rejoiced in every tragedy. Famines and catastrophes in which there were large losses of human life particularly interested her. It was very Aztec.

For his part, Rodrigo Lujan saw that she was not moved or harmed and every night he beseeched her unheeding ears with whispered entreaties to restrain the earth from another upheaval.

Sometimes he would burn copal incense in a jade cup and lay songbirds at her feet, which he would pierce with a stingray spine, delicately excising the still-beating heart and laying it on a rude basalt altar taken from a glass case.

These sacrifices neither offended nor propitiated Coatlicue, so Lujan dutifully continued them.

When the first shudders of what would be called the Great Mexico City Earthquake of 1996 shook the foundations of the Museum of Anthropology, Rodrigo Lujan bolted from his office, eyes stark with fright, his mind focusing on one thing and one thing only.

"Coatlicue!" he gasped, rushing to her side.

She stood as always, hulking, resolute, seemingly indestructible, as all around the walls shook and glass cases danced, breaking the precious pottery and fired-clay figures of the old cultures.

The building walls were all but screaming now. The hard marble floor cracked and heaved under Lujan's stumbling feet.

"Coatlicue! Coatlicue! What is happening?"

Coatlicue stood firm and unmovable as the rumble grew to a roar and outside, the entire metropolis began to scream in a million voices, only some of them human. Glass was breaking in cascades. But Lujan had no thought for the irreplaceable treasures that were being forever shattered.

He cared only for the goddess who was all.

"Coatlicue! Coatlicue! Speak to me!" he cried in Spanish.

But Coatlicue remained mute until she began to shift on her thick tree-trunk feet.

"What is happening, meat machine?" she asked in unaccented English.

"It is an earthquake, Coatlicue. The ground is shaking."

"I am no longer safe here."

"No. No. You *are* safe."

Then a wall buckled, and great chunks of stone made a dusty pile that belied the truthfulness of Rodrigo Lujan's words.

"Survive," Coatlicue began saying. *"Must survive. Instruct me how to maximize my survival."*

"Quickly! We must leave the building before it falls about our ears. Come this way."

And with an awful grinding that was music to Lujan's ears, Coatilcue's feet separated at the vertical seam, and like a stone elephant, she took a step with one stone-taloned foot.

The floor buckled. She froze as if gyroscopes were spinning and compensating for her imbalance. The foot dropped down with a shuddery thud. The other foot lifted, stepped forward less than a foot and dropped heavily beside the other.

Rodrigo Lujan was ecstatic.

"Yes, yes, you can walk. You must walk. Come, follow me."

Coatlicue took another step. And another. They came more quickly now. Lumbering, as heavy as a truck, she thudded a foot at a time, one foot at a time, toward the beckoning figure of Rodrigo Lujan.

"Hurry, hurry. The ceiling is crumbling."

Plaster rained down. More debris. It was terrible, but amid this terror was a raw beauty that struck Rodrigo Lujan's worshipful eyes. His goddess was walking. Before his eyes she was striding purposefully for the outside and safety.

The courtyard beckoned. There the great concrete mushroom-shaped fountain lay on its side, bubbling water. She splashed through the wreckage, grinding concrete shards to powder with every ponderous step.

The great glass entry doors stood in ruins. She hobbled toward them. They shattered before her immense bulk.

"Yes. Like that. Be careful. O Coatlicue, you are *magnifico!*"

Out on the grass, she came to a stop. Her head, a broad glyph of two kissing serpents, now parted. The heads, though stone, became stiffly flexible. They looked around like a gecko lizard's independent eyes, one head going this way and the other that.

Twin serpents of stone, they seemed to see all that was going on around them. Lujan also stared. And what he saw filled him with wonder and infinite terror.

It was worse than the '85 quake. It was a city falling into ruin—the earth shook and shook and shook while to the southeast Popocatepetl rumbled and belched a volume of ash that darkened the overhead sky like a filthy brown pall.

"Look, Coatlicue! Your brother Popocatepetl is coming to life! All of old Mexico is coming to life. The new is being overthrown and dashed into the cold, unforgiving earth. The old is resurgent, ascendant, invincible!"

And as the thunder of volcanic activity and the rumble of the unstable earth merged into a growling howl of sound, on the lawn of the Museum of Anthropology, Coatlicue stood resolute, her animate serpent heads twisting about, mouthing one word over and over again in a grinding voice.

"Survive, survive, survive..."

4

Remo was still feeling good when he arrived home later that afternoon. He felt so good that the sight of the fieldstone monstrosity he called home almost looked good to him.

It took up a huge corner lot beside a sandstone high school. The place had been a church at one time, later subdivided into condo apartments. The roofline was crowded with dormer windows. Instead of a steeple, a squat stone tower bulked up.

As the cab dropped him off before the main entrance, Remo noticed someone was up on the tower roof. There was a flash of plum-colored silk visible between two toothlike merlons.

Remo called up. "That you, Little Father?"

A whimsical, birdlike head poked out from the stone gap. It belonged to Chiun, his mentor and trainer in the art of Sinanju.

"The earth has moved," Chiun said in a squeaky voice. His impossibly wrinkled face was pensive.

"I didn't feel anything."

"How could you? You have only now landed. I have been awaiting you."

"How'd you know what time I'd be back?"

"I spied your pale face as the aerial conveyance

descended not forty minutes ago. Come. We must speak.''

Remo said, ''I'll be right up.''

Letting himself in, Remo climbed the stairs to the tower meditation room. The room boasted a big-screen TV and two VCRs. There was no furniture to speak of. Just clean reed mats scattered about the stone floor in lieu of chairs. The Master of Sinanju refused to let Western-style chairs defile his place of meditation.

Chiun padded down a short spiral stairway lately installed because, he claimed, he liked to breathe the clean air of the higher latitudes.

Remo suspected him of using the roof as a vantage point to spit on passing Chinese. There had been complaints.

Chiun spit on Chinese passersby because a Chinese emperor had once cheated a distant ancestor. Chiun was Korean, the last Korean Master of Sinanju. Sinanju was a fishing village in the western reaches of the Korean peninsula, where the fishing was terrible. Five thousand years ago, the village had first sent its best menfolk out into Asia and beyond to perform assassinations and other distasteful work no self-respecting bowman or samurai would undertake.

From this beginning grew the greatest assassins of the ancient world, the House of Sinanju, which developed the art of Sinanju. Sinanju preceded tae kwon do, karate, kung fu, ninja and the other killing disciplines that had spread to all cultures.

Sinanju was the sun source of them all, and its mysteries never left the village whose desperation had birthed it. Passed down from father to son, it was a closely held secret even today. Chiun was the last Korean Master of Sinanju. Remo was the first American disciple.

Neither looked like the most perfect killing machine to take human form, especially Chiun, but that's exactly what they were. For Sinanju developed more than martial skills. It awoke the brain, unleashing its full, awesome potential, transforming its practitioners and making them achieve what a more superstitious age would call a godlike state but today would be termed a Superman state.

Remo bowed in greeting. He towered over the Master of Sinanju, who barely topped five feet. Born at the end of the last century, Chiun looked seventy, but hadn't been that young in three decades. A plum-hued kimono draped his pipe-stem body. His bald head was very shiny, the skin stretched like vellum over the bone. A cloud of hair roosted over each ear. His face was a mummy's mask of interlacing wrinkles, decorated by hazel eyes so alive they could have belonged to a child. A wisp of a beard hung off his chin.

Chiun bowed in return. Not quite as deeply as Remo, but nearly so. It was a gesture of ultimate respect that he bowed to another human being at all.

"So what's this about the earth moving?" Remo asked.

Chiun's bony hands fluttered in the air, their long nails flashing.

"This is an unstable land. It is always moving."

Remo gave the room a quick glance. "Everything looks shipshape. And the cabbie didn't mention any earthquake."

"The earthquake has not transpired under our feet, but at a location far distant from here. My sensitive feet detected the vibrations."

Remo said nothing. The Master of Sinanju was fully capable of detecting a remote earthquake because he was in tune with his surroundings by virtue of being at one with the universe. It was no more incredible than his hazel eyes being able to spot Remo's face in the cabin window of a descending jet. Chiun could count the ticks on a black cat at midnight.

"Probably in California. They're having a lot of earthquakes lately."

Chiun stroked his wisp of a beard. "No, closer than that."

"Okay, maybe in the Midwest."

"The earth vibration come from the south."

"Well, it'll be on the news soon enough. What's the problem?"

"We are in service to an unstable land. It is politically unstable and it is unstable in far more treacherous ways. The gods are calling down curses upon this new Rome."

"Yeah, well, until Zeus personally tells me to find a new country, I'm not budging."

"Every day it is something new. If not conflagrations, it is typhoons. If not typhoons, it is earthquakes or sludge slides or avalanches of rock or worse calamities."

"That's mostly in California."

"It is connected to the rest of America, is it not? And is it not said that all customs that bedevil America begin in its far western province?"

"Yeah, but earthquakes and firestorms don't migrate like crystal sniffing or color therapy. We have nothing to worry about."

"Yet the earth moved. To the south. Not to the west. If the instabilty to the west has traveled east, then what is to stop it from coming north to topple my fine castle?"

"This is New England, Little Father," Remo explained patiently. "The last time Massachusetts had a major earthquake, the Pilgrims fell off their horses."

Chiun gasped. "So recent as that! I did not know this."

"For crying out loud, that was four hundred years ago!"

Chiun's hazel eyes narrowed. "Perhaps I was too hasty in signing my last contract. Perhaps we should relocate at once lest we be buried under the rubble of this doomed Atlantis."

"I don't believe Atlantis ever existed and, if you'll excuse me, I have a few loose ends to tie up."

Chiun ceased his fussy pacing. He narrowed one eye in Remo's direction.

"You were successful?"

Remo nodded. "The only crack skyscraper in human history has been shut down."

"And the fiend who was called Friend?"

"I threw every computer chip I could find into the Atlantic."

"Good. He will never vex us again."

"Fine with me. Enough vexing goes on around here as it is."

Remo had the phone receiver in one hand and was leaning on the 1 button. It was the foolproof code that connected him to Dr. Harold W. Smith at Folcroft Sanitarium, the cover for CURE, the organization he worked for even though it didn't officially exist.

At length a lemony voice came on the line.

"Remo?"

"It's shut down."

"Did you locate the Friend chip?"

"I found a zillion chips. Chucked them all into the ocean."

"You are certain you got them all?"

"All the big ones, at any rate. Cleaned out the place of other vermin, too."

"Good."

"Okay. My end is done. Now you have to take care of your end."

"What is your wish?"

"I'm still waiting for that replacement car you promised me at the last negotiation."

"I am working on it."

"It's gotta be impervious to these maniac Boston drivers. And I want you to find my daughter, by the way."

The line was quiet for a moment.

"Excuse me?"

"I have a daughter. I need to find her."

"I had no idea you had a daughter. How old?"

"She'd be about eleven or twelve by now."

Smith cleared his throat. "Until recently you had been searching for your parents. Then you changed your mind. Why is that?"

"I changed my mind. My past is my past. I'm looking to the future now. Find my daughter."

"What is her name?"

"Freya."

"Spell it, please."

Remo did.

"Last name?" asked Smith.

"Search me. She's probably going by her mother's last name."

"And what is that?"

"I have no clue," Remo admitted sheepishly.

In the corner the Master of Sinanju shook his head sadly. "Whites," he said under his breath. "They have no sense of family."

"You have no idea who the mother of your daughter is?" Smith asked in an incredulous tone.

"Her first name is Jilda."

"Is that spelled with a *J?*" asked Smith.

"Yeah. I think so."

"It is probably pronounced 'Hilda.'"

"Jilda," said Remo, emphasizing the *J*, "always pronounced it with a *J.*"

"You are positive?"

"I think a grown woman would know how to pronounce her own name, don't you?"

Smith cleared his throat. "Please do not take that tone with me."

"Mind your emperor, Remo," Chiun said loudly. "He is only trying to aid you in your most recent futile search for relatives who have more sense than to associate with you."

Remo slapped a hand over the mouthpiece.

"I don't need any help from the peanut gallery," he whispered.

"It is good we never found your father," Chiun continued, louder than before. "No doubt he would have cast you into the same outer darkness as when you were born, O misbegotten one."

"That's enough," Remo hissed. Taking his hand off the receiver, Remo said to Smith, "Just find them, okay? They could be anywhere. Maybe in Scandinavia. Jilda is from there. She's called Jilda of Lakluun."

"I will do my best," Smith promised.

And the line went dead.

Hanging up, Remo looked toward the Master of Sinanju. And all the anger drained from him.

"I didn't need you chiming in."

"It was necessary to throw Emperor Smith off the scent."

"Smith couldn't smell a limburger-cheese fart if it was piped into a plastic bag tied around his head. All he knows is what his computers tell him."

"If he ever learns that your father lives, there may be dire consequences."

"Yeah, I know," said Remo, his deep-set eyes flickering. "But it's my daughter I'm worried about."

"The words the spirit of your mother spoke to you trouble you still?"

"Yeah. I can't get them out of my mind. She said my daughter was in some kind of danger. The danger was real but not immediate. But I'm not going to wait for it to grow. I need to make sure she's safe."

Chiun cocked his birdlike head to one side. "And if the child's mother prefers that you do not?"

"I'll deal with that then."

"It is difficult being a parent," Chiun said thinly.

"I've never really been a parent."

"It is difficult for you who were born an orphan to know what to do with your feelings. You who had no

brother or sisters or parents now have met the father
you never knew. You have a daughter you have seen
but once in your life. A son, too."

"I don't know about him."

"That truly was your son. He possessed your face
and eyes and uncouth manners."

"Well, he's where Smith can't get at him anymore."

"We will find your daughter, Remo Williams."

"Let's hope so."

Chiun drew near, holding Remo's eyes with his
own. "But have you asked the logical question?"

Remo nodded. "What then?"

"Yes. What then? What will you do? She cannot
live with you. It would be too dangerous, with the
work that we do. We are assassins. We go where our
emperor sends us. Some day we may go and never return."

"I have an idea," said Remo.

Chiun examined his pupil's face quizzically.

"Sometimes a grandparent is a better parent than
the true parent," said Remo.

Chiun's eyes beamed. "You mean me?"

"No. I don't mean you."

"But I am the father you never knew. Who is more
fit to raise your child? Now that you are Apprentice
Reigning Master, destined to assume the throne of
Sinanju if you so choose, perhaps I could ease into
my long-deferred retirement and raise your found-
ling daughter before white ways fully smother her
natural grace."

"Actually I was thinking of *my* father, Chiun,"
said Remo, rotating his freakishly thick wrists absently.

The Master of Sinanju became still. His thin shoulders fell.

"He, at least, is part Korean, as are you," he admitted.

Remo relaxed. He expected the old Korean to take violent offense.

"It's just a thought. First we gotta find her. Then I have to convince Jilda."

"Smith's oracles will show you the way."

"Yeah. Let's hope they come through this time." Remo laughed awkwardly. "For an orphan I suddenly have a lot of family ties."

"If you have family," said Chiun magnanimously, "then I have family. For your blood is the same color as mine."

And Remo smiled through his worry. After all these years, they had learned that much about each other at least.

5

United Nations Secretary General Anwar Anwar-Sadat did not normally accept guests into his Beekman Place home in New York City.

Business was business, and he conducted his business on the thirty-eighth floor of the UN Secretariat Building. Not here among his prized collection of rare Egyptian sphinxes, which symbolized both the secretary general's native country and the prime directive of international diplomacy: keep your damn mouth shut.

But this particular envelope was marked Personal and mailed to his luxury apartments. It enclosed a cryptic black calling card: THE EXTINGUISHER IS COMING.

The follow-up call came the next day.

"Say hello to the answer to all your problems," a voice said.

The voice was definitely male, but had a youthful timbre. It sounded very confident, that voice. Almost cocksure.

"And your name?"

"Didn't you read the card?"

"It said that you are the Extinguisher. But I fail to understand. Are you selling a service? I do not have roaches."

"You have a flash point, the Extinguisher will extinguish it."

"I see," said Anwar Anwar-Sadat slowly, his mind racing. He had many flash points. All stemming from his four-year term as UN secretary general. He had a vision for the world under the United Nations. It was called One World, an idea that surfaced from time to time only to be shot down in ignominious flames by the unimaginative. Anwar Anwar-Sadat was determined that this idea not die when his term of office expired.

"How are you able to help me?" he purred.

"You called for a UN rapid-reaction force tasked to put out every brushfire war and conflict, right?"

"This has been stolen from me. The stubborn and narrow-minded NATO generals have siezed control of my blue helmets."

"That's because you're thinking out loud."

"I fail to follow."

"The U.S. Navy has a quick-reaction force called SEAL Team Six. But they're clandestine. No one knows who they are and where they go until the dirty work is done and Six is on the move to the next hot spot."

"Yes, I am familiar with this SEAL team called Six. But what has that to do with me? Or for that matter, you?"

"This—I'm your personal SEAL team. A multi-tasked army rolled into one guy. I have the know-how, the weapons and most of all, the sheer blind guts."

"You talk boldly for a man who conceals his name."

"Call me Blaize. Blaize Fury"

"I have never heard of you, Blaize Fury."

The voice became suddenly petulant. "You never heard of Blaize Fury, The Extinguisher? The scourge of terrorists the world over?"

"I am afraid I have not. You are obviously he."

"I," said the voice calling itself the Extinguisher, "snuffed your worst enemy."

"I possess many enemies. Who might this be?"

"Mahout Feroze Anin. He had a price on your head. Don't tell me he didn't. You put a price on his head during that UN action in Stomique. Anin got away, chased your peacekeepers out and that left your sorry butt hanging in the wind. He swore to wax you in revenge."

Anwar-Sadat gripped the receiver until his knuckles burned white against his dusky caramel skin. "He is dead?"

"Consider his cold corpse my credentials. Now can we meet?"

"How do I know you are not an emissary of Anin?"

"If I wanted to kill you, my business card would have blown up in your face," the voice of the Extinguisher said flatly.

Anwar-Sadat regarded the ominous ebony card. It was a preposterous claim, but the voice was so confident he found the card slipping from his unnerved fingers.

"Call me tomorrow. If Anin is reliably reported dead, we will meet. But only to thank you, you must understand."

"Signal received," said the voice of the Extinguisher. And he hung up.

Anwar Anwar-Sadat replaced the receiver and walked to the big picture window overlooking the East River.

If the thorn Anin was truly dead, a great burden had been lifted from his life. As for the Extinguisher, it would be useful to meet such a man, if only to take his measure. But as for his preposterous offer, of what use is one man in the pursuit of the new world order? Armies remade worlds, and Anwar Anwar-Sadat controlled the mightiest army on the face of the globe, the UN Protection Force.

If only his colleagues would give him sanction to wage true war in the pursuit of peace, UNPROFOR would be an army to reckon with.

THE NEXT MORNING found the secretary general in his Situation Room in a nondescript building across the street from the UN complex. The room was long and narrow, staffed only by banks of computer terminals. One wall was filled with a global map showing the nations of the world from a politically neutral polar perspective. Nations enjoying a UN peacekeeping presence were rimmed in blue.

He took the accustomed chair proffered by his aide before the computer terminal tied into the international Internet.

The functionary depressed the keys for him as he called out instructions.

"Bring up 'alt.culture.mexico.' "

"At once, my General," the functionary said, using the form of address the secretary general preferred when he was overseeing his far-flung army of peacekeepers.

The computer screen displayed the Mexico Internet discussion group. He scanned the subject headings. Most concerned the simmering insurgency in the southern state of Chiapas.

"This one, then this one, then this one," he said.

"Yes, my General."

The beauty of the Internet, as Anwar-Sadat saw it, lay in how it drew the dispossessed and diaspora of the earth together via fiber-optic lines. These discussion groups often foreshadowed political events and thinking available nowhere else.

"The *insurgentistas* are very busy," he muttered.

"They say that civil war is not far off, my General."

A new subject heading appeared at the end of the column. Anwar-Sadat's eyes fell on it, growing wide.

"What is this?"

"It says 'Earthquake.'"

"I know it says 'Earthquake.' Why does it say 'Earthquake'?"

"May I call it up for you?" the factotum asked.

"Yes, yes, at once, if you please," Anwar-Sadat said testily.

It was a bulletin, originating in Mexico City. In times past such reports would be handled by ham radio. But in the computer age there were more efficient conduits.

"An earthquake has struck the capital," the person wrote. "Power is out in scattered localities. From my window in the Hotel Nikko, I can see smoke rising from Mount Popo."

"What is this Popo?" Anwar-Sadat asked.

"It is a volcano, I believe."

Nodding, he read on.

"Damage appears extensive. This is greater than the 1985 quake."

Frowning with all of his stony Coptic face, Anwar Anwar-Sadat leaned back in his chair, his arms folded across his chest.

"This will further destabilize Mexico," he murmured.

"Yes."

"We must convene an emergency meeting of the Security Council. UN relief must pour in lest civil war break out in the countryside."

"An excellent suggestion, my General."

"And perhaps the authorities in Mexico will at last see the wisdom of allowing UN peacekeepers into the Chiapas area to deal with the insurgent problem."

The functionary frowned. "That might be more difficult."

"Difficult, yes. Impossible, no. For I sense a momentous opportunity here."

"The Mexicans will never allow UN peacekeepers on their native soil. And the U.S. will never allow UN peacekeepers who are not Americans onto Mexican soil."

"We will see about that," said Anwar Anwar-Sadat, signaling that the computer be turned off with an impatient snap of his fingers.

The news was more dire that he had thought.

It was already being called the Great Mexico City Earthquake and it was not confined to the Valley of Mexico. It had shaken the countryside. Tremors had radiated up to El Paso and troubled the waters of the Gulf of Mexico.

Aftershocks were frequent, and Mount Popocate-petl was vomiting a brownish ash as if on the verge of full eruption.

Lost in all this bad news was an official report that the body of former Stomiqui strongman Mahout Feroze Anin had been found in his Nairobi hotel room the previous day, apparently assassinated by persons unknown.

"Yes, yes, I already know about this," said Sadat, brushing the item away as he fielded call after call from his fellow UN ambassadors.

"We must take action at once," he told anyone who would listen. "Mexico must not be allowed to descend into chaos. We must have action. The United Nations is the only hope for this suffering people."

"It is working, Mr. Secretary," the functionary said once the clamor of telephones died down.

"Once we have peacekeepers in the Western Hemisphere, it would be only a matter of time before we have them in this nation."

"And Canada. We must not forget Canada."

"Canada will be more difficult than Mexico."

"What is good enough for Mexico is good enough for Canada."

"I must write that down. Write it down for me. I will use it in a speech at the appropriate time."

"Yes, Mr. Secretary."

By the end of the day, a draft resolution had been laid on the secretary general's desk.

"It reads very well. How can they veto it? It is purely humanitarian. Once my blue helmets bring food in, who would be in a hurry to usher them out again?"

"Only base ingrates, my General."

"Or Serbs," Anwar Anwar-Sadat said, shuddering.

THAT NIGHT Anwar Anwar-Sadat returned to his luxury apartments well after midnight, bleary of eye but buoyant of heart. It was a fortunate turn of events, this Mexican earthquake. It was as if a door of opportunity had opened in the earth's crust.

Switching on the light, he saw a man seated in the overstuffed chair beside his sphinx-filled bookcase.

"Who are you?" he demanded of the seated figure.

The man stood up. He was a tower of black, from the knit balaclava that muffled his head down to his shiny combat boots. His black nightsuit was festooned with popcorn pockets and black leather holsters bristling with implements of violence.

"Enter the Extinguisher."

"Oh, yes, yes. Of course. Very good to meet you. But I have not time for you now. I have had a very trying day."

"Anin is dead. You can thank the Extinguisher for that."

"Yes, yes, excellent. He was a big thorn in my side."

"The Extinguisher makes a speciality of pulling out thorns. Just name one and he'll by waxed and booby-trapped inside of forty-eight hours. Guaranteed or your money back."

Anwar Anwar-Sadat hesitated. "What do you wish in return?"

"Sanctioning."

"You want me to sanction you? As I sanction Iraq or Libya?"

"No, the Extinguisher wants sanctioning. He needs an operational franchise. Free-lance isn't his style. He has skills. They're on the market, but he doesn't want to work for just anybody. He wants to work for the UN."

"Why must you work for the United Nations?"

"The Extinguisher doesn't work for despots or tyrants. He stands for justice. His holy war must continue. But the Extinguisher has to eat like an ordinary mortal, too. We're talking salary here. I was thinking in the mid-five-figure range."

"I cannot pay you a salary to liquidate for the UN. There would be a paper trail."

"We can work something out."

"Also I have no proof you slew Anin. Can you prove this?"

"There are fourteen Hydra-Shok rounds in him. You can check it out."

"I will. But it is not proof. By now the autopsy has been performed."

"The rounds have skull noses. It's the Extinguisher's trademark."

"Yes. Yes. Like the Ghost Who Walks?"

"Who?"

"The Phantom? A very famous figure of justice."

"Look, I'm not kidding here. I—I mean the Extinguisher—wants to work for the UN. With my skills and reputation, we can clean out the international drug lords, the would-be Hitlers and the petty tyrants before they can get started."

Anwar-Sadat shook his head violently. "I cannot sanction any of this, interesting as it may sound."

"How about another dry run?"

"What do you mean by dry run?"

"Name a bad guy. He's gotta be evil. I'll take him out."

"For dinner?"

"No. That means extinguish him."

"I cannot instruct you to assassinate anybody, although there are many obstacles to my new world order."

"Name one."

"There is an insurgency in Mexico."

"Sure. Subcomandante Verapaz. He's welded the Maya peasants into a paramilitary force, and they're all in revolt."

"He is a thorn, for he has taken up arms against the new world order. Not that I would ask you to terminate him, you understand."

The man in the balaclava winked broadly. "Understood."

"Nor do I promise payment should he meet an unseemly end."

"The Extinguisher assures you he's as good as buzzard bait."

"Why must you refer to yourself in the third person?" asked Anwar Anwar-Sadat.

"Because the Extinguisher is greater than one man in combat black. He's a symbol, a force of nature. He is good personified against evil incarnate, the irresistible force all immovable objects fear and a wild-haired warrior for our time."

"Yes. Like Zorro."

"No, damn it! Like the Extinguisher. Stop dragging those other guys into the conversation. They're not real. I am. There is only one Extinguisher, and his true name will never be known."

"But you have told me that your name is Blaize Fury."

"Another alias for the hero with a thousand faces."

Suddenly the man in black strode to the balcony window.

"Where are you going?"

"To Mexico."

"No, I mean at this moment. We are twenty floors up from the ground."

The lower part of the black balaclava shifted as if the mouth behind it smiled.

"Yeah, but only three from the roof."

Reaching out, the Extinguisher grasped a dangling black nylon line with his gloved hands. He cast a final glance in the secretary general's direction.

"Look for me in the newspapers or wherever men sing of blood."

And he was gone.

Anwar Anwar-Sadat walked out to the balcony and looked for the Extinguisher on the pavement below. When he saw no mangled body or stopped traffic, he decided the fool had survived his foolhardy exit.

How very much like Batman, he thought approvingly.

Well, if the fool succeeded, that would be good. If not, there was no political downside. He had given no explicit instructions to kill anybody, and that was all that mattered.

That, and the deniability of the sphinx.

6

Dr. Harold W. Smith had problems.

For Smith's entire life, he had been dogged by problems. Problems were as much a part of living as breathing, eating, sleeping and work. Problems came with the territory. Problems were his life.

Every responsible adult human being had problems. It was part of the human condition. And among human beings, Harold W. Smith of the Vermont Smiths was one of the most responsible.

A U.S. president had long ago recognized Harold Smith's unswerving rectitude and responsibility. Smith was then an obscure CIA bureaucrat who toiled in the then-new field of computer science. Data interpretation and analysis was Smith's specialty. He analyzed shipments of raw materials, changes in the military hierarchies of other governments, food-distribution patterns, and out of these disparate data, forecast coups and brushfire wars with uncanny accuracy.

And he was noticed.

The President in those days was young and idealistic and took up the responsibilities of being chief executive and leader of the free world with great vigor and enthusiasm. Those were the coldest days of the Cold War, but the young President, upon assuming high office, discovered that communism wasn't the direst threat he faced. The real enemy lay within its borders. And America was already all but lost.

A period of lawlessness had brought the nation to the brink of anarchy. In other countries, martial law would have been declared. But this was the United States of America. States could declare martial law. As could cities and towns. Governors and mayors had that power.

The President of the United States could not declare a state of emergency short of civil war or foreign invasion. Not without admitting the unadmittable—that the experiment called democracy, which had flowered briefly among the ancient Greeks and was revived by tavern revolutionaries in a tiny colony of Great Britian, had failed.

In fact, his legal options were virtually nonexistent.

Suspending the Constitution was ruled out.

So the President had conceived an alternative. He called it CURE. It was not an acronym, but a prescription for a society poisoned by corruption, moral decay and organized crime.

That President had plucked Harold Smith out of the CIA, entrusting him with the ultimate responsibilty: save his country through any means, legal or illegal.

"Any means?" Smith had asked.

"As long as the means are secret. Nothing must reach back to this office. Officially the organization does not exist. You will have funding. You may recruit agents and informants so long as they do not know they are working for the organization. Only you and I must know. Save your country, Mr. Smith, and

God willing, we can abolish CURE by the time we put that first man on the moon.''

But by that time the President who had laid the burden of the ultimate responsibility on Harold Smith's shoulders had been cut down by the very lawlessness he had sought to defeat. By that time there were American footprints on the moon, but the greatest nation on the face of the earth was no closer to internal stability than before.

Smith had decided in those days that he would have to take the ultimate sanction. Assassination. Prior to that fateful decision, he had worked through the system, exposing crooked union organizers, corrupt judges, organized-crime figures in ways that dragged them into the remorseless grindstone of the judicial system.

It was not enough. After less than a decade, Smith understood it would never be enough.

So he reached out to New Jersey for an ordinary-seeming beat cop who had been tested in the jungles of Vietnam, and code-named him the Destroyer.

America's supersecret agency that didn't exist now had an enforcement arm who also didn't exist.

Only then did the hand of CURE truly begin to exert its awesome power against America's enemies.

The tide was turned back. True, it constantly threatened to swamp the ship of state, but America now had an edge. More importantly the Constitution survived intact. Smith bent, folded and spindled it on a daily basis. But only the successor Presidents had any inkling of that.

America struggled on.

The problems came and the problems went. Smith disposed of them with a ruthless efficiency that control of the greatest assassins in human history gave them. Invariably the problems always went away. And just as quickly new ones reared their heads.

Lately Harold had his eye on two particular problems. They existed on separate computer files designated Amtrak and Mexico.

Smith was pulling up the Amtrak file as the sun began to set on another day.

It was forty-three items long, he saw with a frown. For some two years now, train derailments had been piling up at an alarmimg rate. Some were passenger-rail mishaps, others freight accidents. Major and minor, they made the papers so often that late-night comedians joked that the nation's aging rail system was itself one gigantic train wreck.

The latest had occurred near La Plata, Missouri. A Santa Fe freight train had gone off its tracks while rounding a bend. A shifting cargo car overloaded with scrap metal was the official cause. Smith's frown deepened.

It was possible, he supposed. Virtually every derailment had its reasonable cause. A split rail. A vandal switching tracks. Poor track conditions. The numbers of people who annually attempted to beat fast-moving trains to crossings and paid for their folly with their lives continually amazed him. These incidents Smith dumped from the Amtrak file as non-aberrations attributable to human error.

Individually there was nothing to be suspicious of. Collectively they suggested a pattern. But no common cause seemed to percolate up from the mass of news-wire extracts and National Transportation Safety Board accident reports.

Smith stared at the slowly scrolling reports, his tired gray eyes behind the glass shields of his rimless eyeglasses skimming mechanically, as if they could perceive what long hours of study could not: a common link.

His old CIA-analyst skills were as sharp as they had been in the long-ago days when he was known in the Agency's corridors as "the Gray Ghost," as much for his colorless demeanor as for his unflagging habit of wearing banker's gray.

But today they failed him.

Smith hit the scroll-lock key and turned in his cracked leather chair.

Through the picture window of one-way glass that protected the most secure office outside of the Pentagon from prying eyes, Smith let his tired eyes fall on the restful waters of Long Island Sound.

Perhaps, he thought, it was time to send Remo and Chiun into the field on this one. If no force or agency was responsible for this unprecedented string of accidents, it suggested America's rail system was either overburdened or so shoddily run it presented a menace to the nation's vital transportation lines.

If so, exposing the dangerous condition technically fell within CURE operating parameters.

Smith turned in his seat, his pinched patrician face grim with resolve. He reached across the black glass of his desktop for the blue contact telephone he employed to reach his Destroyer. It was a secure line, scrambled and completely insulated from wiretapping. It was second only to the dialless red telephone he kept under lock and key in a lower desk drawer until such time as he needed to reach the current President.

This was not a situation that called for Presidential consultation. The President did not control CURE, any more than he controlled Congress these days. The CURE mandate allowed for Presidential suggestions, but not orders. The only order the President was allowed to give was the one that would close down CURE forever.

Smith's age-gnarled hand briefly touched the slick plastic of the pale blue receiver when his computer beeped once.

Withdrawing his hand, Smith addressed the screen. It was buried beneath the desktop's tinted glass surface and angled so it faced him.

The monitor itself was invisible under the black glass. Only the amber letters floating on the screen showed.

The red light in one corner winked insistently. A message beside it said, "Mexico!"

That meant one of Smith's automatic net-trolling programs had picked up something important. Probably an AP story moving across the wires that contained the keyword *Mexico*.

Smith tapped the silent pads of the keyless capacity-keyboard and brought it up.

It was an Associated Press bulletin:

MEXICO—QUAKE
MEXICO CITY, MEXICO (AP)
A severe earthquake struck the Valley of Mexico at approximately 2:00 p.m. EST this afternoon. Initial reports say that damage to Mexico City is substantial, and there is significant loss of life. Eyewitness reports add that Mount Popocatepetl is giving indications a major eruption is

near. It is not yet known whether the volcano triggered the quake or if the quake brought the volcano—which had been showing renewed signs of activity in the past several months—to life again.

Smith frowned. This was not good news. Mexico was his other chief concern these days. The uprising in Chiapas, combined with political and economic instability, had turned America's sleepy southern neighbor into a smoldering political volcano.

Only a few months before, Mexican army tanks had taken up threatening positions on the Texas border, but were quickly pulled back. It had been an ominous move, but relations between the two nations had officially returned to normalcy.

But the strains were still there. Illegal immigration, the devaluation of the peso and fallout from the ill-fated NAFTA agreement had produced a growing animosity between the peoples of the U.S. and Mexico. That their respective leaders were outwardly cordial meant little. In the age of electronic news media, public opinion, not political will, drove policy.

As Smith reflected on this problem, a second bulletin popped onto the screen.

CHIAPAS REBEL
MEXICO CITY, MEXICO (AP)
Subcomandante Verapaz, leader of the insurgent Benito Juarez National Liberation Front, has in the past hour declared that the violent convulsion in Mexico City is a sign from the gods that they have turned away from the beleaguered leadership of Mexico and that the time

has come to take the struggle into the capital. Verapaz, whose true name and identity is unknown, is calling for all indigenous Mexicans to rise up and overwhelm the Federal Army of Mexico.

That decided Harold Smith. The Amtrak matter could wait.

Remo and Chiun were going into the field, all right. But they were going to Mexico.

Subcomandante Verapaz was no longer an internal Mexican problem. He was out to overthrow the lawful government in Mexico City. And a revolution on America's southern border constituted a direct threat to the United States of America.

Harold Smith's gray hand reached out to the blue contact telephone.

7

Remo Williams was watching the Master of Sinanju fillet a fish when the telephone rang.

"I'll get it," he said, starting from his seat in the kitchen. It was a cane chair. Chairs were allowed in the downstairs kitchen. Tables, too, although most of the time they ate at a low taboret, seated cross-legged on tatami mats.

"You will not," snapped the Master of Sinanju.

"It might be Smith."

"It might be a czar or a bey or an emir. But it is none of them. We are about to dine. If Emperor Smith wishes to speak to me, let him call at an appropriate hour."

"It might be for me, you know."

"Smith only calls you in order to reach me."

"Not always."

"You will watch me prepare this excellent fish."

Remo sighed. He returned to his seat and placed his chin in the cup of his hands. He wasn't sure what was so important about this particular fish, but Chiun seemed to think it was.

"Observe the specimen in question. Is it not enticing to behold?"

"If you like sea bass," said Remo. "Me, I'm in the mood for pike."

"Pike is not yet in season."

"That's probably why I'm in the mood for it."

Chiun made a face. His wrinkles puckered into gullies.

In the background the telephone continued to ring.

"That's gotta be Smith," Remo said. "Who else would refuse to give up after twenty-six rings?"

"He will hang up after the forty-second ring."

"Yeah, and start all over again, figuring he might have misdialed."

"We are stronger than he is stubborn. Now, pay close attention. This is the correct way to fillet a fish."

As Remo watched, Chiun held the sea bass by its tail with one hand. The fish hung with its mouth agape, its eyes glassy. It didn't bother Remo. Chiun often served the fish with the head still on. He had long ago gotten used to having his dinner stare back at him.

As Remo watched, Chiun said, "Sea bass makes excellent stir fry. So we must dismember this excellent specimen first."

"This is starting to sound like 'Wok with Wing.'"

"Do not insult me by comparing me to a Chinese television chef. I spit upon Chinese."

"That's the rumor in the neighborhood," Remo said dryly.

The Master of Sinanju's eyes went thin with menace. He blew out his cheeks like an annoyed puffer fish. An eagle's talon, his free hand curled in, then out, ivory fingernails revealing themselves with a slow menace.

Abruptly they flashed, weaving a silvery pattern about the fish. Skin fell away in long strips to land on the newspaper under the head.

The head fell amid the shed skin with a plop.

As if coming back to life, the bass leaped from Chiun's hand and, swapping ends, suddenly hung tail downward. A fingernail went *whisk,* and the tail was sheared off cleanly. The fins fluttered after it.

Then, working in midair, Chiun began to fillet the fish with nothing more that his wickedly sharp and slightly curved index fingernail.

"Hope you washed recently," Remo said as the telephone finally fell silent.

Chiun made no rely. The phone started its discordant ringing anew. Remo switched hands, cupping his chin in the other hand and simultaneously stifling a yawn.

Chiun worked so swiftly the ordinary eye could never hope to follow it. It seemed as if the fish were caught in some troubled ivory web that peeled off long sheets of pale flesh as it thrashed to escape the invisible strands.

When it was over—and it was over in a twinkling—the sea bass lay in two separate piles, discarded internal matter and perfectly boneless fillets of fish.

Remo wondered if he should applaud.

"Why do you not applaud?" asked Chiun.

"I wasn't sure if that was what you wanted."

"And you are correct. Perfection does not require applause."

"Good. I made the right decision."

"Sincerity is the most flattering form of imitation, however."

"I think you have that filleted up."

"Perhaps. But I do not demonstrate the ancient Korean art of filleting fish with no tools other than the natural ones of the body without reason."

"Okay, I'll bite. Why the demonstration?"

"To instruct you in the error of your ways."

"Which are?"

"I am Reigning Master. You are next Reigning Master, currently Apprentice Reigning Master."

"Yep."

"You will follow in my sandals, taking up my kimono after I am gone or retired, whichever comes first."

"I'll have to think about the kimono."

"Kimonos are traditional."

"Kimonos are Eastern. I gotta operate in the West."

"Perhaps in the next century, by Western reckoning, you will operate in the East. Especially if the West falls into the ocean."

"That's not going to happen, Little Father."

"Wherever you operate, you must do so with sublime grace, skill and a perfection that approaches that of your teacher."

"Perfection is perfection. If I am perfect, I will be as perfect as you," said Remo.

"You cannot be as perfect as me, being but half-Korean. It is impossible. Unless you mend your ways, of course."

"Assuming I want to mend my ways, what are you driving at?"

And Chiun lifted his long-nailed fingers, admiring them. "Observe these, the ultimate tools of a Sinanju Master. Are they not graceful? Are they not perfection? No blade of steel or bone or wood can approach their deadliness. It is for this reason that Sinanju has long celebrated them as the Knives of Eternity, for even if broken they will unfailingly grow back to strike terror into the hearts of all enemies of Sinanju."

"They're striking terror into mine right now."

"Now look at your own pitiful nails."

Remo did. They were cut short Western style. The index nail of his right finger was slightly longer. Just enough to score glass or metal. It looked like an ordinary nail. But years of Sinanju diet, exercise and certain honing techniques had imbued it with a sharpness so fine it could slice open thick rhinoceros hide.

"Looks fine to me," he said.

"In Sinanju's eyes, they are maimed and disfigured. If my ancestors—who are your ancestors—"

"Half ancestors," Remo corrected.

"If *our* ancestors could see you with your sacred Knives of Eternity cut to the quick and discarded like mere lemon peels, they would tear out their hair, rend their kimonos and shriek against the whiteness that has tainted you."

"I met a few of them in the Void. Nobody mentioned my nails."

"They were too embarrassed. If you had an extra toe or a hideous scar, would you expect them to point it out?"

"You would."

"I am!" Chiun shrieked. "You embarrass me before your—our—ancestors by clinging to transient Western ways. How can you walk in my sandals when you cannot gouge out the eyes of the enemies of the House properly? How can you hold your head up when you blunt your fingers with crude steel implements? Next you will insert copper studs in your ears or brass rings in your nose as they do in the West.''

''Cut it out, Chiun. We had this argument years and years ago. You lost. Get over it.''

''I did *not* lose. I retreated. Now I am back, more determined than ever before that I will have my way.''

''I just want my dinner,'' moaned Remo.

''When you can fillet your own fish, you may eat fish again. Not until then.''

The phone was still ringing, and Remo, annoyed, jumped for it.

''What is it?'' he barked into the mouthpiece.

''Remo, is something amiss?'' It was Harold Smith.

''Oh, Chiun is just ragging me that my fingernails are longer than your fingernails. Nyah. Nyah. Nyah. Unquote.''

Smith made a throat-clearing sound. ''I need you in Mexico.''

''What's in Mexico?''

''A major earthquake.''

Chiun crowed, ''Hah! I told you so, but you refused to heed my warning.''

''What was that?'' Smith asked.

''Just Chiun busting my chops. He claims to have felt the earth move a couple hours ago. And he was alone.''

''The Mexican situation is precarious, Remo. A nationwide state of emergency has been declared by the Mexican president. Already, frightened immigrants are flooding U.S. border checkpoints, clamoring for refuge.''

"So? Either we let them in or we close down the border. It's our country, isn't it?"

"There is more. You are familiar with Subcomandante Verapaz?"

"Yeah. The rebel leader who thinks he's the next Fidel Castro."

"Exactly. He had called upon his followers to take to the streets. He wants revolution and he sees this as the historic moment. It is time to take him out of the political equation."

"Good."

"I am glad you agree."

"I don't care two fingers about Mexico. I just want someone to take my frustrations out on," Remo said fiercely.

"You have no frustrations," Chiun countered. "I am the frustrated one. I have exalted you above all others and am now forced to endure the sight of your disfigured, impotent fingers as my reward."

"Blow it out your barracks bag," said Remo.

And as Remo watched, the Master of Sinanju flung himself about and ran the perfect fillets of sea bass down the complaining garbage disposal.

"Your tickets to Mexico City will be waiting for you at the Azteca Airlines counter at Logan Airport," Smith was saying. "Connections to the Chiapas city of San Cristóbal de las Casas will be through Aero Quetzal. From there, pick up his trail in the town of Boca Zotz. It is a hotbed of *Juarezista* sympathizers. Verapaz holds most of his press conferences there."

"If we know that, how come the Mexican army doesn't?"

"They do. But liquidating Verapaz would create more political problems than it would solve. This is why we are taking the initiative. Make certain it looks like natural causes."

"Anything else?"

"Be discreet. Relations with Mexico City are delicate. We want no diplomatic incidents."

"Is there a meal on that flight?" asked Remo.

"Yes."

"Good." And Remo hung up. "We're going to Mexico, Little Father."

Chiun did not look up from the sink. "Do not forget to pack your gloves," he said thinly.

"It's jungle down there. I won't need gloves."

"Then allow your fingers to flower like the fearsome thorns they are so that shame-concealing gloves will not be necessary."

Remo rolled his eyes ceilingward.

8

The Extinguisher approached Mexico City airport customs bearing a passport that identified him as Laszlo Crannick, Jr. His hair was darkened to a jet black. Wraparound mirror-finish sunglasses concealed the piercing blue color of his eyes. A gray sport coat thrown over his black turtleneck combat shirt gave him a vaguely Continental look.

He carried a duffel bag, his rucksack hanging off one heroic shoulder.

Divided among them were the nonmetallic components of his Hellfire supermachine pistol, the most sophisticated and versatile hand weapon ever designed.

In the leather holster at the small of his back was a backup pistol made of space-age ceramics undetectable by conventional airport magnometers.

The customs area was equipped with stoplights. You pressed a button. If the light came up green, you were passed through. If red, you were subject to a baggage search.

Striding to the button, he pressed it confidently. It glowed red. No problem. It happened. He'd ace it no sweat.

The Extinguisher dropped his bags on the table

while the customs man sized him up with an unreadable glance.

"Pasaporte, por favor."

"Huh?"

The customs man looked closer, his eyes hard as obsidian.

"American?" he demanded.

"Yes."

He held up his hand. "Let me see your passport, *señor.*"

The passport was offered. Here was the critical moment. If he cleared customs without incident, all of Mexico was open to him.

The customs officer in his dark green uniform looked at the passport carefully. If he knew the real name of the wild-haired warrior who sought entry into Mexico, he would wear a more respectful face. But he did not know he was facing Blaize Fury. He did not know he stood within killing distance of the internationally feared Extinguisher.

When his eyes came up, they were hard.

"I must see other identifications."

He was just being thorough, the Extinguisher decided. Chances were he wouldn't check the baggage. Odds were long he would be passed through without a hitch.

"Here."

The bogus U.S. driver's license was surrendered.

The customs man gave it only cursory examination. He motioned for another customs officer to join him.

The Extinguisher stood his ground. He had no quarrel with these two. If it came to a fair fight, then he would do what was necessary. All that mattered was the mission. Nailing Subcomandante Verapaz. In his war against tyrants, he and Mexican customs were on the same team. They just didn't know it. If they were fortunate, they never would.

He made his voice low and steady as a rock. "Is something wrong?"

The customs man's response was like the soft crack of a whip. "This passport is not valid."

"Not valid! Screw you, taco breath! It says Laszlo Crannick, Jr. I'm Laszlo Crannick, Jr. Just ask my father, Laszlo Crannick, Sr."

All eyes were drawn to the formidable figure of the man in gray sport clothes. Other customs officials approached.

If it came to a fight, he would have to take the customs men out first. Then bolt for the exit. There would be a car, maybe a taxi. After that, it would be easy to blend into the congestion of Mexico City traffic. Urban camouflage was an Extinguisher specialty.

"I must ask jou to step out of line," the senior customs man said sternly. "Jou are being detained."

"You can't detain me!"

"Nevertheless, jou are being detained. Come with me."

Before the Extinguisher could reach for his backup weapon, two pairs of hands came from nowhere to seize his arms. His bags were taken up, and he was marched away under the frightened gaze of American tourists whose faces wondered if they, too, would receive such harsh treatment if the customs light came up red.

The Extinguisher allowed himself to be led way. It would be easier to deal with his opponents behind closed doors, where there were no witnesess and no backup. A master of hand-to-hand combat, he could take them all. There were only four.

The room was a cubicle, and with the door shut, the sounds of airport bustle abated.

As two green uniforms stripped open the zipper of his bag, the senior one said, "I must ask your business in Mexico."

"I'm a tourist."

"Jou come to see the sights, not to do business?"

"I have no business in Mexico City," the Extinguisher assured them in his firm, no-nonsense voice.

Out of the duffel came the barrel of his CIA-designed Hellfire, wrapped in metallic gold-and-green Christmas paper. It might have been a Cuban cigar. Except for its weight.

The chief customs officer frowned angrily. "What is this?"

"A Christmas present."

He extracted more wrapped packages. "And these?"

"More presents."

"Christmas was two months ago, *señor*."

The Extinguisher managed a cool shrug. "So I'm late. People bring Christmas presents late all the time."

"To whom are jou bringing these presents if jou are only a tourist?" the interrogator asked as the others began tearing off the wrappings.

"Hey! You can't do that!"

"We are merely opening these innocent presents of yours."

"You know how long it took me to wrap those?"

"Jou may rewrap them once we are done. Now I must ask for the name and address of the person or persons to whom these presents are intended."

Before he could form the next words, the Extinguisher saw the colorful green-and-gold paper come off the Lucite ammo drum filled with skull-faced Hydra-Shok rounds and decided to shift tactics.

"Look, I'll level with you."

A pistol was in the act of being drawn from side leather. The Extinguisher made sure his hands were open and in full view.

"Speak."

"I'm not Laszlo Crannick, Jr. That's not my true name."

"What is your true name?"

"It's—" he let the pause hang heavy in the air "—Blaize Fury."

The eyes of his interrogator grew darkly sharp. Those of the others went wide in their brown faces. The man holding the ammo drum dropped it to the floor. It rattled like the deadly dice of death.

The tactical advantage belonged to the Extinguisher again.

"I'm here on an important mission," he announced in grim tones.

"State this mission."

"You all know about Subcomandante Verapaz."

Eyes hardened at the despised name.

"Good. I've been sent to take him out. Cold. Savvy?"

"Jou are to kill him?"

"The Extinguisher doesn't merely kill. He extinguishes."

"Can jou prove jou are Blaize Fury?" the chief customs man asked in a guarded tone.

The Extinguisher lifted his arms. "ID cards in the band of my pants."

He was quickly searched. They found the backup pistol before the tiny card case. It no longer mattered. They were all on the same side. Everybody knew that now.

The man who found the card case exploded in his excitement.

"*¡Madre de Dios!* It is true! These cards proclaim him to be *El Extinguirador.*"

The customs official grabbed a card and read it quickly.

"But jou—jou are a myth!"

The Extinguisher allowed a cool, confident smile to warp his lips. "Camouflage. If people think I don't exist, they drop their guard. Then I move in for the kill."

"Jou mean the extinguish, do jou not?" an impressed customs man said.

The chief interrogator snapped, "Who sends jou after the insurgent, Verapaz?"

"I'm not at liberty to divulge the name of my employer. You understand. Deniability."

"Jou must tell us this thing."

"Sorry. It's a need-to-know kind of deal."

"Then jou are under arrest."

"Are you shitting me? We're on the same team."

This time all four side arms were out of leather and aimed at him. One trembled in the hand of the man who pointed it.

"Jou will place your hand at your back, *Señor El Extinguirador.*"

"Look, you don't want to do this. Just let me through, and Verapaz will be a bad memory inside of forty-eight hours."

"Jou will be turned over to the Federal Judicial Police for further questioning and disposal."

"Look, how much will it cost for you guys to look the other way?"

Interest flickered in the senior customs officer's dark eyes.

"How much have jou in mind, *señor?*"

"There's three hundred bucks in my wallet. Take half."

While the guns kept him at bay, a hand fished his wallet from the inner pocket of his gray sport coat.

"It is true, there is three hundred American dollars here."

The senior customs official said something in Spanish, and the money was quickly divided into two unequal piles.

Seeing this, the Extinguisher began to relax. His strong, angular face had a slight sheen of tension upon it.

The senior customs man took the larger pile while the other was divided equally among his subordinates. Then the wallet was returned to the inner jacket pocket. Its weight no longer tugged at the coat's fabric.

"You can't do that. How will I pay my way to Chiapas?"

"Jou will not. Jou will instead cool your boots in a FJP cell."

"You're making a big mistake here," the Extinguisher protested as the cold steel handcuffs were clamped to his unresisting wrists.

"It is jou who have made the mistake, coming to Mexico intent upon mischief as jou have."

"You want this whole country to careen into civil war?"

"Being the man who captured the much-wanted Blaize Fury is more important to me today. I will worry about civil war *mañana.*"

They led him out of the terminal and into the stagnant, smoky air of Mexico City. It tasted foul. But not as foul as the betrayal raising his gorge.

The Extinguisher had been captured. Well, it had happened before. It was always temporary. There wasn't a prison built that could hold him for long.

There was an olive green Light Armored Vehicle waiting at the curb, and he was loaded into this. He noticed the ground was cracked in spots and wondered if the entire country was this badly maintained. Somewhere in the back of his mind, the Extinguisher recalled something the airline captain had announced about the present emergency. He had a really thick accent, so he hadn't paid much attention. Mexico was always having problems anyway.

As he stepped into the back, the Extinguisher supressed a thin smile of contempt. The LAV was small and toylike compared to the Armored Personnel Carriers of major powers. U.S. police SWAT teams had LAVs exactly like this. They were a joke. Their armor wouldn't turn a hollowpoint slug.

The doors clanged shut, and the LAV moved into traffic.

On the other side of the LAV interior, two brown-uniformed soldiers sat as stony faced as Aztec idols.

"You guys always look this happy?" he asked.

They said nothing. Their faces were a dark mask.

"Screw you mothers, then."

They said nothing to that. Only then did the Extinguisher realize they spoke no English.

The traffic sounds were horrendous. Horns honked and blared, and the air coming through the body armor smelled of car exhaust and sulphur. He wondered if it was a muffler hole, or the smog that hung in the Valley of Mexico like a perpetual shroud of death.

The LAV rattled and jounced as it moved through the stop-and-go traffic. It seemed to hit a light every hundred yards.

On the floor the Extinguisher's duffel bag sat unzipped. A soldier noticed the bright-colored packages and reached down to help himself to one.

Seeing this, the other *soldado* decided he couldn't be left out. He took up the rucksack and began rummaging through it.

"Hey! That's not your property."

They pointedly ignored him as they stripped the "presents" of their colorful metallic paper wrapping.

Quickly the true nature of the contents was revealed.

They were soldiers and knew armament. They began to assemble the pieces one by one, as if doing a puzzle. The dreaded Hellfire supermachine pistol slowly took shape.

"That's right, you dillweeds. Put it together. Make it easy for me."

The LAV stopped at a light. Cross traffic hummed all around. The gun ports were closed, so surreptitious visual recon was impossible.

Abruptly the LAV started rocking on its springs. It started as a side-to-side rocking, then shifted to a vertical bouncing. The LAV began pogoing. Everyone grabbed for something to hold on to. Except the Extinguisher, whose hands were pinioned at his back.

"What the hell's going on here?" he growled.

The soldiers swapped startled looks. One dropped the half-assembled machine pistol.

"*Ay!*"

The LAV kept rocking. Outside, something shattered. It sounded like glass. More glass shattered. And suddenly it seemed as if every mirror in the universe was breaking all at once.

One soldier screamed out a word. "*¡Temblor!*"

"What?"

"*¡Temblor de tierra!*"

The other soldier screamed, "*¡Terremoto! ¡Terremoto!*"

"Say it in English, will you?"

"*¡Terremoto!*"

The rocking grew more violent. The Extinguisher's head collided with the LAV roof.

"Ow!"

And the two *soldados* jumped from their seats, throwing open the doors and evacuating the LAV.

"Wait! What's going on?"

The LAV was literally bouncing on its tires now.

The cacophony of Mexico City took on a new ferocious quality. Men screamed. Woman wailed. Glass shattered. Something like stone cracking turned into a protracted splintery rumble.

As if a blind giant were pushing it around, the LAV started swinging on its braked tires. Visible through the open back door, a city falling into chaos was revealed.

"Holy shit! The mother of all earthquakes!"

The Extinguisher sprang into action. He dived for the ground. It shook hard enough to rattle his teeth. Flat on his stomach, he looked around, sizing up the situation.

Almost at once, he decided to get back into the LAV. It looked like the safest thing for miles around.

Outside, as the city shook itself, a thunderous roar came from due southeast. He got down on the cold floor and recovered his weapon by feel. Fingering a thin steel pick from its butt receptacle, he inserted it into the handcuff lock and tried to pick the lock.

The lock aperture kept shaking.

"Damn it! Hold still a minute," he snapped.

The lock refused to cooperate.

The earth was still shaking when he sprung the cuffs. Taking up his Hellfire supermachine pistol, he stowed it into his rucksack, along with the rest of his gear.

When the earth finally stopped shaking, there was a long, terrible silence.

Blaize Fury stepped out.

The great city had been brought to its knees. To the north a building face had fallen to the pavement, exposing the cubbyholes of a multifloored office tower. People shrieked up there looking out at the city that had been whelmed by a force greater than any city ever built.

"Man, this place looks like Oklahoma City in quadraphonic stereo!"

But in the context of his mission, the Extinguisher had drawn a trump card.

Climbing into the driver's seat, he found the keys had been left in the ignition. The engine was still idling. He threw the emergency brake and got moving.

The ashpalt had buckled directly ahead. It was impassable. Traffic lay stopped all around. People were out of their cars, looking up and around and all around again, their varicolored faces slack and dazed, as their eyes tried to take in the enormity of what had transpired.

"Gotta get out of this hellhole," the Extinguisher muttered.

Spotting a stretch of empty sidewalk, he ran the LAV up on it, honking the horn impatiently.

People got out of the way. Not as fast as they should. They were too stunned for that. But a path was cleared.

When he found a stretch of clear road, he jumped for it.

Traffic was stopped everywhere. Life was stopped everywhere. As he muscled the LAV over buckled crevices, around obstacles and through the city, a dirty rain began to fall.

It only looked like rain at first. When the grayish black precipitation touched the windshield, it stuck like snow. But it wasn't snow. For one thing, it smoked.

The Extinguisher threw out a hand to collect a sample. He snapped it back instantly.

"Ouch! Damn it! Motherfucker."

Sucking on his burned hand, he drove one-handed.

Near the broad paved square called the Zocalo, he began to understand. Visible past the forlorn Mexican national flag that was already drooping at half staff was one of the many mountains that ring the Mexican capital city.

It was throwing up a great column of excrement-brown smoke like vaporizing compost.

"Don't look now, but I think that's one upset volcano," the Extinguisher muttered to himself.

Rolling up the window, he drove grimly, as people, covering their heads with newspapers and anything else at hand, fled the burning volcanic ash.

For once the Extinguisher understood he was outmatched. For once his warrior skills meant next to nothing. For once he was no better than any gunless mortal.

"Man, if she really blows her top my *cojones* are guacamole!"

9

The Azteca Airlines flight left the Boston gate on time and, thanks to a brisk tail wind, arrived on the ground in Dallas/Fort Worth International Airport more than an hour early.

"Attention, all passengers," the captain said. "We have landed in Texas in order to refuel. The stewardess will be coming through the cabin to collect the fuel tax."

"Fuel tax?" Remo said.

"I will pay no tax," said the Master of Sinanju at his window seat. He always took the window seat in case the wing showed signs of falling off. He wore an emerald green kimono now, trimmed in ocher.

"Why do we have to pay a fuel tax?" Remo asked the stewardess when the wicker collection basket was placed under his nose. It reminded him of the collection baskets in the church he attended as a boy.

"Because Azteca Airlines is too poor to afford the fuel since NAFTA was passed."

"We will pay no tax," insisted Chiun.

"I'll get it," Remo said. "Anything to get going."

"This is taxation without reservations," Chiun sniffed.

"Actually the slogan is Taxation Without Representation, but I like your version better."

"Señor Ross Perot was correct," said the stewardess after Remo dropped two twenties in the basket. "If jou *gringos* had voted for that giant of a man, Mexico would today be a First World country."

"Yeah, and General Alzheimer would have been vice president."

"It is preferable to that stick of wood who cannot dance."

The plane was in the air within thirty minutes. During that time, a meal was served.

"I can't eat this," said Remo, pointing to the plastic tray loaded with refried beans in a spicy tomato sauce.

"Good. I will eat it, then," said the stewardess, taking back the meal and disappearing into the galley.

When she returned, Remo asked her for rice.

"We have no rice. Only corn."

"What kind of airline doesn't serve rice?"

"A Mexican one," said the stewardess, continuing her rounds.

"Guess I go hungry a while longer," said Remo, who would have settled for corn, but was forbidden to eat it by the Master of Sinanju, who claimed it would turn the whites of Remo's eyes yellow.

"We are going to be late," Chiun said, his tone accusing.

"So what?" said Remo. "Verapaz can wait."

A woman passenger immediately behind them leaned forward. "Did jou say 'Verapaz,' *señor?*"

"No," said Remo.

"Possibly," said Chiun. "What do you know of him?"

The woman clapped her hand to her ample bosom. "He is the handsomest man in all of Mexico."

A notch formed between Remo's dark eyes.

"How do you know that? He wears a ski mask all the time."

"His eyes are handsome. Therefore, his face must be handsome. It is logical, no?"

"It is logical, definitely no," said Remo.

"They say he has green eyes," a woman across the aisle said. "I adore green eyes."

"It is said he is a defrocked Jesuit priest who has taken up arms to liberate his country," the stewardess offered.

"He is a *comunista!*" a man snarled.

"No, he is a pure-blooded Maya who was educated in the states," another man affirmed. "God has blessed this man."

"In other words," Remo said, "none of you know a thing."

"In Mexico," the stewardess said sternly, "the truth is what jou believe because the reality of life is so terrible."

"Tell that to the Kurds," Remo said.

The captain came on the intercom to announce that they were within thirty minutes of their destination. "That is, if the NAFTA tax is paid in full," he added.

"Another tax!" Chiun squeaked.

"It is necessary," the stewardess assured him. "Since NAFTA, Mexico has been impoverished."

"I thought you people were all for NAFTA," said Remo.

"We wanted the good that came from NAFTA. Not the bad things."

"Tough. You bought in. You draw the bad with the good."

"There is no good. We were tricked by our leaders. Your leaders, as well."

"This is taxation without restriction," Chiun said. "We will pay no more taxes."

"That goes double for me," Remo said.

"In that case, we will circle Mexico City until we run out of fuel, or crash," warned the stewardess.

"You wouldn't do that in a million years."

"Sometimes death is preferable to life. It is true for Mexicans ever since the calamity."

"The earthquake?"

"No. NAFTA. Our souls are strong, and we will endure countless earthquakes. Earthquakes can only break our bodies. But NAFTA has crushed our proud Mexican spirits. We have no future because our money is worth nothing now."

"How does that give you the right to hold up Americans every chance you get?"

"*Norteamericanos* are feelthy rich."

"Not for long if we keep getting taxed into the poorhouse," said Remo sourly.

"We will pay no tax," said Chiun firmly.

"The fuel tax is all you'll see from this row," Remo added.

The stewardess went away, and a moment later the captain came back, his face dark with an anger that ran deep into the bone.

"Jou must pay the NAFTA tax if we are to land, *señores.*"

Remo folded his lean arms. "Go ahead. Crash the plane. I dare you."

"Yes," said Chiun, also folding his silk-clad arms, "destroy yourselves. We do not care. We have been taxed nearly to death. You are demanding blood from two stones."

Shaking his fist in their faces the captain vowed, "Mexicans will never bend to American intimidations."

"That wasn't a threat, we just—"

But the captain had already spun on his heel and stormed back to the cabin. The door slammed shut so hard the overhead luggage bins shook in sympathy.

"We win," Chiun said blandly.

"I'm not so sure about that...."

Seconds later the 727 nosed into a steep dive. The engines began howling. Rushing air screamed over the wings and other control surfaces. Standing passengers were thrown off their feet. Anyone seated was jammed forward in his seat. A stewardess coming out of the rear rest room landed on her stomach and, despite her best efforts to grab chair supports, inexorably slid toward the front of the aircraft, her liquid eyes full of fear.

"Now will jou pay the tax?" the captain demanded over the intercom.

"Damn," said Remo, jumping from his seat so fast his seat belt snapped in two. Chiun followed, an emerald specter.

Remo hit the cockpit door. It was locked. He was stepping back to kick it in when the Master of Sinanju floated up and inserted one long fingernail into the lock aperture. He twisted his finger left, then right. The lock went click, and he flung the door open with a grand gesture.

"Thanks," said Remo.

He stepped into the cabin.

The captain and copilot were frozen in their seats. The captain had thrown the control yoke all the way forward. Eyes welded shut, the copilot was making the sign of the cross.

Through the windshield, Remo could see the mountains of northern Mexico coming up to meet the plane like blunt brown teeth.

"Are you crazy!" he exploded.

"The tax or *muerte! ¡Viva Mexico!*"

Remo took the captain by his right earlobe. With his free hand he took the copilot's left earlobe. He squeezed.

"Aieee!" they screamed in stereo.

"Pull up now or the pain gets worse," Remo warned.

And Remo squeezed harder on the earlobe nerve that filled the veins and nervous system with a sensation exactly like that of scalding acid.

Tears squeezing from his eyes, the captain pulled back on the yoke. The plane, shuddering, brought its nose up. The air scream abated. The turbines settled down. They were soon flying level again.

"Jou may let go now, *señor,*" the captain gasped. "I have done as jou have asked."

"You through screwing around?" Remo demanded.

"Sí."

"You going to land the plane?"

"On my mother's honor."

"On the ground is all I care about," said Remo, returning to his seat. Chiun trailed him, saying, "Without me, where would you be at this exact moment?"

"Probably pounding a beat back in Newark," Remo said unhappily.

"That is not what I meant."

"You would be dead if it were not for the elegant Knives of Eternity which grace my perfect hands."

"Okay, I'd be dead. But I'm not growing my fingernails as long as Fu Manchu."

Chiun beat him to their row so Remo couldn't steal the window seat. When he saw that the wing was still attached to the plane, his bony fingers grasped the opposite wrist, and the verdant sleeves of his silk kimono closed over both hands.

After they got settled again, the stewardess came up and said, "Jou must pay for the seat belt jou broke."

Remo sighed. "How much?"

"Thirty dollars. American. We do not accept pesos."

"Figures. How much was the NAFTA tax?"

"Thirty dollars, but it is a coincidence."

Remo handed over three tens and noticed they went into the wicker basket labeled NAFTA.

"I never liked Mexico," Remo muttered.

"The House never lowered itself to working for them."

"Didn't you once tell me the House would have loved working for the Aztecs?"

"I lied. We would only have loved their gold, not their rulers."

"That's really convincing coming from someone who won't take his eyes off the wing because that's the time they pick to fall off. Unquote."

"It will happen to us some day. Mark my words."

When the Fasten Seat Belt sign came on, Remo tied his seat belt about his flat stomach like the sleeves of a sweater. Out the window the ring of mountains surrounding the Valley of Mexico loomed up like a jagged earthen wall.

Almost at once the plane shook as if buffeted by turbulence. Remo knew from past experience this was normal. Thermal updrafts from the valley below were constant.

But the buffeting grew violent. The Azteca Airlines plane dipped on one wing, and through the sealed window ports everyone could hear a thunderous rumble and roar.

"It is another *terremoto!*" a man screamed.

"That means *earthquake*," Chiun translated for Remo's benefit.

"Don't be ridiculous," Remo said. "Earthquakes shake the ground, not the air."

"It is an airquake!" the panicked passenger insisted.

"No," said the Master of Sinanju. "It is a volcano."

No sooner had the old Korean spoken the word than a cloud seemed to swallow the aircraft. The sky outside the window became a hideous smoky brown.

The emergency lights came on. Overhead compartments sprung open. Yellow plastic oxygen masks dropped down on their flexible tubes.

Chiun grabbed his, and Remo decided it was a good idea, so he followed suit.

"Ladies and gentlemen," the captain said in a fear-strangled voice. "I regret to inform jou that Mount Popocatepetl has erupted. We must divert to another airport."

The plane's engines began laboring and straining.

The 727 flew and flew through a realm of roiling denseness, like boiling liquid excrement. Nothing was visible beyond the portholes. Not even the wing-lights.

"Remo!" Chiun squeaked. "The wings are gone."

"If the wings were gone, Little Father, we'd be in a tailspin by now."

"Perhaps they are awaiting the most treacherous moment. Wings are sneaky that way. One never knows when they will choose to fall off."

"Remind me never to fly this airline again," Remo muttered.

"It is all the fault of NAFTA," the stewardess who had slid the length of the cabin said as she adjusted her foundation garments through her disheveled uniform.

"How is this NAFTA's fault?" Remo asked.

"NAFTA has angered the gods of old Mexico," she spit out the words with venom.

"That's ridiculous," said Remo.

Chiun laid a quieting hand on Remo's bare arm.

"Hush, Remo. Lest the gods of old Mexico hear your blasphemous words and wrench the wings from this mighty craft in their malevolent spite."

"Not you, too?"

"There is an old saying in my house. 'One may slay a king, but the wise assassin avoids treading on the bunions of the gods.'"

Remo lifted a skeptical eyebrow. "The *bunions* of the gods?"

Chiun arranged his kimono skirts absently. "That is the saying. I did not make it up. I merely report it."

All at once daylight broke. The plane emerged from the roiling brown clouds of ash to broad daylight as if passing from the twilight zone of dusk and dawn.

On either side the wings shone as if scoured clean by the hot ash.

"Good thing these windows don't open," Remo muttered, removing his oxygen mask.

Chiun nodded sagely. "The gods are not displeased with us. Good."

The captain came on the intercom again.

"Ladies and gentlemen, this is your *capitán* speaking. I am informed by the Mexico City tower that it is inadvisable to land for some time. We will divert to another city. I will now entertain offers as to the most popular city of your choice."

"What did he say?" Remo asked Chiun.

"Quickly! Offer him as much as is necessary to take us to our destination."

"Are you kidding?"

Looking back to where the other passengers were hastily pooling their funds in order to bid on the destination of their choice, Chiun hissed, "Hurry. Lest we are marooned in some godforsaken place."

"Godforsaken," said Remo, coming out of his seat, "just about describes every part of the Mexican experience."

Remo beat two businessmen and a nun to the cabin and shut the door behind him for privacy.

Recognizing Remo, the captain and copilot clapped their hands over their ears in self-defense.

Instantly the yoke tipped forward, and the aircraft went into another dive. Remo reached across, hauled it back and pried the captain's fingers from his ears.

Guiding by the wrists, he forced them to curl around the control wheel again.

"What is your wish, *señor?*" he gasped.

"I'm thinking of San Cristóbal de las Casas."

"San Cristóbal de las Casas is an excellent destination. Do jou not think so, Vergillio?"

The copilot, Vergillio, sat unhearing. Remo pried a hand off an ear so the captain could repeat his statement.

"*Sí*, San Cristóbal de las Casas is very excellent. But we must allow the other passengers to make their offer. It is the democratic way."

"It is the way of Mexico," agreed the captain.

"It's called institutional bribery," Remo countered.

"The way of Mexico," the captain repeated blandly.

Sighing, Remo said, "I'll top any offers."

"Done," the captain and copilot said in unison.

"You take Visa or Discover?"

"*Sí.*"

THE AIRPORT at San Cristóbal de las Casas, it turned out, was neither open nor large enough to accommodate a 727, but for five thousand dollars American the captain and his copilot were willing to risk it.

They dropped airspeed, the turbines spooling down, and lowered the landing gear.

They made a first pass, decided the runway was only a thousand yards too short and came around from the north.

The 727 set down perfectly, rolling and rattling across the weed-grown asphalt. The overhead bins shook. Three popped open, dropping luggage onto passenger heads. Everybody held on for dear life.

Just when it started to look like a good landing, the wings started coming off.

First it was the right wing. It struck a cypress tree and was instantly sheered off. All eyes went to the starboard side of the plane. Faces went white.

And so everyone except the Master of Sinanju missed the startling sight of the port wing as it was yanked free by another tree.

As it turned out, losing the wings was the best thing that could have happened. Passengers realized that when the lumbering cabin was suddenly bumping through what amounted to a lane in a dense green forest.

This went on for what seemed an eternity, but couldn't have been much more than a minute.

In the end the 727 didn't so much brake as run out of momentum.

"Welcome to the Lacadón forest," said the captain in a relieved voice. "Jou have survived another flight on Azteca Airlines. Thank jou and we hope that jou will fly with us again soon."

The cabin burst into applause.

The stewardess threw open the cabin door, and a wave of sultry heat came in, instantly overpowering the air-conditioning.

Remo got to the door first and looked out. There were no air stairs naturally. Below was soft soil. It supported a dense growth of forest that was a strange mixture of tropical jungle and pine forest. Firs jostled cypress trees and weird-looking palms.

Peering ahead, Remo noticed the nose of the 727 had stopped about twenty feet short of a bank of some trees he couldn't begin to classify, because he'd never seen bark so red and peeling.

The captain popped his head out the cabin door.

"Hokay?"

"Are you crazy? You crashed the plane for three grand! They're going to fire you."

"It does not matter. Since NAFTA, my salary equals twelve dollars American a day. On three thousand, I can retire. Happy landings, *señor*."

"You could have gotten us all killed, you know."

The copilot smiled with all of his teeth. "Next time, perhaps. *Adios*."

Remo dropped to the ground and, using the edge of his hand, started chopping away at the bole of a fir tree. He cut it on opposite sides the way lumberjacks did, and when he had the cut he wanted, he took up a position and gave the fir a single hard side-kick.

It splintered, toppling to fall parallel with the cabin.

It was no coincidence that the bole provided the perfect first step for the Master of Sinanju.

Chiun stepped off the plane and looked around. His face was a parchment mask.

"Not bad for a guy with short fingernails, huh, Little Father?"

"Do not forget my trunk," said Chiun, his voice dripping with ingratitude.

Remo's face fell.

"Next time whistle up your own air-stairs," he snapped.

"Next time," said Chiun, stepping off and settling to the ground like a tiny green mandarin making landfall after a long sea voyage, "we will not come to Mexico."

As they prepared to leave the airport, someone accosted them and tried to charge them for cutting down the fir tree. No one seemed overly concerned about the demolished plane, but the tree was another matter.

"Stuff it," said Remo.

The local authorities were summoned, and Remo found himself confronted by a knot of hard-eyed Mexican soldiers in wilted uniforms.

"Jou are under arrest," a sergeant announced.

Remo had one of Chiun's traveling trunks slung over one shoulder. It had been a major miracle to convince the old Korean to travel this lightly, so he wasn't about to complain. Normally the Master of Sinanju insisted that all seventeen steamer trucks accompany him during his foreign travels. This time Chiun had expressed an irrational fear that should America sink beneath the waves in their absence, their precious contents would be lost forever.

Only by personally promising to scour the sunken ruins of Massachusetts for the other sixteen had Remo prevailed. That settled, Chiun had ordered Remo to carry the trunk with the lapis lazuli phoenixes rampant against mother-of-pearl panels.

With infinite care, Remo lowered the trunk to the ground.

"Look, we don't want trouble," he said.

"You wish to avoid trouble, *señores?*"

"Always."

"That will be five hundred dollars American."

"In other words, you want a bribe?"

"We call it *la mordida.* Little favor."

"Five hundred isn't a little favor. It's highway robbery."

"Nevertheless, it will be five hundred dollars or a night in jail. Perhaps two."

Chiun regarded the soldiers with a cold disdain. "Do not pay these brigands, Remo."

"Careful, old one. Or jou may be shot attempting to escape."

"It is not I who will be attempting to escape if you do not step from my path, uniformed one," Chiun warned.

"I'll handle this," said Remo.

Stepping up to the *sargento*, Remo lowered his voice and said, "Can you say *'commotio cordis'*?"

"Eh?"

"If you can say *'commotio cordis'* three times fast, I'll give you five hundred each."

The three soldiers looked interested. They had watched Mexican versions of U.S. game shows where incredible amounts of money were given away simply for correct guesses to simple questions.

"Say this phrase again?" the *sargento* asked.

"Commotio cordis," said Remo.

"Como—"

They made a good effort. One of them almost got the second word out.

Remo reached out and, timing his blow to perfection, struck two of the soldiers' chests during the precise millisecond when their heart muscles were poised for the next beat. This moment was called the T-wave by physicians. Typically it lasted only 30 one thousandths of a second, and humans were completely unaware of this most vulnerable state of the heart muscle, when the cells electrically depolarize themselves before the next contraction.

But Remo was aware. He could hear the pause through the rib-sheathed chest walls. For him it was beyond timing now. It was sheer instinct. He struck swiftly, the chest walls slammed into the quiescent heart muscles and nature took her unforgiving course.

The two coughed, turned blue and collapsed, hearts beating wildly and out of control. Physicians called this ventricular fibrillation. Most people just said heart attack and let it go at that.

The third soldier was on the *o* of *cordis* when his T-wave started. Remo slammed his rib cage with the hard heel of his hand, and he pitched forward to join the agitated pile.

One by one their out-of-control heart muscles, unable to recover normal rhythm, surrendered and went still.

That left their Humvee free for the taking, so Remo carefully laid the trunk into the backseat and opened the door for the Master of Sinanju. Chiun settled into the seat. Remo took the wheel.

"You employed the Thunder Dragon blow," Chiun said. "Why did you call it *'commotio cordis'?*"

"*Commotio cordis* is Latin for *heart concussion,*" Remo explained. "I read about it in a newspaper article once."

"It is the Thunder Dragon blow. Remember that."

"A soldier by any other name wilts the same."

"That is not the saying."

"It's my version, okay?" And Remo sent the Humvee wheeling away to the town called Boca Zotz.

10

As Colonel Mauricio Primitivo of the Mexican federal army saw it, oppression of the indigenous peoples of Mexico had been a mistake most terrible.

It was a five-hundred-year old mistake. And now it had come back to haunt his proud but still-struggling nation.

The uprising in Chiapas was the result.

Oh, there had been uprisings before. Always they were put down harshly and severely. The Indians had always gone back to being the oppressed, and the lords of Mexico had returned to dutifully oppressing them.

It was actually quite a good system. Except it had gone on far too long.

"We should have exterminated them as the *norteamericanos* did their indigenous parasites," he said, pounding the table at Fonda del Refugio, an elegant restaurant in the Pink Zone of Mexico City. They were in the dim back dining room, where the powerful dined and discussed business that could not stand the light of day over sangria and chicken in chocolate sauce.

"There are still *indios* in America," his host corrected. His host wore mufti. But he sat like a military man. He was a very high-ranking general in the Interior Ministry. Alacran was his last name. General Jeronimo Alacran. No more than this did Colonel Primitivo know for certain.

"Yes, in harmless pockets called reservations. The greater portion of them were buried long ago with the genes of future generations that have never come to pass. That is what we should have done. Exterminate the dirty *indios*."

"Let us be politically correct in our speech," General Alacran said softly. "They are *los indígenos*."

The colonel swirled a collop of chicken in its piquant brown sauce as he nodded. "Of course."

"But who would harvest the coffee and the beans if this is done?" the general inquired.

"Those that remain. The totality of *los indígenos* are unkillable. If there were fewer of them, they could be more easily controlled. But there are so many that the men cross the border at will and work in America while the women stay behind to raise the unwanted children. Now the situation is worse. There are so many *indios*, there are more men than work to be done. They sit around idle, drinking pulque and mescal. And in their drunken idleness they turn to revolution time and again."

Primitivo downed the last of his sangria to quench the hateful thoughts troubling his fevered brain.

"And they will be put down again," General Alacran said.

"Not so easily. For now there are foreign media and meddlers from other nations. They will not sit idly by while we exterminate the vermin." Colonel Primitivo shook his heavy head. "It is too late. We are outnumbered."

"These are very interesting sentiments, Colonel. How would you like to go to Chiapas and deal with this unfortunate insurgency?"

"Gladly. But it is too late. I would not be allowed to do my duty. Look at the upstart Verapaz. His communiqués come out of the jungle to pollute our newspapers. His masked face is on every magazine cover now. Women swoon over it, though he may be as pocked of face as the dark side of the moon. He himself gives press conferences to foreign journalists. I say send me to one of these so-called press conferences disguised as a reporter and I will exterminate them all. Especially the *journalistas.*"

"That would be politically unacceptable. If Verapaz is murdered, there would be an international uproar. To say nothing of the problem of the dead *journalistas.*"

"Bah. I care not for politics. Only of my duty to Mexico. No, I must turn down your very tempting offer to go to Chiapas to kill Mayans and others of their ilk. If I succeed, I will be scapegoated. If I fail, I will be humiliated. Mark my words. Chiapas will be the Vietnam of Mexico. And all because the motherless ones who came before us had not the stomach to exterminate the *indios.*"

The general had first spoken to Colonel Mauricio Primitivo about this difficult duty in the spring after the first Chiapas uprising, when Verapaz had been on the cusp of becoming a hero to *mestizo* and *indio* alike.

Now, two springs later, the situation remained essentially unchanged. In stalemate. The new Mexican government, if anything, was more timid on the subject of Verapaz. They were in intense negotiations with the bandit with the jade green eyes. He was all but untouchable now, the repercussions of his assassination too delicate to risk.

The opportunity to deal correctly with him had been lost. At least until a true hombre once again took hold of the reins of power.

Then came the Great Mexico City Earthquake, which shook hacienda and hovel alike.

Colonel Primitivo's phone rang within the hour. It was the general who had first contacted him two springs earlier.

"Colonel, I bring your greetings from the capital."

"It stands?"

"It shakes. I myself am shaking now. I admit it. But my duty calls, so I must steel myself and move swiftly to deal with this crisis."

"How bad?"

"*Muy terrible.* Popo smokes like a bad cigar now. I fear an epic eruption. I need your help, Colonel Primitivo."

"I do not know how to fight volcanos, but I and my men will do whatever is asked of us."

"Then go to Chiapas and exterminate the renegade Verapaz."

"This order comes from *El Presidente?*"

"No, this comes from my lips to your ears. Not even God must hear these words."

"I understand."

"Within the hour, Verapaz has issued a communiqué. He is deserting the jungle and forests. His goal is nothing less than Mexico City—all Mexican cities ultimately."

"He is drunk with pulque and arrogance."

"He understands the central government has been plunged into a crisis from which it may never emerge. Victory may be his if steps are not undertaken. I am ordering you into Chiapas. Find and intercept this man. Kill him. Make it seem as if he perished in the earthquake. That way no embarrassment will attach itself to you or I or *El Presidente.*"

"I spit upon *El Presidente.*"

"That opportunity, too, may arise very soon," the general said dryly. "For all of Mexico is up for grabs, and it is incumbent upon the strong to crush the less strong with all of our might before we fall to the weak."

"I go to Chiapas. Subcomandante Verapaz has issued his last flowery communiqué."

"Go with God, Colonel. Just do not allow Him to witness what you do."

"Understood, General."

That very hour a column of tanks and APCs left Montezuma Barracks in Oaxaca at full speed, heading south into Chiapas, where destiny awaited Colonel Mauricio Primitivo.

Destiny lay in ambush for Subcomandante Verapaz, as well. But it was a different destiny. A cold, wormy one.

11

A funny thing happened to Alirio Antonio Arcila on the way to the revolution.

It was not so much funny as it was tragic. Yet it was also funny. There was no avoiding this. It was a great joke, a cosmic joke. The gods might have conceived such a joke, except Antonio did not believe in any gods, Mexican, Christian or otherwise.

His gods were Marx and Lenin and other dead white European males whose economic philosophy had seized the twentieth century by the throat.

Alirio Antonio Arcila was a Communist. He was a brother in spirit to Che and Fidel and Mao, and so ached to follow in their booted footsteps.

Then came Gorbachev. The Berlin Wall fell. It was a calamity. And the calamity was followed by other, more calamitous calamities. The Eastern Bloc disintegrated. The mighty USSR fragmented into the powerless CIS.

Just as Alirio Antonio Arcila was poised to reap the violent fruit of ten years spent planting the seeds of discontent in the Lacandón jungle, the international Communist movement was no more. There was no more communism, in fact. Democracy had gripped Moscow with its unshakable iron grip. Even the unbending gray mandarins in Beijing were embracing capitalism even as they clutched Mao's little red book.

And those who clung to the socialist path were overnight bereft of sponsors and funding. Havana became a basket case. Pyongyang an isolated embarrassment. Hanoi lurched into the capitalistic camp. And in Peru the Maoist Shining Path had been hurled reeling and broken, by an elected dictator into the mountains that gave them birth.

All was lost. All was for naught.

Except Alirio Antonio Arcila had been trained as a socialist revolutionary. He had no other talents, no marketable skills, no vocation. There was no other path to follow in life. He knew only revolution and its bloody talents.

So even though the cause was lost, there was no reason that he could think of not to throw a revolution anyway.

It was either that or take over his father's coffee plantation. Antonio would never do that. His father was an oppressor. Antonio would rather make futile revolution than become an oppressor like his evil father, who had amassed a fortune on the backs of illiterate peasants and sold his product to capitalists who in turn sold it to others at obscene profits in a cycle of exploitation without end.

For months after that last stipend had come, Antonio brooded in the jungle, thinking that all he needed was a cause. If only he had a cause.

But what cause?

Oh, he had convinced the Mayan peasants that their cause was liberation and economic justice. But those were only words. Antonio intended to liberate them only to deliver them into the hands of the new

Communist rulers of Mexico, of whom one would be no less than Alirio Antonio Arcila.

Then had come NAFTA.

He did not perfectly understand the North American Free Trade Agreement. It involved free trade, obviously. That equaled capitalism. Therefore, it was bad. If not evil.

And so he'd addressed his Maya on this looming evil.

"I have heard this day of a plot called NAFTA," he had told them. "It is a scheme to oppress you as never before."

They regarded him with their sad, stony eyes. Those eyes were the eyes of Mexico, full of soul-deep contradictions and conflicting emotions.

"In this new NAFTA world, the farms of the capital—I mean the *norteamericanos*—will be placed on the same footing as your meager corn and bean fields. This is fundamentally unfair. For they farm with fierce machines while you have but your strong backs and rude hoes. This is betrayal. Worse, this is treason. We must fight this unfairness."

The Maya heard these words and they nodded in their mute way. They were not men for talk. Talk wasted the breath. They knew that their allotted breaths were fewer than those who breathed the machine-fouled air of the cities. This, too, was unfair. But it was undeniable.

Besides, over the years Antonio dwelled among them, they had come to see their light-skinned patron and advisor with the quetzal green eyes as Kukulcan incarnate. According to legend, Kukulcan, the Plumed Serpent, had been a white man come from across the sea to lift up the Maya many *baktuns* ago.

He had given them the gifts of writing, agriculture and other high knowledge only to depart, vowing to return in a future time of great need.

It was obvious to the simple *indio* peasants that their benefactor was Kukulcan incarnate, returned as he had promised.

Antonio did nothing to dissuade them from this belief. After all, it had worked for Cortez when he arrived in Yucatán in the Aztec year called One Reed. He was thought by the original Mexicans to be Quetzalcoatl, the very same Plumed Serpent god, white of skin and heralding a new era, whose return in the next One Reed year had been prophesied by Aztec prophets.

Cortez did bring gifts, in his way. He ushered in the era of the Spanish conquest. The Aztecs were cast down into slavery. The Maya empire had by then fallen into ruin, the survivors retreating into the jungles to eke out simple agrarian lives.

The Maya equivalent of Quetzalcoatl, whom they called Kukulcan, had not returned in Cortez. In Antonio, they had their Kukulcan. And as he was their god incarnate, the word of Alirio Antonio Arcila was law.

The word of Lord Kukulcan was to resist NAFTA by force.

They took up their Uzis and their AK-47s that had been cached all over the jungle, cleaned off the rust-resisting Cosmoline and began training in earnest.

The Maya day of 2 Ik was selected because it corresponded with the 1 January 1994.

"If NAFTA passes, we will strike on 2 Ik," Antonio announced.

The Maya had accepted this. Kukulcan had spoken. His word was absolute. The demon NAFTA would not survive after that date, no matter how fearsome his fangs and talons.

On that day Antonio passed out proletariat red bandanas for the first time. It was a very cold day in the mountains above the lush forest canopy.

"Wear these to protect your faces from the cold and from *federalista* eyes," he said, drawing on a black ski mask with the hole cut before the mouth so that he could enjoy his one solace—a short-stemmed briar pipe.

"From this time forward you are *Juarezistas*. After this day your blood will ignite the jungle, as did the sacrifices of Benito Juarez, the first *indio* ruler of the Mexican republic, whose cause we now take up and in whose name we struggle. And from now on, I will call myself Subcomandante Verapaz, for my personal struggle is for true peace in Mexico. Our peace. No other peace will be acceptable."

The Maya accepted this with passive fatalism. Their lives were short and unhappy. Death came soon enough. They would not seek out death, but neither would they shrink from the bony embrace of Yum Cimil, Lord of Death.

On that first day they seized six towns. On the second day, 3 Akbal, the army descended, driving them out. Many were slain. Subcomandante Luz perished. As did Subcomandante Luna. The survivors slunk back to their mountain stronghold.

"We have failed, Lord Kukulcan," they told him, shame in their low voices. It was the third day, called 4 Kan.

"I am no lord, but your *subcomandante*. I cannot be your lord because I am but a *criollo*. A usurper. You are the Maya, the true lords of this jungle."

But they were beaten lords from the look of them.

It had been an abysmal failure. But because anything was better than working his father's coffee plantations, Antonio racked his brain for another way.

THE NEW WAY CAME to the Maya farm town of Boca Zotz in the form of *journalistas*. The cause was irretrievably lost, so Subcomandante Verapaz agreed to meet with them. Perhaps he could trade safe passage to the Guatemalan frontier in return for a few last defiant quotes.

At the appointed hour, he showed up in a jungle clearing, wearing his black ski mask, his pipe redolent of cannabis—a harmless affectation from his former bourgeois existence. Five bandana-masked *Juarezistas* surrounded him, fingers on triggers, dark, moody eyes alert.

The questions pelted Antonio like cast stones.

"Are you a *comunista?*"

"Never!"

"You are *indígena?*"

"With these eyes? No, I am not *indígena.*"

"Then why do you wage revolution?"

Antonio hesitated. He had prepared for this struggle for so long, the rote worker's slogans almost rose up from his throat even though they no longer had meaning. He swallowed them.

"I fight," he said after taking a long suck on his pipe, "I fight because this has been the struggle of my family for many generations."

The reporters frowned. They understood revolution, insurrections. But this was new.

At that point Antonio blurted out the flowery romantic words to cover the tracks that might lead to the Arcila family. But the *journalistas* were not satisfied with this.

"Tell us more," one invited.

"I am not the first Subcomandante Verapaz. My father was Subcomandante Verapaz before me. And my grandfather, his father, was Subcomandante Verapaz, stretching back I cannot tell how many generations. We took up the cause of righteousness, and consecrated our lives to it. In the name of all oppressed indigenous peoples, Subcomandante Verapaz wages war against oppression."

"Are you sure you aren't a *comunista?*"

"I have denied this. I am but the Verapaz of this generation. When I fall—and all my forebears eventually fell to their foes—my son will take up my gun and my mask and he will be the next Subcomandante Verapaz. Thus, I am unkillable and will never die."

At that point, camera flashbulbs began popping. His *Juarezista* bodyguards almost shot the head off a reporter until Antonio interceded.

The video cameras whirred, their glassy, greenish lenses capturing the dashing masked figure whose manly chest was crossed by bandoliers evocative of the romantic Mexican revolutionaries of the past.

When the press conference was over, Antonio melted back into his jungle cave, that night burning his black ski mask because he knew it was to death to wear it again. All Mexico would know him after this night.

It became truer than Antonio could ever envision.

His face was telecast throughout the world. His muffled head, jutting pipe and trademark soulful green eyes adorned magazine covers from Mexico City to Singapore.

He began to understand when more and more reporters came to visit him. At first he turned them all away. The revolution had sputtered out ignominiously. Chiapas was cordoned off, all escape routes blocked so that no *criollo* with green eyes could pass through alive. And besides that, he had no concealing Subcomandante Verapaz mask.

The entreaties continued to be carried to his jungle stronghold. Farmers by day who had been *Juarezistas* by night, bore the magazines with their glowing articles.

"You are a hero in Mexico City," he was told.

"What?"

"It is said, my lord, the women all adore you. There are toys bearing your likeness. Masks are sold and worn proudly. The students in the universities make speeches in your name. Pipe smoking is all the rage."

"Increíble," he muttered, reading furiously.

But it was true. The romantic fantasy he had spun had been accepted as truth. He was no longer a failed, causeless revolutionary, but a cultural hero to modern Mexicans. Just like Zapata or Villa or Kukulcan.

"What shall we convey to these reporters?" his right hand, a Mayan *guerrillero* named Kix, had asked.

"Tell them," proclaimed Alirio Antonio Arcila, aka Lord Kukulcan, aka Subcomandante Verapaz, "that in return for one dozen black ski masks, I will agree to another press conference."

The masks arrived with astonishing alacrity. Antonio took one, with a knife slashing a hole for his pipe stem, and then distributed the remainder among his *compañeros.*

"From now on, we will all be Subcomandante Verapaz," he proclaimed.

And his Maya wept with pride, never imagining that by donning these masks, they greatly increased the odds that one of them would take an assassin's bullet intended for their leader.

The press conferences became a monthly ritual. Money poured in. Arms. Supplies of other kinds. A revolution that might have been recorded by history as the last sputtering gasp of Third World Communist insurgency was reborn as the first truly indigenous revolution of the century.

Learned articles and dissertations were penned to analyze the phenomenon of a spontaneous revolution with no political or social entity motivating it. The first postmodern revolution, the *New York Times* dubbed it.

And no one suspected the true leader of all the *Juarezistas* who continued to fight and spill their blood in the sacred cause of furthering Alirio Antonio Arcila's celebrity—and incidentally forestalling the hated day he would return to the family coffee plantation and concede to his despised father that he had been right all along.

The successes came often after that. Minor skirmishes were hailed in the press as major engagements. When the old president of Mexico was chased from power, it was hailed as a *Juarezista* victory. When his handpicked successor was assassinated after expressing veiled pro-*Juarezista* sentiments, it lent legitimacy to the cause. And when a new, more liberal candidate replaced him, it was also seen as a *Juarezista* victory.

Every advance for the people and setback for the lawful government was viewed in the light of a handful of Maya *pistoleros* led by the unemployed son of a coffee grower, and although no true progress was made on the battlefield, the mere fact that Subcomandante Verapaz struggled on despite every attempt to capture or kill him added luster to the growing legend.

In the end the federal government declared a unilateral cease-fire and offered to engage in peace talks. They would never give Subcomandante Verapaz any political concessions, of course. But in declaring a one-sided peace, they signaled that Verapaz had grown too great to stop with mere bullets. In death, he could only grow more powerful. He would be left alone if he caused no problems so great it threatened Mexico City.

But Antonio had not spent ten years in the jungle eating bad tortillas and drinking stagnant water only to spend the rest of the century doing so. Ignoring the peace talks, he stepped up his campaign of words and communiqués.

When he had forced the current governor of Chiapas to step down on behalf of a man whom he had blessed, Antonio began to consider the possibility that while he might never conquer Mexico, it was perhaps possible to seize a measure of political control of events beyond Chiapas.

The advent of the Great Mexico City Earthquake all but made that an inevitability.

After all, he was no longer Alirio Antonio Arcila now. Nor really Subcomandante Verapaz. He was Lord Kukulcan, a god sheathed in flesh who had united the polyglot peoples of Mexico in their blind hero-worshiping.

And most rewarding of all, it was tacitly acknowledged in the capital that it would be politically unacceptable to exterminate the people's hero.

The road of conquest had been swept clear.

12

As he followed his god through the cracked and broken streets of Mexico City, Rodrigo Lujan had stripped off the confining necktie. He did not care that the streets lay buckled and cracked all around. Nor that mighty office towers tilted and shed their faces like so many false masks. They were the past. He walked with the future. He walked with serpent-skirted Coatlicue whose remorseless tread seemed to make the Valley of Mexico shudder under her petrifying tread.

Let no one say the word *aftershock*. It was Coatlicue, also called Tonantzin—*Our Mother*—who made the very ground tremble.

He followed her closely down Anillo Periferico, toward the southern outskirts. Toward the mountains. Beyond the mountains lay freedom. Beyond the mountains lay the rich and fecund soil of the Zapotec century to come.

Sturdy Zapotec women dwelt to the south, Lujan knew. In Oaxaca. And when they beheld him approach with the goddess Coatlicue, they would offer themselves—no, throw themselves at him.

He, Rodrigo Lujan, would beget a race of new Zapotec warriors that would sweep across the face of

Mexico to usher in a new sun and a brighter tomorrow.

As he flung away the hated confining suit coat, he could taste their chaste, willing kisses.

As they walked, others followed in their wake.

Lujan's great heart seemed to burst with pride to see them follow like an army of ants that know sugar lies near.

The city of twenty million had been clogged with peasants from the countryside. There were the hook-nosed Aztecs, the cross-eyed Maya and the barbarian Chichimecs with their thick bodies. The Olmecs were no more. No man knew what had become of them. The Toltecs had long before been assimilated.

But Zapotecs and Mixtec were plentiful.

And all of them, whether Zapotec, Maya or Chichimec, fell in behind the striding behemoth that was Coatlicue, crying, sobbing, dancing, their heart pounding with joy.

Some threw themselves before her juggernaut form, praying, begging guidance, seeking deliverance as the city of wonder broke and splintered all around them.

Her tread broke their prostrate skulls, splintering their living bones as if they were kindling. They died, their souls liberated. They died *indio* and so died happy.

Lujan wept proud tears to see their blood run. It was like the old days he had never known. Before the Spanish had spilled Zapotec blood and mingled their own with the blood of the women who survived to beget the modern *mestizo* people of Mexico.

Passing a shattered peasant woman, Lujan paused and reached into the raw kindling that was her rib cage to extract her heart, still warm and beating. And walking backward behind his goddess, he held the dripping, pinkish organ over his head for his growing retinue to behold.

"Behold, children of old Mexico. See your future. The day of the machine is over. The tyranny of the *chilangos* is over. Time has turned in on itself like a serpent devouring its own tail. A new era dawns. I am Zapotec. I call upon all of my blood and related blood to follow me into the glorious past which now stretches out before us."

And they did. In growing numbers.

The *chilangos* were struck dumb by the sight. Dazed and whelmed by earthquake, they had shrunk from the sight of the oppressed of the earth throwing off their yoke. Ladino clothes were cast off. Men marched in their underwear or nothing at all. Women walked bare of breast and unashamed of their rich *indio* skin.

At times police officials, seeing this affront to their so-called civilization that had brought sick air and a quiet desperation of spirit, fell on them.

But their guns held but handfuls of bullets. Some fell. And after they expended their futile lead missiles, they were fallen upon and torn limb from limb by the blood-crazed crowd.

Soon many walked holding the pulsing, bleeding hearts of the oppressor in their hands.

And before them lumbered Coatlicue, implacable, remorseless, all but oblivious to the revolution that she led, her only words the same single-minded incantation droned over and over again: *"survive, survive, survive . . ."*

13

The Extinguisher was making wicked excellent time.

The LAV's lightness was an advantage. It may have been the military equivalent to a Volvo, but it covered road like a speeding jeep. Its light frame meant gasoline went farther, too.

The towns and villages along the Pan American Highway zipped by. No one stopped or questioned him. For the Extinguisher drove a Mexican police vehicle. No one questioned the Mexican Federal Judicial Police.

Out here the Federal Judicial Police were the only law that mattered.

Now with night falling, even that thin brown line of authority was fading. The law of the jungle was supreme.

That was fine with the Extinguisher. The law of the jungle was his kind of law. Of all the predators in the jungle, he was the most predatory of them all.

Eventually his gas ran out. There were two spare jerricans, which he used to replenish the tanks. That bought him another hundred miles. But by the time the lights of Tapanatepec came into view, the LAV was bone-dry.

Out here gas stations didn't exactly rub shoulders fighting for business. It was the end of the line.

The Extinguisher flicked on the dome light and checked his maps. They were throwaway maps, ripped from magazines, but they were good enough.

Also torn from magazines were photographs of his quarry, Subcomandante Verapaz. Since he had made good time, the Extinguisher had time to refresh his battle memory regarding the foe he sought.

The pictures showed a jaunty man in a black ski mask. The soulful poet's eyes were the same in every picture. That was important. That meant while many wore the black ski mask of the Benito Juarez National Liberation Front, there was only one Subcomandante Verapaz. The man may have doubles, but they did not pose for the press to confuse the issue.

Well, that was Verapaz's mistake. If he didn't understand the fine art of confusing the enemy, that was his tough break.

When they at last came face-to-face, the Extinguisher would know those jungle green eyes. There would be no mistaking them ever.

And when it came time to extinguish them, well, that was what the Extinguisher did.

14

The ground had grown quiescent when the retinue of Coatlicue, now thousands strong, had passed through the mountains.

The aftershocks came, making the belly quail, but at greater intervals. Popocatepetl still smoked. The sky hung brown and brooding, and the air below was filled with warm ash. Men, women and children captured the falling benedictions between their hands like children cavorting in their first snowstorm. They smeared their fleshy, half-naked bodies with the pungent unguent in blasphemous parody of their cast-off Ash Wednesday rituals.

The too-warm air awoke the spring wildflowers early. Birds roosted silent and pensive in the trees. Now night fell. The first night of the new sun. The night after which all nights would be forevermore changed.

"We must stop to rest, Coatlicue," said Rodrigo Lujan, walking backward before his goddess. He wore a cloak trimmed in rabbit fur over a cotton girdle that protected his manly loins. The tyranny of confining garments lay in his past, along with his necktie and shoes.

"Survival dictates continued flight. The terrain is too exposed here. And I am presently unable to assimilate another form."

"Nothing can happen to you now, Coatlicue. The ground has stopped shaking."

"Seismic activity has entered a quiescent phase. There is every reason to assume it will resume anew. Aftershocks continue. Continued survival necessitates seeking stable ground."

"Your followers need rest. They have marched behind you all day. Now they require rest and food."

"I do not require followers."

"But what is a god without followers? It is their secret prayers which have awakened you. It is their unheard yearnings that have warmed the many stone hearts upon your breast."

"I had elected to remain quiescent until my foes had ceased to exist, which I estimate would transpire in approximately 60.8 years at the latest. During my inactive state, I attempted to complete all self-repairs possible. This task is ongoing. The seismic disturbance triggered my self-preservation override. That function is presently being executed."

"Stop, Coatlicue. Stop. You must allow us to sacrifice in your name. It will make you stronger."

One serpentine head rolled to fix him with its weird stone orbs.

"How will sacrifice make me stronger?"

"It is the way of Coatlicue. Your womanly strength comes from human sacrifice. Human sacrifice empowers your hearts, feeds your people and keeps the universe running."

"I must keep moving if I am to survive."

And head retracting, Coatlicue lumbered on.

Lujan skipped around to her side, realizing that if he stumbled she would stomp him into a mass of jelly under her cruel tread. That was why he loved her so. She cared not for her subjects. Her subjects must worship her, not the other way around.

"We are yours to command, O Coatlicue. Do you not understand? Do with us as you please. Break our backs, crush our thin skulls, we will follow you anywhere."

Coatlicue made no reply to that.

"O Coatlicue, Devourer of Filth, do you not know that there is safety in numbers?"

"I am the only one of my kind. There is no other than I."

"Yes. Yes. You are the exalted one. No one is greater than Coatlicue. Not that Aztec Quetzalcoatl. Not Kukulcan. Not even Huitzilopochtli, who is your true son. All are less than fleas beneath your cruel shadow."

Coatlicue walked on, unheeding and unconcerned. It stirred Rodrigo Lujan's passions to see her walk so proud and unmoved.

Then out of the west came a trio of federal army helicopter gunships, Gatling guns and rocket rods hanging off them like barbed scorpion spines.

"Coatlicue! Behold! The *chilango* army has come to defeat you."

Coatlicue stopped. Her serpent heads lined up parallel to one another until both regarded the approaching gunship stonily.

No flicker of emotion showed in those basalt slits.

"Coatlicue. Listen to me," Lujan pleaded. "They will soon attack. Let us be your shields."

"Yes. Be my shields."

"Command us to be your shields."

"I command you to be my shields."

And grinning, Rodrigo Lujan turned to his retinue. Truly, it was Coatlicue's retinue. But the authority to command them had been conferred upon him.

"Come. Come form a human shield. Coatlicue needs protection from the *chilango* army."

And they came. The men, the women, the sunbrowned children. They formed a circle that was many people deep. Some climbed atop Coatlicue to shield her stone flesh with their soft brown skins.

"Shoot, army of *chilangos!*" cried out Rodrigo Lujan. "Shoot if you dare! You will never harm our stone-hearted mother."

And the lead helicopter broke off from the others to make its first clattering pass.

It was armed with side-mounted Gatling guns. The multiple-barreled tubes began spinning. Everyone could see them spin.

The hot bullets came like a hard, remorseless rain.

The screams that lifted from the throat of the army of High Priest Rodrigo Lujan were screams of liberation. Liberation from oppression, liberation from poverty and liberation from earthly toil.

The bodies dropped from Coatlicue's shoulder and head like spoiled fruit. They ran as red as pomegranates, as bloody as crushed tomatoes, their juices forming scarlet pools at the unmoved feet of Coatlicue.

All around her the *indios* fell. The bodies formed stepping stones for others to scramble to take their place.

"Yes, yes. Fight to protect Coatlicue, the mother of us all. Come and offer yourself. Liberation is ours! Victory is ours. *Mañana* is ours!"

The first antitank rocket left its pod in a bloom of smoky flame. The screaming device sped toward them unerringly. Its speed was breathtaking.

Men forming a human pyramid clawed one another in their heated desire to be the first to absorb the coming blow. They slithered over one another like brown sweaty earthworms.

When the rocket struck, it exploded a vertical cone of human flesh in all directions.

The cone simply vanished, only to reform in a thudding rain of arms, legs, head and separated torsos.

"*¡Magnifico!*" cried Rodrigo Lujan. "You have done it! You have saved Coatlicue from the rocket!"

Coatlicue stood as before, her double-serpent head parted, one tracking the overflying helicopter, the other focused on the third one, which hung back, poised to let fly more blood and destruction.

"*The meat machines are protecting me,*" she said.

"Yes. We will all die if it takes that."

"*I command you all to die to preserve my survival,*" intoned Coatlicue in an emotionless and very masculine voice. Rodrigo Lujan loved masculine women. He turned to his followers.

"Do you hear? We are commanded to die. To die is glorious. Let us all die to preserve Our Mother," proclaimed Rodrigo Lujan, who had to jump to one side so the stampede of *indios* could rush up and take the place of one dead and he would have an excellent view of the slaughter.

It was better than a bullfight. In the bullring, the bull dies or the matador is gored. There is only so much blood. A spot or two. A puddle at most.

Here it was a whirlwind of blood and carnage.

The *indios* took their places. They formed a dome of flesh. Like locusts, they swarmed over their Mother Goddess until her stone lines were no longer visible. They clung to her and to one another until Coatlicue resembled an upright beetle covered in ants.

The next rocket scored a direct hit. Hot metal flew. Flesh and bone turned to shrapnel. The screams were terrible yet beautiful. It was so incredibly Mexican. It was the most Mexican sight Rodrigo Lujan had ever beheld.

More bullets and then more rockets came, to snap and crump at the human anthill. And the more death gnawed, the more the *indios* strove to join it.

"Death!" they sang. "Bring us death so Coatlicue may live. We live through Coatlicue. Our blood illuminates the world!"

"Your blood illuminates the universe!" Rodrigo Lujan shouted to the dark, impersonal heavens as he crouched by the shoulder of the road, his bare skin now red from the rain that was not rain.

At length the helicopter gunships depleted themselves of missiles.

Perhaps it was also that the pilots had become sickened by the slaughter. For whatever reason, they broke formation, each retreating in a different direction.

"We have done it!" Rodrigo Lujan shouted to the cold stars above. "We have succeeded! We are Zapotecs!"

"And Aztecs," a man reminded.

"Maya," another said.

"I am Mixtec."

"We are all brothers in blood," Rodrigo said generously.

"And sisters," a woman said, licking a smear of blood off her naked forearm.

Others, seeing this and remembering tales of ancestral blood sacrifice, began eyeing the dead not as fallen human beings to be buried reverently in the earth but as something else.

The hungry look in his fellow *indios'* eyes gave Rodrigo Lujan the courage to say and do what in the past he could only imagine down in his deepest Zapotec dreams.

"Coatlicue has reminded us. We are no longer men. We are not women. We are not human. We are her servants. We are meat machines. And if we are but machines made of meat, we may partake of other machines whose meat is no longer of use to them."

And to show the truth of his words, Rodrigo Lujan picked up the severed arm that had only minutes before belonged to a comely Maya maiden and took a ferocious bite out of her warm bicep with his strong white Zapotec teeth.

15

Remo made good time rolling down Highway 195 in
Chiapas State until he ran into a Mexican federal
army patrol.

"Uh-oh," he muttered as the patrol rounded a
bend in the road.

Beside him the Master of Sinanju said, "Pretend
we are innocent of any suspicion. They will not see
us."

Eyeing Chiun's emerald-and-ocher kimono, Remo
said, "I have a better idea."

He floored the Humvee. It surged ahead.

The oncoming armored column consisted of a toylike LAV followed by two light tanks. It slithered up
the winding, mountainous road.

"We can outrun these guys," Remo said confidently.

As he accelerated, the Master of Sinanju reached
out to hold on to the swaying machine. His balance
was perfect. He could have remained comfortably
seated through an ordinary turn. But the Master of
Sinanju was familiar with his pupil's driving. He
knew what was coming and didn't care to be flung
from the vehicle.

Remo took the corner on two wheels. The narrow-
ness of the road made that mandatory. Jerking the

wheel hard to the right, he brought the wide Humvee all the way up on its right tires.

It was an impossible maneuver. Low-slung vehicles can't run up on two wheels unless they are out of control.

In a sense, Remo had thrown the heavy machine out of control. It would have crashed. No question of that. But Remo was master of his own body and balance, and as long as he could control that, he could control the hurtling juggernaut that was the Humvee.

At the apex of the turn, the Humvee was canted at an extreme perpendicular, running on rims of rubber. Chiun turtled his head between his thin-boned shoulders to protect it.

"Okay now," Remo said tightly.

In unison, they shifted left. The Humvee wobbled on its spinning tires, then like a gyroscopically controlled toy began righting itself in a smooth descent that looked like gravity taking hold but was really Sinanju.

When the left-side tires touched asphalt, Remo let the vehicle freewheel a hundred yards, then floored it again.

Behind them the armored column was laboriously turning around.

"They will never catch up to us," Chiun said with satisfaction.

"Not in a million years," Remo agreed.

A whistling came from behind, arced over their heads and landed with a bang that threw up dirt and clods of red soil.

They heard the cannon detonation somewhere in the middle of the whistle.

"They are shooting at us," Chiun remarked.

"Are they crazy? They don't know who we are. We could be on their side, or anyone."

"Yes, anyone driving a pilfered army jeep."

"They call them Humvees now."

"They are trying to stop their Humvee with whistles," said Chiun as another shell screamed over their heads. This one slammed into the road before them. It erupted in a shower of dirt and asphalt chunks.

Remo eased to a halt. Looking back over his shoulder, he threw the Humvee into reverse and stepped on the gas.

The machine responded, barreling back up the road and into the teeth of a tank gun.

"Why are you driving the wrong way?" Chiun asked without evident concern in his voice or face.

"Because I'm hungry, aggravated and most of all pissed off."

"And because of these temporary inconveniences, you have decided to commit suicide and are taking me with you?"

"I left out one thing."

"And what is that?"

"I know something these guys don't."

"Yes?"

"The effective range of a tank gun."

Remo stopped the Humvee two hundred yards short of the booming tank gun. A shell whistled overhead. Their eyes tracked it as if it were a silvery painted balloon floating by on a brisk wind.

A second shell boomed past, to join the one before.

Both tore up the road well beyond the Humvee. The detonations came only seconds apart, the second shell dispersing the dust cloud made by the first.

"If they want to knock us out with that thing, they'll have to back up another six hundred yards."

"And if they do?"

"We'll back up with them, but that won't happen."

"Why not?"

"Because in another minute they'll be out of shells."

It happened sooner than that.

No more shells boomed forth. Instead, the turret was popped, and a handful of Mexican soldiers armed with stubby Heckler & Koch machine guns came trotting up the road.

"I guess this is where we get personal," Remo said, leaving his seat.

Chiun also exited the vehicle.

The approaching soldiers fixed them in their sights and called, *"¡Manos arriba!"*

"You catch that, Little Father?"

"He is saying 'Stick them up.'"

"Must mean our hands," said Remo throwing up his hands because Chiun had taught him it brought the enemy closer.

It didn't work this time.

From the light tank a commanding voice called out one ripping word. *"¡Disparen!"*

Chiun started to say, "That means—"

The soldiers lit up their weapons, but Remo had already spotted their trigger fingers turning white the moment before the muzzle began flashing.

Chiun faded left. Remo dropped into a sudden crouch so the first vicious burst could pass harmlessly over his head.

They started moving in on their attackers.

There were only three. Their weapons had a high rate of fire, and clips began running empty.

It takes almost as much time to extract an empty clip and ram a fresh one into the receiver as it does to empty the first clip to begin with, Remo knew.

That was plenty of time when shooting at the unarmed or engaged in sporadic firefights from shelter. But it was fatally long when facing two Masters of Sinanju.

Remo arrowed up and ahead when the empty clip started dropping free. Less than a second transpired.

He had cleared the halfway point when the empty clip clinked to the roadway. He made a fist.

The soldier was whipping out a second clip from a belt pouch, and his speed was good. He wasn't taking chances even though he was trying to shoot an unarmed foe who had surrendered on command.

At the exact moment the soldier's fingers gripped the fresh clip, Remo's fist started up from his belt line.

It was a short blow. It struck the hovering gun barrel, which cracked off and jumped into the soldier's gaping mouth. The mouth shut reflexively.

It would have been comical except the metal fragment kept going, taking out the cervical vertebrae in the neck via a newly excavated exit wound.

The soldier dropped, and Remo turned to deal with a second soldier, who was popping bullets one at a time in an effort to conserve ammunition.

One at a time was easy. Remo struck a pose, making a teapot handle with one crooked arm so the first round had an empty space to pass through. The soldier kept trying to correct his aim, but Remo corrected his stance each time.

Stubbornly the soldier kept trying to perforate Remo's exposed chest, but the bullets only managed to speed by past his inner elbow. His face grew dark with rage as he put out snarling round after snarling round, wondering why his bullets insisted upon hitting a triangular patch of empty air instead of his taunting target. A triangle that seemed to grow in size with each shot fired through it.

He never realized the triangle was growing in size because he was so concentrated on his task he didn't sense the approach of two-footed doom.

"Can you say 'mandibular dislocation'?" Remo asked.

The soldier's response was to clench his teeth and redirect his weapon in Remo's direction.

So Remo showed him the harmless palm of his open hand before it slapped his jaw off its hinges to land in the dirt like a fresh-cut lamb chop.

When the soldier's remaining face hit the road, his dangling tongue hissed as it came into contact with a hot shell casing. He moaned.

Stepping up, Remo put him out of his misery with a hard heel that opened his skull like a cantaloupe.

He turned just in time to watch Chiun make a point about correct grooming. The Master of Sinanju was methodically flaying his antagonist.

The flayee seemed unaware of his plight at first. It was hard not to notice elongated strips of one's own flesh as they came off in long, thin peels, but the soldier's mind was obviously elsewhere.

Mistaking Chiun for a pushover, the soldier had dropped his submachine gun and pulled his combat knife out. It was a bad error in judgment. Chiun might have put him down with a quick blow otherwise, but the soldier gave him an irresistible opportunity.

"We don't have all day," Remo called over as the Master of Sinanju deflected a knife thrust and stripped the soldier's forearm skin on the return.

The soldier started to notice he was losing strips of hide. But he was game. He shifted hands. Chiun obligingly shifted hands, too.

The rest was a forgone conclusion. It was only one knife against ten fingernails.

Chiun extended a deadly sharp fingernail and parried every blow. The clash of tempered steel and flexible nail sounded like metal on horn. The thin, bamboolike nail gave just enough not to break.

The blade gave not at all. That was its undoing.

In the middle of a flurry of parries, the blade just broke.

The soldier heard the brittle snap and mistook the sound for imminent victory.

Grinning, he took a step back, preparing to plunge the blade into the old Korean's thin chest.

Then he noticed his blade was not sticking out from the handle anymore. A comical expression crossed his face. He looked down the way a man looks down when he hears the clink of a quarter falling out of his pocket.

The Master of Sinanju floated into the opening and inserted his fingernail directly into the man's navel.

Chiun turned his hand like a key.

The soldier's feet left the ground in his torment. He screamed and wailed, and as Remo stood off to one side with his arms folded, tapping a foot impatiently, the Master of Sinanju looked over his shoulder to see that Remo was paying attention.

Remo made a snap-it-up motion.

And Chiun turned the key the other way.

If right was pain, then left was oblivion. The soldier made a disordered pile of khaki at the Master of Sinanju's feet.

Padding back, Chiun made a show of displaying his bloodless nail, blowing on it the way a Western gunfighter blew gunsmoke from the muzzle of his Peacemakers.

And that was the end of the grooming lesson intended for Remo's benefit.

"Show-off," said Remo.

"I merely demonstrated techniques that will cease to be practiced if the next Reigning Master continues on the path of stubbornness."

The muttering light tank started up. It clanked toward them. The steel tracks rolled over the fallen, breaking their bones and shredding dead flesh.

Remo and Chiun patiently watched their oncoming doom.

At the last moment they casually stepped out of the way of the steel hulk, each going in a separate direction.

The driver was not happy with this. Jockeying the vehicle, he attempted to follow the Master of Sinanju. Walking backward, Chiun led him toward the side of the road.

Meanwhile, Remo slipped up to the back and gave one spinning track a hard kick.

The tank rolled off its track, leaving it behind like a discarded serpent of segmented steel.

After that the tank rolled in slow impotent circles.

"Jou are under military arrest, *señores!*" the driver said angrily once he got his steed stopped. He was peering out from a crack in his half-opened hatch.

"What's that?" Remo asked.

"I said, 'Jou are under military arrest.' "

"Can't hear you over the echo. You'll have to come out."

The soldier eased the hatch higher to see up the road. The rest of his column had continued on, thinking he had the situation under control. Now they were too far away to help him out of his predicament.

"I am not coming out," he said flatly.

"You can't arrest us until you come out," Remo said firmly.

"Jou are under arrest anyway."

"Fine. We're under arrest. We'll see you later. Come on, Little Father. This guy is too chicken to arrest us."

"I am not chicken! Jou come back here. At once!"

"Make us," taunted Chiun.

The tank driver popped his hatch all the way and came out clutching a Belgian-made FAL rifle.

"See? I am not afraid of *gringos*. As I say, jou are under arrest."

"Guess he's got the drop on us, Little Father."

"We are captured." And Chiun shook his aged head in mock defeat.

The soldier advanced, and Remo and Chiun awaited him, their hands loose-fingered by their sides.

"Stand steel!"

"I think that means *stand still,*" said Chiun.

"Jou are under arrest."

"You wouldn't know where we can find Subcomandante Verapaz?" asked Remo.

"Jou are *Juarezista?*"

"No. Verapaz owes us something."

"What is that?"

"His life."

"Hah! I do not know where the masked one is. But jou are both under military arrest."

"And you are under cardiac arrest," returned Remo.

"¿Que?"

The soldier didn't see Remo's hand come up like a striking serpent that threw his rifle skyward. Nor did he feel the malletlike fist of the Master of Sinanju strike his rib cage over his wildly beating heart.

The soldier felt the air go out of his lungs and his heart go into overdrive. Then he fell onto his back and lay there jittering until the heart muscle burst from the strain.

"That is how the Thunder Dragon blow is properly delivered," Chiun said to Remo as they walked back to the waiting Humvee.

"I'll take that over Fu Manchu fingernails any day."

"The day will come when the lack of talons will be your undoing."

"Not as long as I have you by my side, Little Father."

"That day, too, is coming," Chiun said aridly.

Remo said nothing. It was the truth. Nobody lived forever. Not even a Master of Sinanju.

16

The president of the United States of Mexico had never seen such times. He had never heard of such times. His beloved Mexico had suffered much in times past. She had suffered incredibly. Sometimes, during the centuries since the conquest, it seemed that she was cursed to endure endless cycles of hope and desperation, desperation and hope. Every time the golden sun came within reach, she was cast down into perdition. Each time she had sunk into the lowermost depths of Hades, a ray of light would filter down to stir that cruel demon hope once again.

The straining toward the sun would resume, and so would the casting down into torment.

It was *muy* Mexican. It was quintessentially Mexican.

The president of Mexico knew that conundrum now. He felt it keenly as he paced his ruined office in the National Palace, fielding the frantic telephone calls as he saw through the shattered windows the city that was his capital lying in ruins under an ashy shroud.

It was a gray city now. Its whiteness was all gone. It was like the end of the world. Pompeii must have resembled this landscape. But Pompeii had never suffered so before being extinguished.

Mexico City suffered interminably, and the boon of extinction refused to come over it.

The initial earthquake had been the worst ever. Aftershocks ran as high as 6.9 on the Richter scale. This number was repeated over and over into his numbed ears. No one could say what that meant. Damage was extensive. Many of the same buildings that had been weakened in the 1985 convulsion were crushed once more. The dead were beyond counting.

Then after the earth had settled down, Popocatepetl had erupted in warning, and the earth shook anew.

Buildings that tottered precariously had fallen into rubble. The survivors, trapped but awaiting rescue, had been snuffed of all life. Fires not yet banked had roared anew.

Then came the ash.

Mercifully it had cooled somewhat while descending. It burned hair and blistered flesh, but did not consume. There were scattered fires as a result. But people could breathe the brown air if they held wet cloths to their faces. They could see if they blinked often enough.

The shroud of gray covered everyone and everything.

There was no escaping it for long because the aftershocks resumed soon after. People who had fled into their homes seeking shelter soon flowed back into the streets to brave the ashen rain rather than be crushed by stone and concrete and stucco.

And the fear that clutched at every heart took the form of an unanswerable question: Will Mount Popo truly erupt this time, raining lava and fire and meteors of death?

Meanwhile, the direct-line telephone to the National Center for the Prevention of Disaster kept ringing.

"Excellency, we have no power in San Angel."

"Excellency, there are looters in the Zona Rosa."

"Excellency, what do we do?"

To each of these pleas the president of Mexico could only offer soothing words of encouragement while inwardly cursing the cruel fate that had granted him the ultimate political power he had sought all of his adult life, only to precipitate the avalanches of NAFTA, devaluation, inflation, unemployment, rebellion and now earthquake upon his insufficient shoulders. It was more than his predecessor could have imagined. If only, he reflected, these things had transpired on the watch of the Bald One, now enjoying a comfortable but undeserved exile in the United States.

Then came a call that seemed to be delirium given voice.

"Excellency, this is General Alacran."

"Yes, General."

"Coatlicue walks again."

"What is this?"

"The stone statue. From the museum. You will recall the rumors of her previous escape."

The president did. Vaguely. There had been whispers that the great idol had disappeared from the Museum of Anthropology only to be found at Teotihuacán some time later, broken and shattered. It had been a national treasure in a nation in which the dominant culture and the subservient culture had been smelted together in a kind of schizophrenic amalgam.

"The city lies is ruins and you talk to me of statuary? We will find it later—if there is a later."

"She is not missing, Excellency. For I have found her."

"Then what is the problem, Alacran?"

"She is on the Pan American Highway. She is walking. She is leading a veritable army of *indios*. They walk half-naked and singing, casting their crucifixes under the feet of the idol."

"The stone statue walks like a man?"

"No, Excellency. Like a god. It is like nothing you can imagine. If my sainted mother, who was Aztec, could see it now, she would swear that the old gods of Teotihuacán had returned to this land."

"You are drunk!" the president accused. "Are you drunk?"

"Before God, I am not drunk. I have film. Cameras do not hallucinate."

"If the earthquake has liberated the old gods, then that is beyond the scope of my duties. I preside over a nation of men and must see to their mortal needs. I will view this film another time. Thank you for your report."

"There is more, Excellency."

"Speak. I listen."

"I ordered rocket attacks against this walking Coatlicue."

"Why?"

"Because I do not believe in the gods of old Mexico. Thus, I surmised it was something to be suppressed."

"Pray continue."

"The antitank rockets failed. The machine guns were to no avail, either."

"How can this be?"

The *indios* threw themselves before this living Coatlicue with great abandon. They were slaughtered by the rockets and machine-gun bullets. You should have seen the blood. *¡Madre!* It is river. And the flesh and the bones. They litter the highway as if it were the road to a slaughterhouse."

"Enough," said the president, sickened by the things his dark Mexican imagination brought before his eyes.

"The *indios* worship Coatlicue. They will do anything for her. And they are thousands strong. This is a dire security threat. As even now the *subversivo* Verapaz is reported headed this way."

"Yes, yes. I see. Tell me, General. What do the *indios* do at this moment?"

"They feast."

"Where do they find food on the highway?"

"They find food among the slain," said the general, whose voice very suddenly sounded sickened, as well.

"If they move, inform me."

"And if they do not?"

"If they do not, we will deal with them some other way than slaughter. There is death enough in our country this night."

"I fear that death has only begun to dance across the face of Mexico, Excellency."

17

By the time night had clamped down and the drunken Mexican moon had climbed into the night sky, the Extinguisher abandoned his borrowed vehicle and took to the jungle.

He was in his element now. The jungle was his realm. Long ago the Extinguisher had experienced his baptism by fire in the war-torn jungles of Southeast Asia.

Pausing by a pool, he blackened his angular face with camo paint until it no longer shone. His Hellfire supermachine pistol hung from a Whip-it sling under his right armpit. His backup pistol gleamed snug at the small of his back. A Randall survival knife was jammed into one boot.

As he moved, he clinked. But that was okay. In the jungle it was good to clink. Clinking was not a jungle sound, but clinking would scare off predators. The Extinguisher had no quarrel with the natural predators, only the two-legged ones. He preferred to avoid the natural ones.

Especially jaguars.

Tucked into his war book was an article ripped from the library copy of the *World Book Encyclopedia*. It was all about jaguars. They were a cat to be respected. The Extinguisher had no interest in crossing fangs with any jaguar.

And so he clinked with each step.

As the night deepened, it grew cool, then cold. Spring was still weeks away. But this was the Lacandón jungle. The Extinguisher had expected warmth. His Intel said nothing about pine trees and damp, chilly jungle breezes.

His nose began to go numb. And his ears.

"Son of a bitch!" he hissed. "I'm freezing my tailbone off here."

Reaching into a slash pocket of his black combat suit, he extracted the black balaclava that protected his identity when he was in full-Extinguisher combat mode. He drew this on. It muffled his entire head, except for a V-shaped slit that framed his icy blue eyes.

Soon the warm wool absorbed his body heat, warming his cool skin in return.

The Extinguisher moved on.

There was a calculated risk to wearing the feared mask where the ski-masked forces of the insurgent *Juarezistas* were being hunted. But since the Extinguisher was one of the hunters, that shouldn't matter.

Maybe he would stumble across one of the unlucky bastards, take him hostage and extract the whereabouts of Subcomandante Verapaz from his trembling body.

The mission would go a lot more smoothly with better intelligence, he reflected. God knew there wasn't a lot of raw Intel to be found lying around in the jungle. It was worse than fucking Stomique.

The night wore on, and the Extinguisher grew thirsty. Reconnoitering the area, he found a pool of water. He looked it over with the aid of a penlight. Not brackish. It didn't seem poisoned. He scooped up a cupful with a tin cup taken from his rucksack. Into this he dropped two haldozone tablets. He let the water sit awhile, then drank his fill.

Then the Extinguisher moved on.

After a while, he realized he had to take a whiz real, real bad. No problem. There were plenty of trees.

The Extinguisher was in the act of relieving himself when the ominous click of a hammer drawing back reached his sensitive, battle-honed ears.

Warily he looked right, then left.

As the warm stream petered out against the base of a fluted mahogany tree, he saw why he had heard it with such distinctness.

There was an FAL rifle pointed at his right temple and another pointed at his left. Behind them loomed two men in uniform.

Hard words rattled at him. He froze. They were repeated. The language was Spanish but spoken so fast nothing registered. Nothing sounded like the phrases he had memorized from *Wicked Spanish for the Traveler.*

He wondered what to do—zip up or raise his hands?

He decided to zip up first. The Geneva Convention must cover this situation. Somewhere.

It was the wrong move. A rifle swapped ends and slammed into the back of his skull. That was actually good. The wool balaclava protected his scalp.

Unfortunately there was no protection for his abdomen, which took the full brunt of the follow-up blow.

"Ooof!"

The Extinguisher went down, hands scrambling for his Hellfire pistol.

A hard boot stamped his wrist, pinning it to the ground. A hard knee leaned over two hundred pounds of *soldado* weight against his opposite elbow.

"Bastard! Get off me! You want to break something?"

A hand snatched away the balaclava, unmasking him.

A light seared his eyes. He tried to turn away, but strong fingers seized his hair, yanking his head around. The light held steady.

Beyond the light there were only man shadows.

"You could have let me zip up, damn it!" he cursed.

The men muttered something in Spanish.

"¿Habla Espanol?" one asked.

"No savvy," he said. *"No comprendo."*

While the boots and knees held him to the cool ground, other hands reached in and stripped him of his gear.

"Look, anybody savvy English?"

Someone spit in his face.

That was a mistake. No one spits in the Extinguisher's game face.

Twisting, he angled one knee between the legs of his tormentor. He moved it a short distance, hard and swift.

"¡Hijo de la chingada!" a man screamed, clutching himself.

In any language the meaning was plain.

The rifle stocks began raining down on his head after that, and for the Extinguisher the night and the jungle and, most merciful of all, the thudding, pounding, relentless pain all went away.

18

The first startling word reached Comandante Efrain Zaragoza in Chiapas Barracks by field telephone.

"Sir! We have captured Subcomandante Verapaz."

"Alive or dead?"

"Alive."

"How do you know he is Verapaz? Has he confessed?"

"No, he is unconscious. But it is him. He has blue eyes."

"Verapaz has green eyes."

"So they say. But his *Juarezistas* are all *indios*. They possess brown eyes. Therefore, it stands to reason that this blue-eyed masked one is Verapaz himself, and not one of his *insurgentistas.*"

It was typical Mexican logic. A triumph of desire over evidence. But it sounded logical to the zone commander, so he ordered the prisoner brought to Chiapas Barracks while he called the excellent tidings up the line until he reached the Interior Ministry General Jeronimo Alacran in the beleaguered Federal District.

It was a miracle that the connection went through. It was a miracle whenever the connection went through on a good day, never mind on this night of turmoil when aftershocks could be felt all the way to Chiapas and the brownish haze in the evening air spoke of troubled winds from the north, carrying the cooling ash of Smoking Mountain.

"You are certain of your facts?" General Alacran demanded.

"He wears a ski mask and possesses blue eyes."

"Verapaz's eyes are green," the general said stubbornly.

"Do we know this for a fact?"

"Our intelligence indicates this. And there are photos in magazines."

"Photos in magazines show colors imperfectly," the zone commander pointed out in a reasonable voice. "Perhaps he wears colored contact lenses when he poses for the press. After all, what manner of man possesses eyes the exact hue of the quetzal bird's plumage?"

"This is an excellent point. And you are very clever to offer this theory. My congratulations. Keep your prisoner safe, for I have already dispatched Colonel Primitivo to Chiapas to deal with this Verapaz."

"This is unnecessary. I have Verapaz in my custody."

"No, you do not," returned General Alacran. "You never had Verapaz."

"But I have him now. He sleeps off the blow that brought him to heel."

"I will repeat myself. You do not have Verapaz. You never had Verapaz. And when Colonel Primitivo arrives, you will surrender this prisoner you do not have and never had."

"But," Comandante Zaragoza sputtered, "what about my credit?"

"You may have the credit if you wish to accept the blame for what follows," the general said coolly.

"What blame?" asked Zaragoza.

"If you would know the blame, you must accept the consequences that attend this knowledge."

"I prefer no blame and no credit, if that is okay with the general," the zone commander said hastily.

"The general finds you a wise man. One who understands that we never had this conversation."

"What conversation?" said the zone commander, realizing even as he terminated the connection to Mexico City that there were worse things in life than losing credit for a duty fulfilled.

Among them, losing one's life, which was shortly to be the fate of Subcomandante Verapaz, the mysterious one of the chilling blue eyes.

COLONEL PRIMITIVO HEARD the excellent news over his field telephone.

He drove the lead LAV. He always took point. He prided himself on taking point. He would not lead men where he would not go himself first.

And in the pursuit of his duty, Colonel Primitivo would enter Hell itself. Not just any hell. Not the hell of his Spanish forebears, but the awful Aztec hell called Mictlan, where the dead had their bones sucked of their sweet marrow by demons.

Colonel Primitivo was unafraid to enter that hell.

So he did not shrink from tearing along the highway that wound through the Lacandón forest that was, although considered Mexican soil, nevertheless enemy territory.

THE PRISONER WAS LOADED into a wooden coffin.

This made perfect sense. He was soon to die, and since the prisoner in Chiapas Barracks was destined to become henceforth a state secret, what better way to conceal the still-living but certainly short-lived body than to load it into a coffin?

Colonel Primitivo blew into the barracks at the head of an armored column. He trailed a choking cloud that this night was more ash than road dust.

The air was becoming difficult to inhale comfortably. Much like the air of Mexico City on a humid summer's night.

Colonel Primitivo snapped a salute. "You have something for me?"

His mouth tight, Comandante Zaragoza motioned to the waiting coffin lying on the ground.

"Dead?"

"That is up to you," he said smoothly.

The colonel nodded. He ripped out a sharp command, and the coffin was loaded into the back of the lead LAV. The rear door clanged shut.

Engines rumbling like drag racers before the checkered flag, the colonel's unit turned like a land dragon and vanished into the jungle night.

"Well, that is done," said Zaragoza, who would have felt much better about the end of the Verapaz matter had it not been for the regrettable lack of credit and the fact that word coming out of the capital bespoke a crisis far worse than the others of recent vintage.

They were saying in the capital that there had been no earthquake. Only a minor spewing of Mount Popocatepetl.

That was very bad to hear. When there was a crisis in the capital, the official line was invariably that were was no crisis. Denial mated with deniability. It was very Mexican.

Now they were saying there was no earthquake when news broadcasts clearly showed the damage and the dead and the unbelievable hellish anguish of it all.

Comandante Zaragoza shuddered at the thought that there might no more be a Mexican government after these calamitous events.

19

The Extinguisher heard the raucous jungle sounds coming as if through a haze. He opened his eyes. They saw nothing. Only darkness.

Was he blind?

He felt confined. His head hurt. He moved it. It pounded. He moved it the other way, and although his eyes were open and he saw only darkness, the entire world of darkness spun and spun and spun until in his pain, he stopped biting his cheek and let out a wounded howl.

"What the hell is going on?"

He was in a box. It opened.

A lid clapped to one side, and he saw stars. Real stars. Shadowy heads intercepted the starlight, and dark eyes looked down on him without warmth or fear.

"Let me out of here," he said, grasping the box's edges so the lid couldn't drop back.

A rifle barrel was pressed to his chest. He subsided. He still lived. There was always opportunity to fight if he could find no other way. He made his voice flippant.

"What's shaking, *compadres?*"

"Subcomandante Verapaz," a man hissed. The

Extinguisher recognized the silver stars of a Mexican colonel on his shoulder boards.

"I'm not Verapaz. I'm the Extinguisher."

"*¿Que?*"

Searching his mind, he recalled the *nom de guerre* he'd heard back in the city.

"*El Extinguirador.*"

More heads came into view. Everyone wanted to see the dreaded Extinguisher now. That was good. It meant he had their attention. Soon he would have their fear. After that he would hold their miserable Third World lives in his capable hands.

Hands reached down to pull him out. He surrendered to them.

They stood him on his feet. He swayed. The fresh air made his skull hurt. He looked around.

The first thing he noticed was the long wooden box he had just occupied.

It was a coffin.

Cracking a smile, he said, "It'll take more than a pine box to keep the Extinguisher down."

The colonel stepped up to him while two others held him on his feet. "Jou call yourself the Extinguisher. Why?"

"That's who I am."

"Your true name, then."

"Blaize. Blaise Fury."

"Jou lie!"

"I *am* Blaize Fury, dillweed. Get used to it."

"Blaize Fury is a fancy. A hero in books."

"That's what I want my enemies to think."

The colonel looked him up and down. "Jou are a military man, *señor?*"

"I'm a warrior born, forged in hellfire and baptized with gun smoke."

"I have read many of the adventures of Blaize Fury when I was jounger. Jou are not Blaize Fury."

"Prove it."

"When I was jounger, Blaize Fury was my age. I am over forty now. Jou are jounger than twenty-five, if my eyes see not lies."

"Blaize Fury is ageless. He is eternal. The Extinguisher will fight evil as long as there are good fights to be fought."

"Señor Blaize Fury served in Vietnam," the colonel shot back. "With the Green Berets."

"So?"

"If jou are Blaize Fury, then jou were a Green Beret."

"I'm not saying I was or I wasn't."

"If jou are a Green Beret, Blaize Fury, what is—"

Brow furrowing, he consulted an aide in low Spanish.

"Emblazoned," the aide whispered in English.

"Yes. What is emblazoned on the flash of the Special Forces beret?"

The Extinguisher thought quickly. His mind raced.

"That's easy. A service knife between crossed arrows."

"No, that was the later flash. I refer to the original flash. Blaize Fury was one of the first Green Berets. He wore the flash before it was changed."

"I don't remember," the Extinguisher said. "It was a long time ago. I fought many battles since then."

"Jou lie! The flash was the Trojan Horse. Jou would know this if jou were truly *El Extinguirador.*

But jou are not. Jou are too young. Jou are a fake, a fraud and, most damning of all, jou are really Subcomandante Verapaz. Now we know your secret. Jou are a renegade American.''

"I am a citizen of the world. And I'm not Verapaz."

"Jou have the blue eyes of Verapaz."

"Recheck your Intel, salsa breath. Verapaz has green eyes."

"A low trick. Jou wear colored eye lenses to make your blue eyes green for photo opportunities. We are chasing after a green-eyed man when all along they were blue. Your deceptions are exposed, and your life is at an end."

"You can't kill the Extinguisher. He will refuse to die."

A hard hand slapped out, rocking the Extinguisher's head.

He spit blood. "Do your worst, Mexican."

"I will do my worst. I find jou guilty of subversion, insurgency and treason and sentence jou to be stood up against a tree and shot dead for your sins and your crimes against the sovereign government of Mexico."

They hauled him over to a pine tree, slamming him against it. The rough bark bit into his back.

All of a sudden the situation looked grim.

"Look, it's not what it looks like," he said quickly. "I'm here to wax Verapaz. Just like you."

"A likely story."

"It's true."

"Who do jou work for, then?"

"The United Nations."

And the soldiers of Mexico laughed, the colonel most boisterously of all.

"That is not even a preposterous lie. It is unbelievable. UN soldiers are not allowed to shoot in combat. Not even in self-defense. Jou expect me to believe the blue helmets employ assassins?"

"It's the truth. I'm unofficial right now. On probation. But as soon as I nail Verapaz, I have a job."

"A yob? The Extinguisher does not require a yob. He fights for freedom and yustice everywhere. He takes no pay. Like how you say? *El Lanero Solitario.*"

"Never heard of him."

An aide whispered in the colonel's ear.

"Jou have never heard of the Lone Ranger?" the colonel said.

"Up yours, Tonto. Besides, that's in books. This is real life. I gotta do it the way I'm doing it."

"And jou will do it no more because now your miserable life is at an end."

The firing squad was assembled. Five men. Their rifles were a motley mixture of Belgian FALs and carbines. No last words were solicited, and they didn't even offer him a blindfold.

"Ready," said the colonel.

The rifles came up. "Aim."

The rifle barrels fell into line. Sweat oozed from the Extinguisher's forehead. This was it. This was real.

"Fire!" shouted the colonel at the top of his lungs.

His heart in his throat, the Extinguisher shut his blue eyes and hoped they all somehow missed.

After all, this was Mexico, and the FAL wasn't exactly the best rifle money could buy. Scuttlebutt was they were subject to wickedly fierce muzzle jump.

20

The lush mountains of the Sierra Madre del Sur lay enshrouded before them, unseen yet palpable, silently calling out in the old tongues, summoning back the scattered Zapotec and Mixtec nations to reclaim the land of their ancestors.

High Priest Rodrigo Lujan heard the mountains call to him, but if his ears heard the past, his eyes saw the future.

The future walked clothed in basalt flesh. The future was named Coatlicue, she who strode like a stone elephant, ponderous but beautiful. But she had changed.

Glints of gold and silver showed in her rude flesh. They had begun appearing after they had left the capital. Miraculously.

It was the third miracle. The first was the Reawakening.

The second Lujan had dubbed the Miracle of the Crosses.

This manifested itself as the followers of Coatlicue flung their pagan gold-and-silver crucifixes in her path, that she might crush them and banish the false religion from the land.

Coatlicue's clawed feet blindly pressed them into

the asphalt, leaving deep cruciform impressions in the ground.

But when Lujan looked into these, the impressions were empty of metal. Every cross pressed into the holy soil left a distinct mark but mysteriously vanished.

That was when the glints began to appear. This miracle Rodrigo Lujan called the Absorption.

As Coatlicue strode tirelessly on, the gold and silver seemed to emerge from her skin like holy eruptions. At two points that he could see, actual crosses surfaced, proving forever his surmise that Coatlicue was reclaiming the very gold idols the Spanish pillaged and recast into their own religious icons. No more. The gold and silver was destined to return to its original purpose. High Priest Rodrigo Lujan vowed this.

Now, as she rested from her inexorable walk so that her followers could eat, Coatlicue had a question.

"Why do you consume your fellow meat machines?"

"It is the way of old Mexico," Rodrigo Lujan explained, picking a shred of calf meat from his teeth. "In the old days war parties raided rival cities, taking hostages. Often of royal blood. These were sacrificed to keep the universe in motion, after which the flesh and tasty organs were eaten."

"The universe is a dynamic construct of electromagnetic forces, cosmic dust and the nuclear furnaces called suns if they are near and stars if they are not. Killing insignificant meat machines can have no direct effect upon its workings."

"But this is our most sacred belief. The flesh of enemies gives us power."

"Consuming animal flesh does fuel the body and impart the stored nutrients of the consumed," Coatlicue admitted. *"Although given the long gestation and childhood periods of human meat machines, this is an inefficient allocation of resources. The proteins absorbed by this practice are more easily obtained from four-footed meat machines and plants. If humans cannibalized other humans on a steady basis, in time the population would be depleted until humans were forced to eat other things or die off as a species."*

"Perhaps this is what did in the Toltecs," Lujan said thoughtfully.

They were in Oaxaca State now. The drab helicopters buzzed the horizon, but no longer approached to do harm. All they did was record the earth-shattering migration with their cameras. This was good. It would communicate fear and dread to the doomed civilized cities now reeling under their own unsupportable weight.

"Coatlicue, I tell you as a man who has never eaten human flesh before this day, I am reborn. My Zapotec spirit soars. My muscles quiver with delight. I feel a strength greater than any since human meat has passed into me."

"This is not explainable by the mere consumption of human flesh whose proteins are inferior to those of lower animals."

"I say it is true. I feel invincible!"

"Your heart rate and respiration show a 7.2 percent increase in efficiency therefore I must accept your claim."

"Good. Good."

"And because I believe you, I will do the same. For I will need all resources obtainable to survive the present situation."

Rodrigo Lujan took an involuntary step backward. He bumped into a prostrate man. The man was on hands and knees, bowing in the direction of the stone golem that spoke a language he did not understand, but had the shape of a Mexican goddess.

Lujan reached down and, taking the man by the hair, exposed his reverent face.

"You look Chichimec," he said.

"I am Chichimec. My name is Pol."

"Chichimec, your Mother desires to know you better."

"I thrill to serve her."

"Let me instruct you that you may best serve her. Place your fine skull at those formidable feet that she may test your faith."

The man scuttled forward on all fours.

"Coatlicue, I worship you," he said in his native tongue.

"He is saying you must eat him," Rodrigo told Coatlicue in English, a tongue not understood by the Chichimecs.

The ophidian heads angled down to fix upon the willing victim like the twin bores of a double-barreled shotgun.

"Crush his skull like a coconut, for the brains are especially delectable," Lujan said.

And lifting one foot, Coatlicue brought it down like a massive nutcracker.

The face was jammed into the dirt. The head actually turned into an oblong under the incredible pressure and when it split, blood and curdlike brain matter gushed from nose, mouth and ears.

When Coatlicue took the dead one, it was all the further proof Rodrigo Lujan required to accept her divinity.

Her mouths did not approach. A blunt elephantine foot pressed down, and as a thousand incredulous eyes watched, the body was taken into the stone like liquid being drawn up a straw.

The foot, an admixture of basalt and precious metals, suddenly marbled with human fat.

"More," said Coatlicue. *"I will have more meat."*

21

"There's one bright spot to being in Mexico," Remo was saying as he piloted the Humvee down the winding road north of San Cristóbal de las Casas. Night was falling. The smells of the Lacandón jungle night were coming to the fore, among them the sharp tang of allspice and pine straw, and another odor that made him think of burnt corncobs. It made Remo remember he hadn't eaten since breakfast.

"And what is that?" asked Chiun.

"We're not in Mexico City."

"Mexico City is a terrible place," agreed Chiun. "The air is foul."

"That's on a good day," said Remo.

"I do not like to think about that place," said Chiun. "It holds terrible memories."

"Yeah. Last time we inhaled so much polluted air we were thrown completely off our game. And we had to fight Gordons."

"Another hateful name," said Chiun. "But that is not why the memories are so terrible."

"No. Then what?"

"It was there that I learned of the wonderful Aztec empire."

"Yeah, it was a great. If you like human sacrifice and kings who drank blood."

"I was not thinking of that. I was thinking of all the gold that was denied the House, for we knew nothing of the Aztecs."

"And they were only what, a four- or five-year sail from Korea?"

"It matters not how long one journeys from one's village, only the weights of gold that one bears upon him on his return," Chiun said aridly, flicking a gnat off one silken knee.

"That's easy for you to say. You weren't Wang or Yang or any of those early Masters who had to walk a few thousand dusty miles in their sandals just to reach India."

"India was a magnificent empire. We carried away much Indian gold. As well as Egyptian and Persian gold. These empires were most worthy in that wise. But of Aztec gold, we had none."

"Alas and alack," Remo clucked.

Chiun sniffed the air. "Perhaps there may yet be Aztec gold lying about, awaiting rescue."

"The only thing yellow I smell is burnt corncobs."

"Close your nostrils to its siren call," said Chiun. "Once you start on the path of corn eating, next you will be drinking its intoxicating juices. The path to slothfulness and ruin is paved with corn and pared fingernails."

"I'd settle for cold rice," Remo said dryly.

A road sign appeared, saying Chi Zotz. There was no milage or direction indicated.

Remo pulled out a map. "Boca Zotz is supposed to be around here, but it's not on this map."

"Perhaps it is near Chi Zotz," Chiun said. "We will stop at the next village and inquire."

"Suits me. Let's hope we can get a line on Verapaz while we're at it. It's a big jungle."

"Bristling with all manner of high dangers and low corn," added the Master of Sinanju sagely.

22

When the harsh rattle of autofire came, it sounded amazingly far away.

Maybe it was the terrible sound itself that contributed to the momentary amazement that seized the wild-haired warrior's helpless body.

Always in the past, the Extinguisher had been in situations that would break a lesser man. Many were the traps, ambushes and deaths engineered for him. Yes, he fell into a good many of these. No warrior is perfect. But always and invariably the Extinguisher mustered his jungle-honed combat skills and saved the day—not to mention his battle-hardened butt.

The percussive sound of autofire meant that this was one time that wasn't going to happen.

In the brief moments before the bullets ripped into his steely muscled form with their hot, fatal kisses, the Extinguisher said a silent combat prayer to the red god of battle. This was not the way he had ever imagined it ending. Not here. Not now. Not so soon, with so many battles to be fought and the enemy in this campaign as yet unvanquished.

But war is hell, even a wild-haired warrior's private war.

His prayer done, he tensed. If it was quick, good. If not, then he would spit out a final curse against the foes who had robbed a troubled world of its one pure protector. That would be good, too. Not as good as living, true, but—

A low moan ascended to the low-hanging moon.

The rustle and thud of a body falling into vegetation came next. Then another. More moans, followed by a confused rustling and thudding.

A final burst of autofire cut off a muffled curse.

The Extinguisher froze, not knowing what to do. He heard it all. The moans. The sounds of sudden death. The dropping bodies.

But none were his own. He still stood erect against the execution tree.

A slow, measured rustle came from the west, and he sensed a nearing presence, soft and stealthy.

Popping open one eye, he saw the firing squad curled up in the high grass like insects whose bodies had been doused with gasoline and set aflame.

A slow movement caught his eye.

Approaching was a cautious figure wearing a brown uniform, a black ski mask muffling the head. It was a very large head, bloated, almost pulpy, as if it concealed a monstrously deformed skull.

"Shh," the figure hissed. The eyes were luminous in the dark, like black opals.

A knife came out. His bonds were sliced apart.

"Thanks," he hissed, rubbing his wrists.

"Shh. *¡Vamos!*"

That last word he understood. It meant *come on*. Grabbing his gear, the Extinguisher followed the wary figure, casting frequent glances over his backtrail in case pursuit materialized.

None did.

The Extinguisher would live to fight another day.

And if this was one time he hadn't saved himself, what the hell? Breathing was breathing. Besides, there was only one witness, and he wore the guerrilla garb that marked him as a *Juarezista*.

Once in the clear, it would be child's play to turn the tables on this jungle revolutionary and have his way with him.

It was unfair—cold turnabout. But this was war. And the first thing tossed out the window in war was gratitude.

23

Coatlicue and her worshipful train were on the move once more.

With each thunderous step, they grew stronger. The earth, still racked by aftershocks, seemed to quake in sympathy with the goddess's mighty tread. And out of the villages and farms, they poured.

Aztec, Zapotec, Mixtec, Chocho, all united in one mystic purpose.

"We go to liberate Oaxaca, seat of the Zapotec empire," High Priest Rodrigo Lujan proclaimed to one and all. "We go to cast off the *chilango* yoke. Join us, become one with us, partake of the bounty of your reclaimed homelands. Shrug off your false saints. Tear down your crosses, your churches, your hollow religion that offers you breads and wines with transparent lies that you eat the blood and flesh of your dead god. That falseness is no more. Coatlicue offers no such things. When you follow Coatlicue, you eat real meat, you drink true blood and, in doing this, become one with your forefathers."

They came, they followed and some who heard that all they need do was lay their heavy bodies on the road before the lumbering one and be absorbed into her did that, too.

Coatlicue crushed them in her brutal mercy, without regard to sex or age or other of the so-called civilized niceties.

As they approached the town of Acatlán, she stood ten feet tall.

Once through it, having emptied the town of *indio* and *mestizo* alike, she topped twelve feet.

By the time she lumbered on through Huajuapan de León, her wary serpent heads straining to reach fifteen feet in height, the rude stone had softened to a warm brown that suggested flesh marbled with fat.

Striding alongside, Rodrigo Lujan reached out to touch her writhing skirt of serpents. It felt pleasantly warm. It was night now. The sun was down. Radiating heat could not explain away the sensation of warmth, nor the sinuousness with which the stone flowed as Coatlicue walked onward.

When he took his finger away, he had to pull hard.

And when he looked at it, Lujan saw he had left behind his entire fingerprint, as men who lived in subzero climates sometimes did when they stupidly touched their moist flesh to cold metal.

Only no phenomenon of cold could account for the patch of Rodrigo's skin that had become one with Coatlicue. She absorbed all flesh that came into contact with her.

Making a mental resolution not to touch or be touched by his goddess again, Lujan quickened his pace. It was harder to keep up with her seven-league strides now that she was growing and growing and growing.

Deep in his heart, he wondered if there was any limit to her ability to increase in size and mass.

Or for that matter, her appetites.

24

"Hold up!" the Extinguisher ordered.

The *Juarezista* guerrilla froze.

"*¿Que?*" The voice was soft, like a jungle breeze.

"Something's wrong," he said, grabbing his stomach.

"What is it?" the *Juarezista* asked, creeping back along the jungle trail to join him.

"I think I'm wounded," he gasped.

Lifting his combat shirt, he exposed his flat abdomen. There was some blood, but no sign of a entry wound. They could be very small, he knew.

Turning around, he asked, "See any sign of an exit wound?"

"No, *señor*."

"Damn. My gut feels like it's on fire."

"Jou are an American?"

"Fury's the name. Blaize Fury," he said.

"I have never heard of you."

"You shitting me?"

"I do not know the name. I am sorry."

"Never mind." The Extinguisher was doubled over now. "Man, what is wrong with me?" he moaned.

The guerrilla hovered solicitously. "Jou are not wounded."

"I feel terrible. It's like someone stuck a cold Kabar in my gut."

"Did jou drink of the water?"

"What? Oh, yeah. A while back."

"Ah...*la turistas.*"

"Don't call me a tourist. I'm a warrior."

"I am not. Jou are suffering from the tourist disease. The water does not agree with your belly."

"I don't feel like I'm going to throw up."

"That is not the hole through which the disease seeks release, *señor.*"

"What are you talking about?"

Then he knew. The sharp pain in his stomach traveled south and became an urgency in his bowels.

"Wait here," he said in a strangled voice.

The Extinguisher left the jungle trail and did his business in the dark, where no one would see. He was at his business a long time. Twice he started to pull up his pants, but had to resume squatting as more of the disease flooded from his beleaguered body.

"Oh, man. I hope this doesn't blow the mission."

When he was done, he stowed his emergency reading material back into his rucksack. To his surprise, he discovered his balaclava. He pulled it on. It seemed to give him strength to face what lay in store.

When he returned to the jungle path, he was the Extinguisher again, erect, proud and unbowed by the cruel rigors of the Lacandón jungle.

The eyes of the *Juarezista* went wide at the sight of his capable, manly figure.

"Jou are—"

"Yes," he said. "Now you understand. I am the Extinguisher."

"*¿Que?*"

"The Extinguisher. *El Extinguirador.*"

"I have never heard that name."

"You've never heard of the Extinguisher, savior of the oppressed? Where have you been living, in a freaking cave?"

"No, but now that I see that jou wear the mask of a *Juarezista,* I am proud to know you. That is, if jou are truly one of us."

He nodded, letting his body language relax. He stepped closer. This was going to be easy. The *Juarezista* stood about five-three and weighed no more than 130 pounds. He was a little thick in the hips, too. Out of shape. No match for the Extinguisher, who balled his fist, intending to coldcock the walking intelligence source before he knew what hit him.

The impulse to strike ignited in his brain.

Some jungle instinct must have seized the *Juarezitsa* because his hand suddenly reached up. He was moving to block the blow. Good luck to him. The Extinguisher had once been a Golden Gloves boxer.

In the brief seconds before the Extinguisher's fist connected, the *Juarezista* tore off his black ski mask and his face was revealed in the blazing moonlight.

The silver light showed an oval face, full, sensuous lips and a cascade of the most gorgeous shimmering black hair he had ever seen.

The fist connected. White teeth clicked shut, and the most gorgeous pair of dark eyes imaginable rolled up in the guerrilla's head as he fell backward, splaying across the jungle trail like a beached khaki starfish.

He lay there breathing rhythmically.

Then and only then did the Extinguisher see that he had a nice set of tits, too.

25

Colonel Mauricio Primitivo awoke to the sound of a screech owl. It perched in a tree branch directly over his aching head. It looked down upon him and gave out an ungodly moan.

The Maya called it a moan bird. But to Colonel Primitivo's eyes, it looked like the ghostly soul of death as it regarded him with its slow-winking eyes.

The colonel took stock. He lived. Obviously.

Memories came back to him.

He remembered giving the command to fire. Remembered, too, the rattle of automatic fire that distinctly came from the wrong direction.

The hot breath of supersonic rounds zipping by him had made spiteful sounds like glass rods breaking. His firing squad had crumpled before his eyes, and then he became aware of a dull pain at his own back.

The pain was still there, he realized.

It was the last thing he remembered before his senses were robbed from him and the first thing he felt now.

He tried to stand up. And failed.

Rolling over, he propped himself up on one khaki elbow. Good. He could do that. He could not be mortally wounded and have such strength after lying bleeding into the jungle floor for God alone knew how many hours.

Stripping off his uniform blouse, he exposed an entry wound in his abdomen above the pelvic saddle. It was an angry red. He gave it a ginger squeeze, and it oozed blood like a small, fleshy volcano.

There was no pain. So he reached around, gritting his teeth as he sought the inevitable exit wound.

What he found was actually smaller. It burned when he gathered up the surrounding flesh and squeezed it. His fingers came back crimson. They kneaded the flesh, seeking hardness and bringing a grimace to his face. But no hardness was to be found.

This was good. It meant the bullet had passed cleanly through the flesh, not striking bone and, it was to be hoped, carefully avoiding organs great and small.

A searing pain racked him as Colonel Primitivo clambered to his feet. He winced, his thick whiskbroom mustache bristling. Well, pain was a sign of life after all.

He stood on his booted feet, swaying slightly.

Men lay all about him, dead. They were very dead, he saw. He gave one a kick for deserting him in the hour of national emergency and then, dripping blood from the clearly God-sent wound, he stumbled off toward Chiapas Barracks.

Never again would he take offense if a woman playfully punched his growing paunch and joked about his love handles.

They had saved his life.

26

When he realized he had sucker-punched a woman, the Extinguisher raged, "Damn, damn, damn, what a stupid idiot I am!"

It was not his way to strike a woman. It was against his personal code. But he had done it, and there was no recalling the blow.

Kneeling, he checked her pulse. She breathed. Of course. Before he struck, he had calculated the force of the blow in advance. It was possible to kill a human being with one well-placed punch. But that was not the Extinguisher's way, either. The dead give up no Intel.

Cradling her limp head in his lap, he checked her mouth. She hadn't bitten or swallowed her tongue. That was good. No broken teeth, either. Also good. Women were fussy about their teeth.

For over an hour he squatted in the unfamiliar jungle protecting the female *Juarezista* guerilla, wondering what to do when she woke up.

Somewhere an unseen animal vented a fierce screech.

"Hope that wasn't a jaguar," he said to himself, snapping the Hellfire pistol up in its Whip-it sling.

If it was, the animal didn't approach.

At length, his conquest began to stir.

A cold shock of fear went through him as the Extinguisher realized the acute difficulty of his position.

Carefully he laid her head on a stone and stood up, his mind racing.

An idea struck him in a bolt of inspiration.

Unsheathing his Randall survival knife, he used it to slice open his left bicep, just enough to produce blood.

Then he jammed the point of the blade into a nearby tree. Two tough mahogany trees stubbornly refused to take the blade, so he plunged it into one with a reddish trunk with bark that hung in long pale strips like peeling dead skin.

Then the Extinguisher stood over her, waiting.

Her eyes fluttered open, roved dazedly, finally falling upon his boots. They looked up.

"¿Que?"

He pitched his voice to its lowest register. "You had a close call."

She shook her head as if to clear the cobwebs of sleep. Abruptly she took it into her hands as the pain told her shaking was a bad idea.

"What happened to me?" she moaned.

"Someone threw a knife at you. The only way to save your life was to knock you out. I caught the bite of the blade along one arm before it hit that tree."

Her eyes went from the streak of blood showing on his arm to the knife hilt protruding from the weird peeling tree.

"Jou—jou saved my life."

"Why not?" he said casually. "You saved mine back there."

With his help she found to her feet again.

She looked around perplexedly. "The one with the knife—where did he go?"

"He didn't get a second throw," the Extinguisher told her, patting his Hellfire.

"You are a brave warrior. You have come to join the Juarez National Liberation Front obviously."

"I fight alongside the good people of this earth wherever I find them," he said truthfully.

Her eyes shone with a mixture of gratitude and frank admiration. It was a look the Extinguisher had seen many, many times. He met it directly, with neither embarrassment nor false modesty.

"Well spoken. My name is Assumpta. I am from a village near here. I go to join the *Juarezistas,* even though I am but a woman."

"You are a brave woman."

She threw back her head proudly, lifting a defiant chin, tossing her hair with the motion. It was very thick and black. It explained why her head had seemed so large under her ski mask.

"The men of my village do not believe women can fight, nor that they should fight," she explained. "But I go anyway to avenge my brother, Ik, who perished at the hands of the *federalistas.*"

"Where you go, I go."

And in the darkness they shook hands firmly.

The Extinguisher had an ally. Whether circumstances would force him to betray her was unknown at this time. But for the moment they were a team.

"Subcomandante Verapaz, it is said, is marching on Mexico City," Assumpta said. "That is where I go."

"Lead the way. This jungle is new to me."

As they started off, the Extinguisher recovered his survival knife, sheathing it with a curt "Souvenir. Might come in handy."

They had donned their black masks again. The jungle accepted them into its cool, treacherous embrace. They moved as one, the *Juarezista* named Assumpta taking point. It was not the Extinguisher's way to let a woman take point, but it was her jungle so he figured it would be okay this time.

Besides, from the rear, he could better keep watch over her.

Not to mention the fact that he was really getting into the easy sway of her olive drab hips.

27

The market town called Chi Zotz was nestled in the shadow of a tablelike mountain range. The air was clean and sweet, laden with budding wildflowers.

An English sign said WELCOME TO CHI ZOTZ. TURNING FOR PALENEQUE RUINS. FOOD, COLD SODA AND SAFE CAR PARKING. BIRTHPLACE OF SUBCOMANDANTE VERA-PAZ.

Near the entrance to the town, a shawled woman stood outside an adobe home preparing a chicken dinner. She had the struggling chicken by the neck and, spreading her legs apart, wound up her arm.

She spun the bird in a circle twice. The neck snapped on the second revolution.

Examining the now-limp bird with satisfaction, she turned to reenter the home when Remo called out to her.

"Excuse me. Is Boca Zotz near here?"

"Boca Zotz is no more, *señor.*"

"Damn. What happened to it?"

"It has been renamed. It is now Chi Zotz, which means Bat's Mouth."

"Boca Zotz is this place, right?"

"No, this place is Chi Zotz. Boca Zotz is no more, *señor.*"

With that, the women vanished into the shadows of her home.

Remo drove on.

The town looked deserted. No one was in the tiny town square or walked the dirt streets. Painted slogans marred almost every blank surface available. Remo didn't need to understand much Spanish to understand defiant phrases like *¡Solidaridad! ¡Libertad!* and *¡Viva Verapaz!*

"I caught you eyeing that fowl," Chiun said sharply.

"I was just thinking I could go for some duck right about now."

"I do not know what duck inhabits this land, but I would not eat it. Nor the fish. We will have rice, which is always safe to eat. Besides, chicken is unclean and unhealthful."

"People eat chicken all the time."

"Yes. Unknowingly."

"What do you mean unknowingly?"

"Chicken are incapable of urinating. This failure of hygiene fouls the fowl's tissues. To eat chicken is worse than consuming the flesh of pork."

Remo parked outside a dingy Spanish colonial building that suggested a restaurant because it sported a painted oval sign that looked exactly like a beer label. It said CARTA BLANCA. Soft *ranchera* music floated out.

When they entered, not a single glance came their way.

All eyes were glued to a flickering black-and-white TV set in one corner of the room. Chairs had been pulled up in a semicircle around the flickering TV light, but many people also stood around.

"Wonder what they're watching?" Remo asked Chiun.

"I do not know, but the odor of fear rises from them."

"Smells like chili and tacos to me," Remo grunted.

As they watched, he noticed a man in a white Texas hat make the sign of the cross.

"Could be coverage of the big earthquake," said Remo.

"I will ask."

Lifting his voice, the Master of Sinanju rattled off a rapid question in Spanish.

"El Monstruoso," a man called back, making the sign of the cross himself.

"Did he say monster?" Remo asked.

"He said monster."

"You'd think with their capital in ruins, they would have better things to do than watch an old monster movie."

"¡Ay! El Monstruoso esta estrujando el tanque," a man cried.

"The monster has crushed a tank," Chiun translated.

"¡El Monstruoso devora el tanque!"

"The monster is eating the tank," Chiun said.

A man began weeping. Others began weeping, too.

"The special effects must be really something," Remo said.

"They are saying that the monster is coming this way."

"They sure take their movies seriously down here," said Remo, grabbing a chair. Chiun joined him.

The waiter was nervous. He sweated. He handed them menus and asked them their preferences in Spanish.

Remo pointed to an item of the menu. *Cabro al cabrón.*

"What's this?" he asked the Master of Sinanju.

"Grilled goat."

"How about *pastas de tortuga?*"

"Turtle's feet."

"You're making this up so I don't get any meat, aren't you?"

"No," said Chiun, who then told the waiter, *"Arroz."*

"If that's rice, make that a double," said Remo in English.

Chiun translated for the waiter, and within a few minutes bowls of steaming rice were laid before them.

They ate quickly. Remo finished first.

The commotion from the TV was distracting, so Remo wandered over and tried to see past the close-clustered heads of the TV viewers. The viewers in the back row were standing on stools. Even getting up on his toes didn't help much.

Getting no cooperation, Remo flicked at the earlobe of a man ahead of him, causing him to glower at the man beside him.

Remo caught a brief glimpse of the screen.

"Huh!" he grunted.

Returning to his table, he whispered to the Master of Sinanju. "Speak of the devil."

"Verapaz?"

"No. Gordons. I just saw him on TV."

Chiun's hazel eyes widened.

"What!"

"Yeah," Remo said casually. "He's the monster."

Chiun eyed his pupil stonily. Remo looked back, a poker expression on his face. Finally he let his face come apart, grinning from ear to ear. "Fooled you."

"It was not Gordons?"

"Well, it looked like him. Or like the form he last assimilated."

"The ugly Aztec woman monster?"

"Yeah. Curlicue or whatever the name was."

"How do you know it is not Gordons returned to life?"

"Three reasons," said Remo. "One, we shattered Gordons into loose rock while he was in that form. He's deactivated. Two, Smith made us leave the corpse after the Mexican authorities stuck him back in their big museum. If he's still there, the roof has fallen in on his head by now."

"Those are not convincing reasons, Remo."

"I was getting to number three. Three, the monster on the TV had to be twenty-five feet tall. Gordons isn't twenty-five feet tall. The statue was only eight."

"Therefore, it is not Gordons."

"Can't be."

"Yes, you are right. Besides, how can it be Gordons when Gordons was vanquished by the Reigning Master of Sinanju?"

"I helped, too."

"I found his dense mechanical brain and broke it in his head."

"And I delivered the *coup de grace*."

Chiun made a face. "You wasted a blow. He was already dead when you struck."

"Could be. But I was making sure. He came back to haunt us too many times before."

"But he is dead now. Long dead."

"If he wasn't, he'd have come back long before. And in a form we wouldn't recognize."

"I spit on his memory," Chiun said bitterly.

When the bill came, it was for five-hundred pesos.

"How much is that American?" Remo asked Chiun, who asked the waiter.

"Only seventy-five dollars."

"For two bowls of rice?" Remo complained.

"Jou are forgetting the water. It is not free."

Remo reached into his chinos. "I'm kinda low on cash. Discover card okay?"

"There is a thirty percent surcharge for all major credit cards."

"I'd get upset, but it goes on my expense account."

The waiter smiled broadly. The smile seemed to say *This is what we count on,* señor.

"By the way, we're looking for Subcomandante Verapaz."

"He is not here."

"I'm a reporter with *Mother Jones* magazine."

"Another?"

"You get a lot of reporters, I hear."

"*Sí*. But not a lot from *Mother Yones*. They only come once or twice a season now. I think they have a little circulation problem."

"Subscriptions have been picking up. So, where can I find him?"

The waiter made his face sad. "Jou cannot, *señor*. For he is like the wind, unseeable and unfindable unless he wishes otherwise."

"How much?" Remo said wearily.

The waiter's sad face brightened. "For fifty dollars cash I will point you in the correct direction."

Remo counted out the money.

"You go north along the Pan American Highway, *señor*. Drive to Mexico City."

"Mexico City?"

"*Sí*. Subcomandante Verapaz even now leads a drive to wrest Mexico City from the oppressor. Jou will undoubtedly find him somewhere along the road, crushing his enemies and lighting joy in the hearts of Mexicans everywhere."

"Thanks. You're a big help."

"May I sell you an authorized Subcomandante Verapaz doll, *señores?* An autographed picture? Get them now because if Verapaz either dies or succeeds, the price will surely double."

"No, but you can tell us why you changed Boca Zotz to Chi Zotz."

"That will be five additional dollars."

"Forget it."

"It is a very interesting story."

"Tell me the story, and I'll pay you what I think it's worth," Remo countered.

"*Boca* is Spanish. We live no longer under Spanish yoke. *Boca* becomes *Chi* so that now we will live in the Mouth of the Bat."

"So what's *Boca* mean?"

The waiter showed Remo his empty palm.

Remo was thinking it over when the Master of Sinanju said, "It is Spanish for *mouth*."

"You changed the name from Bat's Mouth to Bat's Mouth?"

"No, we change it from Bat's Mouth to Mouth of the Bat. It is a very great difference to the people."

"It is a very great pain in the *boca* to find this dump," said Remo on his way out the door.

"The *soldados* all say this, too," the waiter said smugly, folding Remo's money into his pocket.

28

"It is called the give-and-take palm," Assumpta was saying as she broke a wicked needlelike thorn off the weirdly barbed tree. "It is called that because to touch it improperly will cut you. But the bark of the give-and-take plant makes a wonderful bandage with which to bind the very wound it causes, or any wound."

As the Extinguisher watched, she stripped off the bark on long, gauzy rolls almost like Ace bandages.

The moonlight was spectral and it made her black hair shine. Her body was as supple as bamboo. She smelled faintly of coconut.

With sure movements she bound the knife wound and, using one of the long, tough thorns, speared the loose end, cinching it tight.

"The father of my father taught this to me. He was a H'men, which is the same to you as a doctor, but one who uses the plants and herbs of the forest to heal the sick."

The Extinguisher grunted his thanks. It would be something to remember.

They moved on. As they picked their way, she taught him how to recognize the trees of the Lacandón rain forest, which was a weird conglomeration of semitropical vegetation coexisting with oak and pine trees.

"The red-bark one was known as the *turista* tree, because it sheds its bark the way a sunburned *gringo* sheds his skin," she explained. "That is the ceiba. And that the Manzanillo."

"Speaking of the *turistas,*" he said. "Give me a minute, will you?"

She waited patiently as the Extinguisher did what had to be done, thinking that this having to drop one's pants every two miles was one hell of a way to win the trust of an enemy.

Rejoining her, he discovered her hacking a gnarled vine in two. She drank from it as if it were a garden hose. They continued on.

He said little, so she filled in the silences.

Her full name was Assumpta Kaax. She had been raised Catholic in the village called Escuintla, which meant Place of Dogs.

"It was a well-named place, Señor Fury. The dogs, who need little to sustain themselves, did well. The Maya did not."

She was thirteen when Subcomandante Verapaz had come to the village with his knowledge and his medicines and his wise words. He politicized the village, and politicized Assumpta, too. When she came of age, she had two choices. Marry a village boy she did not like, much less love. Or join the *Juarezistas*.

"Not that this last was a choice," she added hastily. "I ran away from my village to do this. I ran from poverty to a new life. Now I am Lieutenant Balam— which means *jaguar*—a true follower of Lord Kukulcan."

"Who?"

"It is the name by which some Maya call Subcomandante Verapaz. Kukulcan was our god many *baktuns* ago. He came bringing corn seeds, writing and other knowledges that uplifted the Maya of that cycle."

"Are you trying to tell me Verapaz is a god?"

"This is what many believe."

"What do you believe?"

She was quiet for a long, pensive period. The only sounds were the peeping of tree toads and the soft rustle of their own bodies bruising foliage.

"My heart is torn two ways," she admitted finally. "The knowledge he brings has caused me to cast off the saints of the priests of the oppressors, as well as the demons of my ancestors. Yet Subcomandante Verapaz is godlike in his way. Like Kukulcan, he has uplifted us, politicized us, opened our minds. Now he leads us to our certain destiny."

"That's not an answer."

"The only answer I can truthfully give is that my heart is torn, but my mind is clear. I would die for my lord Verapaz."

"I understand," the Extinguisher said. And he did. Because his heart was torn, too. He was falling in love with this jungle she-jaguar....

And unwittingly she was leading the Extinguisher to an inescapable rendezvous with betrayal.

29

"It is twenty-five feet tall!" the voice shouted into the ears of the president of the Mexican United States. It was the defense minister.

"What is twenty-five feet tall?" asked the president, holding on to his desk as yet another stomach-churning aftershock rolled through.

"Coatlicue. She is growing!"

"Do not call it a she. It is a statue. Imaginary. Sexless."

"She grows by the hour. And the *indios* pour from the villages to follow her. They flow behind her, a river of humanity."

"She—I mean it—is heading south?"

"South, *sí.*"

"With no objective in mind?"

"None that we can discern, Excellency. She follows the Pan American Highway without deviation."

"Perhaps she will walk into the sea."

"Why would she do that?" the defense minister wondered aloud.

"Because if there is a true God in heaven, that is what He will compel her do," said the president. "Otherwise, I do not know what will happen. I can spare no units. I would not know what orders to give if I could. Coatlicue is a national treasure, a symbol of our joined *mestizo* heritage. If she were to be destroyed, we would have total revolt. I would sooner slap the pope in the face with my own hand.''

''There is one hope,'' the defense minister said in a slightly calmer voice.

''And what is that?'' asked the president, holding his deskblotter over his head to keep the falling plaster out of his hair.

''If Coatlicue continues as she does, she will inescapably reach Chiapas State.''

''This could be good or this could be bad,'' the president mused.

''Subcomandante Verapaz virtually controls Chiapas. Perhaps she will become his problem.''

''If there is any way to urge Coatlicue to do this, I will not complain about the result. For if only one irritation cancels out the other, it would be a boon.''

''Yes, Excellency.''

30

The Extinguisher called a halt.

"We gotta give it a rest," he told Assumpta.

"*¿Que?* What do you mean?"

"I'm beat."

"That is no way for a *guerrillero* to talk. We will never be beaten. Our spirits are indomitable."

"My knees are weak. I think that last time under a sapodilla tree I dumped my balls with the rest of my load."

"Ah, you are weak from sickness, not fear."

"The Extinguisher doesn't know fear."

"Perhaps. But he knows sickness and requires rest like any other man. Come. There is a village near here. They will take us in."

"No. I can't afford to be seen."

"Then we will go no closer than it is necessary and I will obtain food from the village and bring it back to you."

"All right. But be careful."

"I return soon, *El Extinguirador.*"

"Call me Blaize."

The Extinguisher watched her go. She moved like a jungle cat, slipping between trees until she was only a shadow, then a shape, then one with the eternal jungle night.

He unlimbered his pack, picking through it carefully. The way things were going, he'd have to jettison extra gear if he was to make it to his destination—wherever that was.

Digging into his pack, he discovered something important was missing.

There was only one Extinguisher novel. He had brought two. Worst of all, the missing one was the one he hadn't finished.

"Damn it. Musta left it behind last time I took a dump."

Repacking his gear, he left the surviving book out.

It was too dangerous to sleep. Time enough for sleep when Assumpta returned.

Breaking out his waterproof poncho, he tented it over his head, making sure the skirts came all the way to the ground. Clicking on a flashlight, he began reading

The Extinguisher #221, *Hell on Wheels.*

Massachusetts State Trooper Edward X. Mac-Ilwraith thought he'd seen everything in his twenty-eight years cruising Bay State highways until the day he pulled over the cherry red Eldorado and found himself looking into the bore of a .50-caliber Browning gutripper. . . .

The Extinguisher grinned happily. "Looks like a good one. . . ."

31

Colonel Mauricio Primitivo was not accustomed to the jungle.

He knew enough to stay away from the Manzanillo tree, whose easily bruised bark leaked a thick, milky sap that made the skin erupt in ferocious rashes and boils.

The give-and-take palm was also to be avoided, although it was not as vicious as the Manzanillo.

The night wore on. The darkness was both impenetrable and absolute. The wild calls of unseen things abroad in the forest were disturbing. Colonel Primitivo clutched his Heckler & Koch MP-5 submachine gun more tightly.

The dark plots of bean and cornfields that had been scorched black to prepare the land for the spring planting gave off an odor that called to him.

It meant a village. In Chiapas a village meant *indios*. *Indios* meant *Juarezista* sympathizers. And sympathizers inescapably suggested a safe haven where the Masked One might go to lick his wounds.

Releasing the safety on his H&K, Colonel Mauricio Primitivo picked up his pace. His thick mustache quirked upward in a slow anticipatory smile.

He would find what he sought or there would be a slaughter this night.

Perhaps a slaughter might transpire even if he found his quarry. All things were possible in lawless Chiapas.

32

"We're getting nowhere," Remo said, pulling over to the side of the road.

It was well past midnight. They had been driving for hours and they hadn't come across a single *Juarezista* to interrogate.

"I say we head into the forest," Remo suggested.

"You must carry my trunk," said Chiun.

Remo eyed the steamer trunk with the blue phoenixes in the back seat.

"Can't we leave it here?"

"It will be stolen by thieves."

While they were arguing, an armored column roared past.

The faces of the soldiers were grim. And they were in a fierce hurry.

They blew on past without stopping to ask questions.

"Maybe they're on the trail," said Remo.

"Let us follow them," Chiun suggested.

"Beats walking," said Remo, getting the Humvee in gear. He sent it back up the road. They fell in behind the armored column.

They followed a half mile before it abruptly left the highway and disappeared up a winding road.

"Here goes," said Remo.

The road led to a military installation. It was ablaze with lights, and soldiers were climbing into armored vehicles parked in front of it.

The column screeched to a disorganized stop, and men started piling out, blocking the way out.

"Looks like they're getting ready for war," Remo told Chiun. "Wait here with the trunk."

The new arrivals began yelling at the soldiers preparing to leave. They were being yelled at in return. All of it was in Spanish, and Remo understood none of it.

It was a great, noisy confusion in which his "Anyone here speak English?" was completely lost.

Noticing a main building, Remo entered. No one tried to stop him. They were too busy arguing and trying to get their vehicles lined up so the fresh soldiers could depart by the one winding access road.

Remo found the commanding officer fussing at his desk. He was digging through a sheaf of communications while trying to talk into two phones at once, one perched on each shoulder. His nameplate said ZARAGOZA.

"You speak English?" asked Remo.

The commander looked up.

"*Sí.* Now go away."

"Can't."

"I am very busy with the present emeryency."

"It's about Subcomandante Verapaz," said Remo.

"You are too late," the commander said distractedly. "He is defunct."

"Dead?"

"That is what I have heard. But it is only an unsubstantiated rumor. Go away now. I have no time for *gringo journalistas.*"

"In that case, I demand to see the body. Inquiring minds want to see it all."

"You cannot see the body because there is no body," the commander hissed. "Officially."

Remo came around the desk and relieved the commander of his telephones, his disorganized papers and his ability to rise from the chair of his own volition by squeezing his spine.

"Now, you listen very carefully," Remo said. "I've had a long day. I've traveled a long way, eaten expensive food and been soaked by every Mexican whose path I crossed. Not counting the ones who tried to shoot me."

"I understand."

"Good. I'm looking for Subcomandante Verapaz. I don't care if he's alive or dead. I just want to find him. Once I find him I can go home. *¿Comprendo?*"

"*Comprende.* The proper tense is *comprende.*"

"Thank you for the Spanish-grammar lesson. But stay with me here. I want to go home very badly. In the next hour if possible. So if you'll kindly point me in the right direction, I won't place you under cardiac arrest."

"Cardiac—?"

"Also known as *commotio cordis.*"

"*¿Como—?*"

"Don't bother. You'll only get tongue-tied like everybody else."

The commander spread his helpless hands. "I cannot point you to the body, *señor.* I am most sorry.

Colonel Primitivo took this Verapaz from my hands and out into the jungle for summary execution.''

"He come back?''

The commander looked helpless. ''How can he come back if he is dead?'' he asked plaintively.

"I meant the colonel, not the *subcomandante.*"

"Ah, I understand. No, the colonel did not come back. He is not—how you say?—attached to Chiapas Barracks, which this is. He has done his duty, now he is gone forever, no one being the wiser.''

"Except you and me,'' Remo corrected.

"It is a military secret, *señor.* I hope you will keep it.''

"Cross my heart and hope to spit, as the Beaver used to say.''

"*¿Que?*"

"Never mind. Look, if Verapaz is dead, what's all the commotion?''

"We go to battle the monster.''

"What monster?''

"The monster on the TV, *señor.*"

Remo followed the commander's pointing finger.

In a far corner of the room sat a TV set. It was on. The sound was off.

On the screen was a thirty-foot-tall stone monster striding through the night. Helicopter searchlights played over it. It was the same monster movie that had been playing in Chi Zotz hours before.

Remo thought the special effects were pretty good, but the camera work and editing were terrible.

"You going to fight *that?*"

"*Sí.* It is a terrible emeryency up in Oaxaca. All my forces have been called up.''

"Good. You have a nice monster fight. I just have one last question."

"What is that?"

"Where did the colonel take the body?"

"Into the jungle. But I would not go into there."

"Why not?"

"Because this is Maya country and it is after dark."

"So?"

"After dark Kamazotz comes out."

"Kamazotz?"

"Yes. Kamazotz is the bat god of the Maya." The commander shook his head slowly. "Terrible. He will drain your blood and do other unpleasant things to you."

"Thanks for the warning. I'll take my chances."

"You are very welcome, *señor*. But there is one thing more I ask of you."

"What's that?"

"Could you undo the thing that you did to my neck? I would like to use my legs to join my men to fight the monster."

"Oh, sorry," said Remo, returning to release the cervical manipulation that had disabled the commander's vertebrae.

Outside, the soldiers were still fighting. The column looked like a wagon train trying to get itself pointed west. Only no one knew west from south.

Taking the wheel, Remo met Chiun's quizzical gaze.

"They're off to fight the monster."

"What monster?"

"The one on the TV."

"But that monster is not real."

"You're talking about an army that's afraid to go into the forest after curfew because the bat god lives there."

"I fear no bats," sniffed Chiun.

"That's good," Remo said, gunning the engine, "because we're about to hit the jungle. Verapaz is out there, maybe dead, maybe alive."

"It does not matter."

"Why do you say that?"

"Because we are not paid by the slaying. If someone else has felled our victim, we will still be paid."

"Me, I like my work. And I still have a few frustrations to get out."

"Perhaps you suffer from ingrown cuticles," Chiun said aridly. "They can be very painful unless pointed in the proper direction."

"The proper direction of Verapaz is the only direction I care about right now," said Remo, chasing his own bouncing headlight beams.

33

Rodrigo Lujan was worried. He was very worried.

The federal army no longer worried him. They had hurled their all into the teeth of the goddess Coatlicue.

And their all had been hurled back into their own teeth, breaking them.

Military barricades had been erected. No one dared man them, but the roads were blocked by all manner of obstacles.

Massed tanks. These had been trampled and crushed as if by great stone pistons.

Burning wood and fuel had been next. She strode through that unfazed. Not so fortunate were the *indios* who willingly followed her in the conflagration and were consumed.

The smell of their roasted flesh was that of roast suckling pig. Rodrigo veered closer, and spying a rigidly raised fire-crackled arm, stopped and yanked on it.

The cooked black flesh slid off in his hands, exposing pinkish meat, but by struggling he succeeded in pulling the arm from its socket, carrying it away for later consumption.

Farther along, a great ditch had been dug and covered with thin wood and camouflaged to resemble in the darkness a patch of unpaved road.

One great foot touched the ruse, sensed its unnatural hollowness and responding, lurched over the snare and onward.

All obstacles were defeated. Coatlicue was prescient and indomitable. Everyone knew this. So the army had curtailed their futile operations and withdrawn totally. Coatlicue made wonderful progress until she reached the outskirts of Oaxaca.

The *chilango* army had all but ceded the old seat of the Zapotec nation to Coatlicue the invincible. Victory was assured.

That was not what concerned Rodrigo Lujan.

It was Coatlicue's voracious, all-consuming appetite.

The *indios* continued to pour out of the zinc-roofed huts and village hovels. They replenished the newly fallen.

The problem was those who fell, fell not to the enemy but to Coatlicue herself—now a crazy quilt of marbled flesh, stone and armor. She continued feeding. Her appetite was insatiable. It was said of the Aztecs that in the days before the Spanish came, they were sacrificing hearts to the sun at a ferocious rate, far more than were required to keep the universe continually in motion.

Rodrigo Lujan did not wish to become one of the sacrificed.

That was one reason he had commandeered a green Volkswagen taxicab. Should Coatlicue become blindly hungry, she could not take him into her immense body as long as he stayed behind the wheel.

He was following his goddess at a decorous pace when the brilliant notion birthed in his brain. He pressed the accelerator to the floor. The little bug pulled up and was pacing the striding deity that shook the earth that was already shaking.

"Coatlicue! I have the most brilliant idea!"

Coatlicue did not reply. That was good. Sometimes it was good not to be noticed. Also gratifying.

"Coatlicue, I know how you can ensure your survival."

The behemoth took another step and stopped, bringing the trailing clawed foot in line with the first.

The two reticulated serpent heads rolled down. One mouth parted, issuing a grating word. *"Speak...."*

"You must cease consuming your followers."

"This is contradictory. I grow larger and stronger by assimilating them."

"Yes. But now you are strong enough. For to grow stronger would make you a greater target to your enemies."

"I am greater in size, mass and volume than any bipedal meat machine. This equals survival."

"In the jungle it is said that the lowly mouse lives longer than the monkey. For the mouse's small size allows it to hide from predators who would otherwise eat the little mouse."

"I have attempted the survival strategy of feigning an inoperative state. This has failed. My new strategy appears to be working. My enemies have withdrawn because they fear my vast size."

"Yes. They fear you. But you are also striking fear into the hearts of your worshipers. This is not good."

"Previously you encouraged this survival tactic."

"I did. I do. But now it is different. You have all the vastness you require. And now you must emulate the survival tactics of the jungle *guerrilleros.*"

"That word does not match any in my memory banks."

"I am thinking of the greatest master of survival in all of Mexico. By name, Subcomandante Verapaz. He dwells in the jungle, and although the same forces that have so miserably failed to destroy you also seek his destruction, they have never succeeded."

"Explain these survival tactics to me."

"Verapaz surrounds himself with loyal *compañeros,* much as you do."

"Thus, my strategy is equal to his."

"Yes, except that Verapaz does not eat his loyal ones."

"Nor do I. I assimilate them. None are converted into waste products for disposal. The absorbed become inextricable from my present form. Nothing is wasted."

"This is good. For waste is bad. But having consumed your fill, is it not better to permit your followers to protect you with their numbers, their courage and their willingness to sacrifice themselves for you?"

"They appear to be gratified by the sacrifice."

"Yes, we must have sacrifice. I agree. Let us sacrifice others. Let us from this moment forward vow solemnly to sacrifice only our enemies. For my ancestors understood that to eat the brains and flesh of their enemies imbued them with the strength and skills of the vanquished."

"This is reasonable."

"*Bueno.* I am glad that you agree, Coatlicue. Now, come. Oaxaca lies behind this mountain before us. We must reach the seat of your temporal power on earth, where you will rule inviolate."

"Yes, I will rule. For ruling brings me followers and power, and these are the elements that will ensure my survival."

"And mine," muttered Rodrigo Lujan under his breath.

34

Blood hung in the air.

Remo and Chiun picked up the metallic taste in the still jungle air. The ground under their feet rumbled slightly.

"Aftershock," said Remo.

They moved through the jungle with the stealthy ease of jungle cats, following the scent. It was strong. Stronger than the pungent scent of crushed onion grass left by the trampling feet of their quarry. Their careful feet picked bare spots to land, crushing no grass and leaving no trail. They had abandoned the Humvee.

"It is the blood of men," Chiun intoned.

Remo nodded. "I smell gunpowder, too."

"We near our quarry."

"Maybe. Maybe not."

They came upon the dead bodies in a clearing. They wore the khaki uniforms of federal Mexican army soldiers.

"Shot," said Remo, looking them over.

There was a coffin. But no one inside.

"Looks like they had Verapaz in that coffin, took him out to execute him but were ambushed first," Remo concluded.

Chiun's hazel eyes were intent upon the ground. Starting from the coffin, he began walking in a widening circle.

"The footprints of men go this way," he said, pointing to the west.

Remo joined him.

"I count three."

Chiun nodded. "Two are hours old, one more recent."

Remo checked the bodies. "The commander said something about a colonel. There are blood spots here and the impression of a body, but no body. I think the colonel was wounded but got up."

"Yes, these are the prints of a colonel's boots."

"Now, how can you tell that?"

"Because I am Reigning Master and I have fingernails of the correct length."

Remo grunted skeptically. He looked around. "I guess we have a hike ahead of us."

"You may continue to carry my trunk."

"Thanks," Remo said dryly.

And taking the trunk up on his shoulder, Remo faced the Master of Sinanju, saying, "If I see a locker anywhere, I'm stashing this for the duration."

"Do not dare."

"You're just busting my chops, hoping I'll cave in to your little blackmail scam."

"You will," said Chiun.

"I will not."

"The night is young, and the trunk will only get more heavy."

"Actually it's pretty light. What did you say was inside?"

"I did not say. But in exchange for a solemn vow to free your nails, I will allow you to peer inside."

"No, thanks."

"I will not make this generous offer again."

"Good. Because I'm not falling for it."

They continued on. His curiosity aroused, Remo laid an ear against a lapis lazuli phoenix. A faint sound came from the trunk. It was hard to place, but Remo had a growing suspicion that he was carrying approximately five million loose toothpicks.

Well down the trail, they spotted other spoor.

"Smells like something died," Remo said, protecting his nostrils by switching to mouth respiration.

"Or a man's bowels have rebelled against his stomach."

"Yeah, now that you bring it up, that's exactly what it smells like. *Pheew.*"

"No doubt the ill one was a corn addict."

"Corn doesn't cause diarrhea," Remo said.

"Is it not said when the bowels fill with water the surest cure is rice?"

"Yeah . . ."

"And is not corn the opposite of rice?"

"That, I don't buy."

"It does not matter that you buy this or do not, only that it is true. Corn befouls the bowels, which in turn softens the stools. Avoid corn, Remo, if you wish to boast of substantial stools."

"I don't care two shits about my stools."

"You must be aware of these things if you are to achieve my sublime age."

"I can't really imagine myself getting to be one hundred years old."

"Nor can I, who am only eighty."

"Too late, Chiun. I know better. You were born sometime in the last century. You admitted it once."

"That does not mean I am the age you think I am."

Remo stepped over a fallen tree that was perforated by termite burrows. "It does unless you've pulled a Rip Van Winkle when no one was looking."

"Koreans do not reckon time as do Westerners."

"Whatever you say," said Remo. "Is this trunk filled with toothpicks by any chance?"

"No."

Farther along the terrible smell came again.

"I wonder if that's our man?"

"If it is, you may dispatch him," sniffed Chiun. "I do not care to soil my perfect nails with the task."

"Another reason to keep the nail clippers close by. Hey! What's this?"

Chiun froze in place. "What is what?" he hissed.

"That," said Remo, pointing.

Chiun's wide eyes tracked toward the base of a tree. His parchment wrinkles tightened. "I see no foe."

"I didn't say anything about a foe. Isn't that a book?"

"Yes. So? Books are common."

"Not in the jungle," said Remo, laying down the lacquered trunk. "Hold on."

At the base of the tree, Remo examined the book carefully without getting too close. In Vietnam commonplace objects were often dropped along jungle paths by the Vietcong to lure unwary GIs into stepping on buried mines.

This particular book made Remo think of Vietnam. But his sharp eyes detected no trip wires or telltale depression in the ground to suggest a buried antipersonnel mine.

It looked safe, so he knelt and picked up the book. A paperback, it came open in his hands as he regained his feet.

A slow look of surprise came over his face.

"Check it out," said Remo. "Who would read these in the jungle?"

"What is this?" said Chiun, drifting up.

Not taking his gaze from the title page, Remo lifted the book so the Master of Sinanju could examine the cover. It showed a grim-faced man wearing tiger-stripe camouflage paint.

Eyes frowning, Chiun read the title aloud:

"Deadly Death?"

"Guess they ran out of good titles a couple hundred books back," said Remo.

"I do not understand your infatuation."

"This is an Extinguisher book. We used to read these by the ton back in Nam."

"You read this junk?"

"It wasn't junk! At least, it didn't read like junk back then. I don't know about now. This first paragraph is kinda dull."

Flipping back, Remo found the copyright page.

"It's a new one. Boy, I didn't think they still published these."

"It says it is number #214. Is that the number that are printed?"

"No, Little Father, that's the number of adventures in the series."

"You are joking."

"I guess they're still pretty popular."

"Throw it away, it will give you bad ideas."

Remo dropped the book where he found it.

"Okay, but only because we have work do do. But they used to be pretty exciting. I remember one where Blaize Fury single-handedly—"

"Who is Blaize Fury?"

"The Extinguisher's real name. He was a fire fighter whose entire family was burned to death by Mafia arsonists and decided to hunt them down."

"It has taken him 214 adventures and he had not yet succeeded?"

"Actually he got the arsonists in the first book, but it wasn't enough. After that he decided to wipe out the entire Mafia. He would go from city to city shooting practically everyone whose name ended in a vowel."

"No wonder he still struggles. He employs a boom stick and wastes his wrath upon soldiers. Any fool understands if you cut off the head, a snake will quickly die."

"The Mafia had a lot of snake heads in those days. Besides, it's only fiction."

"One man wrote all those books?"

"I don't know about now, but back then, yeah."

"What was his name?"

"Cooper, Carter, or something like that. He was good. But after five or six books, you kinda noticed he was repeating the same three plots over and over again."

"Just like Gordons," sniffed Chiun.

"Now that you mention it, yeah, just like Mr. Gordons. All he was programmed to do was survive, but he lacked one essential ingredient. Creativity. Even when he finally got his programming fixed, he was still as naive as a six-year-old. Last time out, we pulled the wool over his eyes pretty easily.''

''What do you mean 'we,' round-eyes?''

''It was a team effort, okay? Stop busting my chops.''

''I do not like to hear about Gordons.''

''He's out of commission, so what's the problem?''

''He robbed me of my most precious possession.''

''Oh, here we go again....'' Remo groaned.

''Yes, scoff. Minimize. You are a minimizer of tragedies.''

''Right now,'' Remo said, hoisting the trunk up onto his right shoulder, ''I'm just a beast of burden.''

''And I am the last pure-blooded Master of Sinanju. It was my responsibility to sire the next in my line. But I am unable to fulfill this sacred duty because of the accursed man-machine Gordons.''

''Actually he was an android, not a machine.''

''He was a cruel monster. Fashioned by a white lunatic to bring horror to the world just as he brought horror to my formerly serene life.''

''He was created for the space program. To go where human astronauts couldn't. To survive at all costs so that he could send back telemetry of what he found. But I agree with you about the lunatic part. The idiot who built Gordons programmed him to assimilate anything living or not so he could take whatever form maximized his survival.''

''Instead, he maximized my grief by robbing me of my precious seed. An undeniable fact that you persist in minimizing.''

In the jungle darkness Remo rolled his eyes to the interlacing jungle canopy.

In his mind's eye, Remo remembered a previous encounter with the survival android whose creator had named it Mr. Gordons after her favorite brand of gin. It had been shot into outer space, but had returned to earth orbit and assimilated a Soviet space shuttle. The shuttle carried in its cargo bay a doomsday satellite called the Sword of Damocles. Designed to orbit earth indefinitely, the Sword had to receive an annual radio signal or it would activate, bathing the planet in microwaves designed to sterilize the human race. No one would be killed, but eventually humanity would die out from lack of offspring. Showing more malevolence than foresight, the Kremlin had engineered it as a final revenge in the event the USSR ever fell to a Western nuclear strike.

They had successfully neutralized Gordons, but Chiun had been subjected to the rays. Ever since, he swore up and down he'd been sterilized.

The fact that he hadn't attempted to have children throughout the fifty to seventy years before that meant nothing to the Master of Sinanju. It was an injury that cut to the quick of his pride, and whenever the subject came up he wouldn't let Remo hear the end of it.

"I am childless, barren. Doomed forever to bring forth no sons. Though maidens throw their fecund wombs at my feet, I must spurn them, for they are of no use to me."

"Yeah, maidens throw themselves at your feet all the time. Refresh my memory, Little Father. Exactly when was the last time that happened?"

"This they no longer do because they can read the barren emptiness in my eyes. It is written across my features in lines of indescribable pain and sorrow."

"Well, at least you got your revenge."

"Gordons deserved to die a thousand times a thousand ignominious deaths."

"He never really lived, so I don't think it matters much."

"Now the future of the House has fallen upon shoulders that care not whether they sire a child or not. You hoard your precious seed like a miser."

"I gave at the office," Remo grumbled.

"You have squandered your seed. A grown son you did not know exists and a young daughter you never see. It is the end of the pure line of Sinanju. The sun is guttering in the sky, and you fritter away your time on nonsense."

"I have enough Sinanju blood in me and enough seed that when the time comes, I can make all the grandsons you could ever want."

"There is no such number. And it is never too soon to begin."

Noticing Remo shifting shoulders again, the Master of Sinanju asked a pointed question. "Is my precious trunk growing more heavy?"

"A little," Remo admitted.

"That is because its contents grow more heavy with each childless step you take."

"What contents?"

"Guilt."

"Oh, give me a break!"

"I can tell you the truth now. The trunk is empty of all but your burgeoning guilt."

"What have I got to be guilty about?"

"That your offspring do not know their father, just as you did not know yours. The cycle repeats itself. They will carry this burden into the generations to come, and the seeds of the House of Sinanju will be scattered to the four quarters like the seeds of the wayward dandelion."

"I wish a wind would carry this trunk away."

"If it does," Chiun warned, "be certain that it carries you away with it, else you will face my wrath."

"Just as long as it carries me to someplace peaceful," sighed Remo.

35

Assumpta Kaax, aka Lieutenant Balam of the Benito Juarez National Liberation Front, slipped along the jungle trail, following the bitter smell of scorched cornfields.

The air was very bitter this night. The burned-field stink mixed with the strange sulphuric smell coming from the sky.

She looked up. The clear skies were closing. It was difficult to say if this was from rain clouds or the troubled air rolling down from Mount Popo in the north.

The air did not smell like rain, but neither did it smell like air. Not the good clean air of the Lacandón jungle, where the falling rains cleansed everything, making it new again.

In the capital, she understood, the rain fell full of metals and poisons from manufacturing plants and factories that had nothing to do with her life or the lives of her people.

A snap of a branch made her drop to the spongy jungle floor. Crouching, she waited, dark eyes catching faint starlight.

Nothing moved in the direction of the snap.

Careful to remain crouched, she turned her supple body, the better to widen her field of vision.

Another snap came—this time to her left.

She squeezed her weapon, as if for reassurance, and she trembled. She had killed before, but only soldiers. She did not wish to kill a Maya by mistake.

The third snap seemed farther away. It was not the sound of bare feet or the soft Maya sandals. It was the hard sound of heavy boots breaking jungle detritus.

It might be a *soldado,* but it might also be the sound of a *Juarezista* creeping toward a midnight rendezvous.

The latter possibility was sufficiently important that Assumpta decided the risk of the former was worth taking.

Slowly she came to her feet and moved toward the sound.

"YOU HEAR THAT, CHIUN?" said Remo, head swiveling toward the sudden sound.

The Master of Sinanju's quick, birdlike head movement copied that of his pupil. Their eyes pointed in the same direction.

"Yes. The snap of a twig under a boot."

"Okay if I leave the trunk here for a sec?"

Chiun nodded. "Only because we both know your guilt will follow you whether you carry it or not."

They slipped toward the sound, two wraiths, silent and nearly impossible to see in the night.

COLONEL MAURICIO Primitivo crouched behind the sapodilla trees where he could not be seen. In his hands were dry branches he had picked off the ground.

With his thumb he snapped them one at a time, pausing more than a minute between snaps.

The *Juarezista* he had spied from afar would be drawn to the sound, he knew.

He gave the next branch a clean snap, and in the brief echo that followed he heard a soft footfall. Then another.

Yes, closer, he thought. Closer, my unsuspecting *Juarezista*. Come to your doom. For whether you are Subcomandante Verapaz or one of his tools, you will lead me to my heart's desire, I promise you.

He kept one eye on the ground near where he stood. It was the logical approach path. He had picked this spot for that very reason. The sapodilla tree afforded excellent shelter, thick enough to absorb high-velocity rounds.

A dull black boot pressed into the earth not three feet from his own waiting boots.

Dropping the twigs, he brought up his H&K, hissing, "Do not move, *Juarezista!* Or you will surely leave your bones for the tapirs to gnaw on."

The *Juarezista* froze. His training was good.

"Ah, *bueno*. You understood even if you cannot see me. Now, slowly step into the light that I may see you, rebel."

The boot hesitated.

"I can shoot around this tree more swiftly that you can bring your weapon to bear upon me. You know this. If you turn and run, I will pepper your fleeing back. You know this also."

There was no response to that. Colonel Primitivo took this as a sign of assent.

"Good. Now, into the light."

The second boot inched forward, and Colonel Primitivo's eyes went up to the head. A black ski mask enveloped it.

"Let me see your eyes," he said.

The face turned. If the eyes were green, he would obliterate them without hesitation.

But the eyes, large as a deer's, were *mestizo* brown.

Cursing inwardly, Colonel Primitivo snarled, "Now drop your weapon, *insurgentista*."

The weapon remained in the trembling hands.

"Now!"

The weapon was dropped. It struck the jungle floor with a flat finality.

"Now your hands. Raise them that I may search you for concealed weapons."

The hands were elevated.

"Now kneel so that you cannot run away."

Trembling, the *Juarezista* knelt.

When that was done, Colonel Primitivo knelt, too. He laid his right lower leg across the lower limbs of his captive, pinioning them.

Then, holding his own weapon away out of reach with one hand, he employed the other to pat down the rebel.

He found softness where he expected the hardness of a jungle *guerrillero,* and when his hand felt around to the front of the khaki uniform blouse, he discovered the soft mounds of a female.

"What is your name!" he hissed.

"Lieutenant Balam."

"Hah! You are no stalking jaguar on this night, eh *chica?*"

"I am ready to die if necessary."

"And I am prepared to kill you. But I will give you a chance. Subcomandante Verapaz is abroad, here in this zone, on this very night. Tell me where he is and your life may be spared."

"I do not know the answer to your question."

He brought his lips to her ear and made his voice low. "I think you lie, *chica*. Do you lie to me?"

"No."

"Yes, you lie. Your breasts tremble in your blouse. I know how a woman's breasts tremble when she mouths untruths."

The *Juarezista* said nothing. She only trembled more.

"There is a village near here. Perhaps he hides there."

"No, he does not!"

"Hah! You are too quick with your answer."

And stripping off her ski mask by its pom-pom, he exposed a fear-drained face. Long black hair cascaded down. He took up a fall of it and brought it to his nostrils. Sniffing, he detected the scent of coconut.

"You smell good for a jungle girl. You use coconut milk for shampoo. It smells enticing."

With a sudden savage gesture he grabbed up a thick twist of lustrous hair and yanked the girl to her feet even as he came to his.

Placing the stubby snout of the H&K into the small of her back, he ordered her to march toward the village.

The *guerrillera* complied, her steps leaden and defeated.

"Go ahead and cry, *chica*. I think you will need a head start, because after this sad night, this entire jungle will weep because Colonel Mauricio Primitivo has come to visit the rebels.''

"Cabrón," she said thickly.

"Ah, Subcomandante Verapaz has taught you the proper curses of the city, I see."

"¡Chinga tu madre!"

He laughed. "Perhaps later, you and I, we will do what you suggest. Without my mother."

After that the *guerrillera* was silent.

They walked steadily toward the smell of burned corn husks, Colonel Primitivo looking back every once in a while.

He saw nothing. Thus, he knew he was not being followed.

He was wrong. He *was* being followed. But what followed him could not be seen by ordinary eyes or defeated by ordinary arms.

36

Remo Williams gestured to the Master of Sinanju to keep his distance.

They were coming up on the village they had smelled earlier. The Mexican colonel was taking his prisoner directly to it.

"This guy may be doing our work for us."

"As long as he takes no credit," said Chiun, "I will not mind."

"Wonder who the girl is."

"A wench who thinks she is a soldier. What manner of barbarians give a female killing weapons?"

"Women can do a lot of things men can do, Little Father," Remo said dryly. "Scientists discovered this just recently."

"That is not what I mean," Chiun hissed. "What idiot would place a dangerous boom stick into the hands of a creature whose moods swing with the waxing and waning moon?"

"You may have a point there, but right now I think the colonel's in no danger."

They moved on, slipping from tree to tree, becoming one with each bole they attached themselves to. Every time the colonel looked back—which was fairly often—he saw only unmoving trees.

Finally the colonel was tramping through the burned cornfield, making enough rustling sounds to awaken the village.

If that was his plan, he succeeded.

A sleepy head emerged from a shack with a thatched roof.

The colonel casually sighted across the shoulder of his captive and shot it to pieces.

A woman screamed inarticulately, and Remo said, "Damn it, Chiun! That guy was unarmed!"

But the colonel heard them not.

The shots brought new heads sticking out. Switching to selective fire, the colonel popped them like birds on the wing.

Sleepy, surprised faces materialized in the gloom, and were as quickly obliterated.

The colonel raised his voice to a shout. "Verapaz, I am come for you! Show yourself!"

Remo was moving by then.

He cleared the space between himself and the colonel in less than five seconds flat, even with having to skirt various exotic trees.

Even then he was not as fast as the guerrilla, who had dropped to the ground, turned like a dog in the dirt and was kicking out at the colonel with her khaki-clad legs.

"*¡Puta!*" he snarled, bringing his submachine gun down to perforate her belly.

Remo reached him then. One hand drifting out ahead, he broke the weapon in two with a hard downward chop.

The colonel had been holding his weapon steady with both hands. Now they flew apart, each holding a different end.

His eyes went wide at the sight of his bifurcated weapon.

Then Remo was in his face.

"What the hell kind of soldier are you! Those people were unarmed."

"Who are jou?"

Remo relieved him of the weapon parts, tossing them in several directions. The colonel started to grab his combat knife.

Remo let him. When it lifted, Remo took it away from him, held it in front of his face with one hand and used his free index finger to tap the blade. Three taps, starting just back of the point. With each tap, a section of the blade broke off clean until there was no more blade.

Remo handed the colonel back the useless hilt.

To show his gratitude, the colonel tried to shoot Remo in the face with a hastily pulled side arm.

Remo clapped his hands once, abruptly. They came together with the tightly gripped weapon between them.

The colonel felt the sting of the converging hands on his gun hand, flinched and told his brain to tell his trigger finger to squeeze the trigger.

His finger refused. Then the pistol began falling apart in his hands as if every screw had melted.

When he was left with only the cartridge-packed handle, but no breech or barrel, his gun hand began turning red as if sunburned. He stared at it with wide-eyed disbelief.

"Can you say 'vascular disintegration'?" asked Remo.

"I do not know those words."

"Think of the veins on your hand turning to mush and letting all the blood seep into your tissues."

The colonel suddenly screamed. Not from the realization of his maiming but from the pain signals that finally caught up with his brain.

Reaching for his neck, Remo squeezed a nerve that cut off the pain. He wasn't in a hurry; he let some pain seep through.

"I'm looking for Verapaz."

Through gritted teeth, the colonel said, "As am I! We are on the same side, yes?"

"We are on the same side, absolutely *not,*" Remo shot back. "I don't kill noncombatants."

"You are obviously American. CIA?"

"UNICEF."

"The children's fund?"

"That's right. We're looking after the welfare of children everywhere. We also take donations. Dollars, not pesos."

"You are loco."

"If *loco* means I'm mad enough to break your neck, I have no quarrel with *loco.*"

"Jou might have your wish, for I believe Verapaz to be in this very village." He gave the prostrate guerrilla a nudge with a black-booted toe. "This *Naca,* she knows."

Reaching down, Remo brought the guerrilla to her feet.

"Where's Verapaz?"

"I know not."

"She is obviously lying," said Chiun, who had materialized at their side.

"I have said this," Primitivo said.

"You stay out of this," Remo said.

The Master of Sinanju drifted up to the girl, making his voice sympathetic. "Poor child. They give you the tools of death when you should be the bearer of life."

"I do not need your advice, even if you saved my life," she spit.

Remo said, "Look, we have no problem with you. We just want Verapaz."

"I would sooner die than surrender him to you. Go ahead. Shoot me if you must."

Turning away in disgust, Chiun said, "Go ahead, Remo. Shoot her. Her milk has been soured by war. She is spoiled for motherhood."

"I'm shooting nobody." Remo faced her. "There's an easy way and a hard way. Which do you want?"

"The third way. The way out of this nightmare. How dare you come into my land to seek my Lord Verapaz? This is no affair of *gringos.*"

"That's another story. Look, we have a job to do and then we're out of here. I don't want to hurt you."

"I am not afraid of you."

"Damn," said Remo. Turning to Chiun, he said, "Your turn, Little Father."

"I am no harmer of females. That is your job."

Sighing, Remo told the girl, "This is going to hurt me as much as it hurts you."

"Hurt her as much as you wish," said Colonel Primitivo, dark eyes flashing with anticipation.

Remo took her left earlobe, where a sensitive nerve was located, and pinched it. The guerrilla seemed to surge up out of her boots and squeezed her tearing eyes shut even as she gnashed her lower lip to a crimson rag.

"I do not know!" she wailed.

"She lies," spat the colonel.

"She's telling the truth," said Remo, releasing the girl's earlobe.

Gasping for air, she shrank back into her uniform, saying, "Kill me now if you must."

"The next person who touches her," a cold voice said from the jungle thickness, "eats angry subsonic rounds!"

37

The commanding crack of a voice came from the west.

Remo's gaze veered toward the sound.

The ranks of trees were clustered tightly, and clotting darkness held sway between them. The gathering clouds above had almost swallowed the last fading starlight before the approach of dawn.

But there was enough starlight for Remo's eyes to capture and magnify.

Deep in the murk, a figure in black resolved itself out of the shadows. The head was muffled except for a slash surrounding the eyes, which were darkened with burned cork.

Remo saw the eyes. Blue.

"Bingo!" he said. "There's our man, Chiun."

"The eyes should be green."

"Blue—green. They're close enough for government work."

"Come out, come out, wherever you are," Chiun called.

"Step away from the girl!" the crack of a voice said.

"Make us," taunted Chiun.

"I'll wax you all."

"You wax us and the girl dies, too," Remo pointed out.

"That's a chance I'll take."

The guerrilla stiffened and held her breath. Otherwise, she didn't look very worried.

Remo lifted his voice again. "Sorry. No sale. She doesn't think you'll do it, and neither do we."

"You are finished, Verapaz," the Mexican colonel called out.

"Shut up, tostada face. I'm not Verapaz."

"Then who are you?" Chiun demanded.

"Ask your colonel."

Remo eyed the colonel.

Primitivo shrugged. "He claims to be *El Extinguirador*."

"Who?"

"You might know him as Blaize Fury."

"Yeah, I know who Blaize Fury is. How come you do, too?"

"Because I have read many of his pulse-pounding adventures in my carefree jouth."

"Same here."

Primitivo showed smiling teeth. "Then we are allies."

"Blaize Fury wouldn't shoot unarmed civilians in the face and neither would I. Sorry. Consider your fan-club membership permanently revoked."

To Remo's surprise the colonel looked completely crestfallen.

The commanding voice sounded again, a distinct whiplash of a sound. "The Extinguisher doesn't say things twice."

"The Extinguisher is a sissy," Chiun called out.

"Who are you calling a sissy?"

"The Extinguisher. The sissy who extinguishes."

Remo called out. "Look, we're not backing down, so you better come out so we can straighten this out."

A long silence developed. Remo had his eye on the shape in the forest murk. Abruptly it moved to one side.

The Extinguisher thought he was being stealthy, but Remo tracked him easily. He saw that Chiun had him fixed in his sights, too.

At a nod from Remo, the Master of Sinanju faded back into the jungle, his emerald-and-ocher kimono blending in with the vegetation.

After that, Remo folded his arms and waited.

The Extinguisher moved in a semicircle, keeping them in sight at all times. When he reached a tree, he unhooked a small folding grapnel from his web belt and affixed it to a black nylon line. Swinging it up, he snared an overhanging branch. Then like a nimble black spider, he went up, hand over hand.

His grip was not what it should have been. He slid down twice.

Floating across the space came a soft curse or two.

Finally he reached the branch and started to grab for it.

Perched directly above, the Master of Sinanju calmly reached down and sawed the nylon line with one swift fingernail swipe.

The man in black landed in the dirt like a sack of sausage.

Remo was on top of him seconds later. Reaching down, he pulled off his gear and threw it every which way.

"You can't do this to the Extinguisher!"

"Watch me," said Remo, flinging away the web belt and reaching for the black leather shoulder sling supporting a machine pistol.

It broke under the strength of his hard yank, and Remo prepared to toss it away, too, when he noticed amid all the projecting clips a Lucite ammo drum.

"What the hell is this?"

"My Hellfire pistol. It's the only one of its kind."

Remo's eyes looked strange. Dropping the weapon, holster and all, he took hold of the ski mask and yanked it straight up.

The last of the starlight disappeared then. But Remo didn't need it.

The exposed face was young and angular, the short hair dirty blond. And to Remo's eyes it looked very familiar.

"Chiun, I think we have a problem."

"It is not my problem," Chiun said from the branch above. "For he is not my son, but yours."

38

Remo dragged the man who called himself the Extinguisher to his feet.

The Master of Sinanju dropped from his branch, as light as a green parachute descending, to land beside them.

"This idiot isn't my son," Remo said in a disgusted voice.

"Hey, I resent that!"

"No son of mine would parade around tricked out like a walking Swiss army knife. Or pretend to be some phoney dime-novel superhero."

"The Extinguisher is a legend. How do you know he isn't real?"

"Because I have a working brain. Your name is Winston Smith. Until last year you were with the Navy. Now you're AWOL."

"No. Wait. Think about it. Everybody knows the Extinguisher's name. It might be a cover to con the bad guys thinking that they have nothing to be afraid of."

"They do not," Chiun retorted. "For we spied your clumsy clanking and clunking and ambushed you before you could unleash your ridiculous toy gun upon us."

"Hey, I have an excuse. I have the trots."

"What is this witless one talking about?" Chiun asked Remo.

Winston Smith lowered his voice. "The screaming shits to you."

Chiun sniffed the air delicately. "Is it you who has befouled the jungle?" he asked.

"Not my fault. I drank some bad water."

"This is Mexico," Remo said. "All the water is bad."

"Yeah, well, now I know. That doesn't change who I am."

"Kid, I was reading Blaize Fury when I was in Nam and your highest ambition was to crawl up a fallopian tube."

"You were in 'Nam? Cool! What was it like?"

"It was hell."

"You're lucky. I missed out on 'Nam."

"You missed out on common sense too. What are you doing down here?"

"He is a *Juarezista*," the girl inserted.

"That true?"

The Extinguisher looked away. "Let me talk to you in private, okay?"

Remo took him by the arm and into the jungle. In a thick part of the woods, he spun him around.

"Let's have it."

"I'm only pretending to be a *Juarezista*."

"Like you're pretending to be the Extinguisher?"

"No, I'm really him. I mean I took on the *nom de guerre* to further my work."

"What work?"

Smith whispered, "I'm gonna wax Subcomandante Verapaz."

Remo looked at him. In the darkness Smith waited expectantly, his grimy face shining with an inner pride.

"Why?" Remo asked.

"What do you mean—why? It's what the Extinguisher does."

"If you don't stop referring to yourself in the third person, I'm going to shake you so hard your nuts are going to drop out your nostrils. Now, answer my question."

"I'm on assignment," Smith said grudgingly.

"Working for who?"

"That's classified."

Remo gave Smith's bicep a hard squeeze. Smith gritted his teeth, and sweat popped from his forehead. But he fought back his pain with such grim determination that Remo relented slightly.

"No. Really, I can't say who sent me. It's the first rule of black ops."

"The first rule of survival is to tell the truth when a bigger dog has you by the hind legs. Meet the bigger dog. Me."

"Okay, I'm with the UN."

"Nice try. No sale. Try again."

"It's true. I'm working for the UN. It's quasi-official right now. If I dust Verapaz, I'll have a solid gig."

"Well, you can dust off your résumé. Verapaz belongs to us."

"Us! what do you mean us? Who are you guys?"

"That *is* classified," Remo snapped.

"You're kidding, aren't you? I mean, my Uncle Harold sent you down to haul my sorry butt back to Folcroft, didn't he?"

Remo shook his head. "He's not your Uncle Harold, and we're here after Verapaz. Never mind why."

"Look, we'll team up. How's that?"

"I need a partner like you need an imagination. Forget it."

Smith turned. "Okay. Fine. Let me go and may the best man win."

Remo arrested him by the collar. "Look, you were a SEAL, right?"

"Yeah. What's it to you?"

"You should know the score. You're a foreigner in a war zone loaded down with enough gear to get you stood up in front of a firing squad."

Winston Smith cracked a lopsided grin. "Yeah. That chicken-shit Mexican colonel tried that already. I still live."

"That girl save you?"

"She's not just a girl. She's guerrilla. There's no shame in being saved at the last minute by an ally."

"She saved your sorry butt and you conned her into taking you to Verapaz, am I right?"

"Right."

"And in the middle of making formal introductions, you're going to whip out that overgrown Pez dispenser of yours and blow them both away, right?"

"No. Just Verapaz."

"Then what?"

"What do you mean?"

"You heard me. After you blow Verapaz away, what are you going to do about the girl?"

Winston looked at his boots. His voice lost its bluster. "I haven't thought that part all the way through yet," he admitted.

"What if she pulls out her weapon and nails you?"

"She wouldn't do that! Would she?"

"You ask me, she's half in love with you."

Smith brightened. "You really think so?"

"Can the high school stuff. You shoot Verapaz, and she'll either nail you or make you shoot her. Is that what you want?"

"I don't know yet. This is only my second mission."

"Okay. Listen up. From now on, you follow my lead. Understand?"

"What're you planning?"

"Just follow my lead and stay out from underfoot."

Pushing the boy ahead of him, Remo rejoined the others.

The villagers were hanging back in fear. The dead were being pulled out of the shacks, and a fresh-blood smell hung in the air like a jungle miasma.

Remo lifted his voice for Assumpta's benefit. "Looks like we're joining the *Juarezistas*, Little Father."

And keeping his face way from the others, the Master of Sinanju, whose sharp ears had heard every word, winked broadly.

"I have always desired to defend the downpressed."

"It's *oppressed*," Winston said dispiritedly.

"Jou are friends of *El Extinguirador*?" Assumpta asked.

"He thinks he's my father," Winston said.

"He is," Chiun said.

"Is he?" asked Assumpta.

Remo and Winston looked at one another.

"No way," both said in unison.

Turning to Assumpta, Remo asked, "Can you lead us to Verapaz?"

"If you are truly friends of Señor Blaize Fury, I will do this, for I trust him with all of my heart."

Remo shot Winston a glance. Winston looked everywhere but back.

"Okay," Remo said. "One last loose end and we're out of here."

"What is that?" asked Colonel Mauricio Primitivo.

"You."

The colonel squared his shoulder boards. "I am no loose end. I am a colonel in the Mexican federal army."

"No, you're a war criminal in a civil war." And Remo whistled for some of the lurking villagers to come padding up.

"Jou cannot do this. It is uncivilized."

"It is justice," Assumpta spat out the words.

A knot of Maya surrounded Colonel Primitivo. Assumpta spoke to them in a musical tongue that was not Spanish by the quizzical look on the Master of Sinanju's parchment face.

Someone dropped a rock on the colonel's head, knocking him out cold. Others grabbed his ankles and pulled him back into the village.

"What's going to happen to him?" Winston asked as they started off.

Assumpta shrugged. "He may be flayed while living, or burned with the old corn."

"Kinda drastic."

"It is what happens to all who oppose the righteous justice of the *Juarezistas.*"

Winston Smith looked uncomfortable.

39

Oaxaca in the valley was all but empty of men when the flowing train of Coatlicue lumbered in.

The federal government had ceded the capital of the entire state. The immaculate city in the valley was virtually deserted.

Dust still hung in the air from the departed vehicles.

They stood in the center of the broad, tree-ringed Zocalo, the plaza that all Mexican towns and cities possess. This one was not as great as that of Mexico City, but to the eyes of High Priest Rodrigo Lujan, it was holy. Because it belonged to him.

Towering above him under a sky dark with sinister clouds was Coatlicue, in whose name he had taken the city built over sacred Zapotec soil. Her skin resembled that of an armadillo now, covered in steely plates absorbed from the army tanks that she crushed and absorbed. No conquistador was ever so formidable, Lujan thought proudly.

"We are victorious!" he sang out.

"*We are not alone,*" Coatlicue said, her voice ringing hollowly, her eyes peering from armored slits.

"What!"

"*I detect the body heat of meat machines in the*

surrounding structures. A high probability of a trap is indicated.''

"But no trap can possibly harm you, Coatlicue," said Rodrigo, stepping into the shelter of the living idol he worshiped above all.

"You must investigate this situation."

"I?"

"You promised to protect me."

"Very well," said Lujan, adjusting his feathered cloak. He had acquired more festive garments along the way. Others had, too. Nearby stood a knot of Aztecs in the brine-stiffened uniforms of the Jaguar Company. Eagle Knights were nearby, bedecked in feathers both real and artificial. They carried weapons ranging from the obsidian-bladed spears to heavy hardwood clubs capable of dashing a man's brains from his skull.

"Jaguars. Investigate these buildings."

They moved with alacrity. And why not—for they understood that loyal service meant that they needn't be eaten. Not that they would turn away from the prospect. But there were other ways to serve Coatlicue, their Mother.

The Jaguars came back hauling trembling Zapotecs.

"Release them, for these are my people."

Going among them, Lujan blessed them with his hands upon their trembling heads, saying, "Welcome to your new life. For as long as you serve Our Mother, you will eat meat and live in splendor."

Then, lifting his voice in joy and triumph, Lujan called, "Come out, my people. Join the ranks of the new lords of Oaxaca. Come, come, do not be afraid.

The world has turned upside down, and you have happily landed on the correct side. Come, step forth."

Slowly they came. Carefully. Zapotecs were in the majority, but a sprinkling of others showed their faces, as well. Mixtec, mostly. Lujan did not bless them. Mixtec invaders had usurped the old capital of Monte Alban, casting down the Zapotecs who had built it. That was many centuries ago, true, but in his heart Lujan decided these latter-day stragglers would not enjoy the best of the new Zapotec order. After all, someone had to take out the garbage.

In the middle of this rumination, a priest emerged from Santo Domingo Church.

He approached with a trembling certitude. His white cassock with the barbarian purple cross on its front swayed with each step. He walked behind a heavy gold crucifix, which he carried aloft before him.

Lujan welcomed him. "Padre! Come. Approach."

"I do not know from what hell you have emerged, Coatlicue, but in the name of the Father, the Son and the Holy Ghost, I banish you. *Viva Cristo Rey!*"

"You play your role well, Padre," Lujan called out. "You remind me of the padre who is in all the old monster movies. He comes full of faith and fear, just as you do. He is brave. He is true. Despite the awful power of *El Enormo*—or whatever the monster is called—he believes his faith will shield him from the demons from hell."

"I banish you, creature of superstition."

"Do you hear, my people? This padre calls us superstitious. Us! We who stand in the protecting shadow of Our Living Mother. You, priest. Where is your god? Have him appear."

"His spirit is in us all. It permeates the air."

"Look above you. The air is dark and roiled. Terrible powers are abroad. A dark new day has dawned. Your crosses of gold will be melted down and reshaped into braziers and idols. No more confessions. No more commandments. Coatlicue rules now."

The priest stood still, his arm lifted as high as humanly possible. It shook and shook in his great, satisfying fear.

"No," Lujan called. "Do not stop. Approach. Coatlicue will not eat you. For she has had her fill. Is that not right, Coatlicue?"

Coatlicue said nothing. Her armored serpent heads separated and homed in on the priest, very much like the cobralike death-ray dealer in the movie called *The War of the Worlds*.

The priest was speaking Latin now, his words coming faster and faster, the vowels and consonants blended together.

"What is the matter, priest? Your white magic does not work. Coatlicue stands supreme, despite your useless prayers."

When the priest ran out of prayers and strength, he dropped to his knees sobbing. Then his head tipped forward and struck the stone flags of the Zocalo. High Priest Rodrigo Lujan ordered his Eagles to seize him.

They laid him at the feet of the unmoving and unmoved Coatlicue, and as an obsidian dagger was handed to Lujan, the Jaguar soldiers stripped apart the cassock to bare the heaving, helpless chest.

The heart of the priest seemed to beat through his ribs and skin. It called to Rodrigo Lujan, asking, pleading, begging for release.

And with swift, sure movements of the wickedly sharp black blade, Rodrigo Lujan released the pounding heart and held it up to the brownish sky, his blood-spattered face beaming.

Coatlicue looked down through her armored eye slits and boomed, *"No, thank you. I am full."*

40

The word came down from the north.

"There is terrible news, Lord Kukulcan!"

Alirio Antonio Arcila stood up in his jungle encampment. He had expected bad news. They were in Oaxaca State now. They had passed from Chiapas without challenge or incident. It was suspicious. Almost as if the army had let them pass this far. A trap was likely. And so he asked, "The army is massing now?"

"Yes! No!"

"Speak, faithful Kix."

"The army is massing, yes. But that is not the terrible news, no."

"What is it, then?"

"Coatlicue walks the earth again."

Antonio frowned under his ski mask. "What is this you say?"

"The mother god of the rude Aztecs has returned to life. She walks, twenty or thirty feet tall, and hurls back the army like wooden toys."

This time Antonio glowered under his ski mask. Was this *indio baboso* drunk on pulque? "Where do you hear this?" he demanded.

"In the village of my people. It is all over the television. It has even preempted the *telenovelas*."

Antonio's masked mouth dropped open. This was serious if Television Azteca preempted the soap operas. They did not do that even for national catastrophes, of which this past day was the greatest since the conquistadors came ashore.

"I must see this for myself."

Going to a pack mule, he unearthed his chief intelligence-gathering device. A portable battery-powered TV.

"Coatlicue is on Television Azteca," Kix panted. "That is Channel Cinco."

The set took a moment to warm up, during which Antonio fiddled with the rabbit ears. The mountains were a problem, but if he pointed the antenna correctly most of the snow went away.

On Television Azteca he saw the shifting images of destruction.

"This is a monster movie!" he objected, derision in his voice.

"No, this is real. Coatlicue walks."

It was true, he saw after careful study. This was live coverage. The creature was the familiar one from the National Museum of Anthropology. It was easily thirty feet tall.

The army had barricaded the road before it. The statue, somehow animate, stony yet flexible at the same time, crushed the armored vehicles under her remorseless golem tread.

"See! She is invincible!"

"Where is this coming from?" Antonio demanded.

"Ciudad Oaxaca, Lord."

"Oaxaca city means nothing to me. Let Coatlicue have all of Oaxaca State. It will be a buffer state for Chiapas."

"No, no. Do you not see, Lord? If Coatlicue is back, can Tezcatlipoca and Huitzilopochtli be far behind? He is your mortal enemy."

"Tezcatlipoca is the mortal enemy of Quetzalcoatl."

"But you are Quetzalcoatl. The Aztecs call you this in their attempt to steal you from us. They cannot, for we have prior claim, but they have tried."

"I do not care about this," Antonio said impatiently.

"But the television says that all *indios* follow Coatlicue."

"What is this?"

"It is true. Aztec. Mixtec. Even some Maya."

This, Antonio cared about. He came to his feet trembling. "That lumbering rock is usurping my revolution!"

"You must wage counterrevolution."

"Mexico City can wait. We're going to the city of Oaxaca."

"These Aztecs will rue the day they stole our religions, our gods and our women!" Kix swore.

Antonio assembled an advance unit of twenty men to go ahead of the main group.

"This way we will travel faster," he told them. "I, of course shall lead."

If anyone would have told Alirio Antonio Arcila only a day ago that he would willingly lead men in combat against a thirty-foot foe, he would have scoffed.

He was not the first revolutionary to be seduced into madness by his own press.

41

Dawn broke over the Lacandón jungle. The sky was clearing. A few stars still hung in the bluing sky.

"See that star?" said Assumpta, pointing.

"That is no star," Chiun said. "That is Venus. A mere planet."

"That star is the heart and soul of Kukulcan in whose name we fight."

A moment later a shooting star fell.

"And that," she said, "my ancestors believed to be a cigar thrown away by the old gods of the Maya."

"Your gods smoke tobacco?" Chiun asked skeptically.

"This is what was believed."

"No wonder the women of your tribe carry boom sticks."

Remo paused to look behind them.

Winston Smith was bringing up the rear. He clinked and jingled with every step like an itinerant silverware salesman.

"Anytime you want to ditch some of that gear, feel free," Remo called back.

"No chance. These are my warrior's accoutrements."

"You'll catch a bullet jingling like that."

"The round hasn't been cast that will drop the Extinguisher."

"Watch that—"

"Oof!"

"—tree root," finished Remo.

"Be patient with him," Assumpta said. "He suffers from the *turistas*."

Chiun waited for Winston to catch up. He fell in beside him, hands tucked into the sleeves of his kimono.

"You are a disgrace to your bloodline."

"Get stuffed, Wong."

A fingernail drifted out instructively. It seemed only to tap the spine, but the results were noisy.

"Ooowww!"

"Apologize to your grand uncle," Chiun chided.

"You're not my grand uncle."

"I am ashamed to admit it, but it is true. I am a distant relative of your father."

Winston Smith's eyes fell on Remo walking ahead. He dropped his voice. "Hey, what's his name anyway?"

"That is classified," said Chiun, quickening his pace.

The day was in full cry now. The jungle birds were awake. As they marched along, a red macaw watched them with detached curiosity, its scarlet head swiveling like a feathered tracking device. Remo carried Chiun's recovered trunk on one shoulder.

"No, I'm serious. What do I call him?"

"Ask him."

Smith caught up with Remo.

"You know, we've never been really introduced."

"Tough."

"I told you this was my second mission. You never asked me what the first was."

"Ask me if I care," said Remo.

"I did Mahout Feroze Anin, the warlord of Stomique."

Hearing this, Chiun hurried up to join them. "Did you get paid?"

"No, it was a freebie."

"Pah! You are hopeless."

"Look, I had to establish my rep."

"You establish your reputation by the amount of gold received. Do you know nothing about the art you practice?"

"I'm a warrior. I fight. Payment is optional. Besides, my reputation is the greatest one a man could have. Just mention the dreaded name Extinguisher and see the bad guys go white."

"You look a little pale yourself," Remo said.

Smith looked momentarily weird. "Oh, shit. Excuse me a second."

"Hold up," said Remo impatiently. "The dreaded Extinguisher has to take another bathroom break."

"He is very brave to march on weak bowels," Assumpta said.

"How long you known him?" asked Remo.

"Only since last night. Did you know they publish his manly exploits in books?"

"Do tell," said Remo. Chiun yawned.

"It is true. He has told me they have sold forty million copies all around the world."

Chiun's hazel eyes exploded. "Is this true, Remo? Forty millions of copies?"

"That's what that book I found along the trail said."

Chiun's eyes narrowed.

When Winston Smith returned from his assignation with a ceiba tree, all eyes were upon him.

"Do you receive royalties?" Chiun demanded.

"On what?"

"Your foolish adventures."

"No."

"Idiot."

They continued on.

"You guys will learn to respect me for what I do," Smith said plaintively.

"We respect those we respect for their skills and their gold," Chiun said. "You have neither."

"Some day I'm going to have a book published about my actual adventures, then I'll retire on my royalties."

"Don't count on living that long," said Remo.

"I've been writing it all along. Check out my rucksack."

Dropping back, Remo did. He pulled out a black school notebook. On the cover was the stenciled outline of a fire extinguisher spitting bullets through its nozzle.

Remo opened it.

"Looks like a diary."

"It's my war journal."

"You write everything down?"

"Sure!"

"What if you're captured?"

"I get captured all the freaking time. Nothing bad ever happens."

Remo tossed the notebook into the jungle.

"Hey! You can't do that! That's private property."

"Rule number one—don't write anything down. If you're captured, they'll hang you with your own words."

"The rope hasn't been woven that—"

"You're a menace to yourself," said Remo, noticing something drop from a frayed popcorn pocket of Smith's black uniform. He picked it up.

It was tiny plastic fire extinguisher.

"What's this thing?"

"Icons. I wax a kill, I leave it in his hand. Sometimes in his mouth. Strikes fear like crazy into the guys who find him."

Seeing another one drop onto the trail, Remo said, "You might as well leave a trail of bread crumbs behind for the enemy to follow."

"Listen, you just don't understand my profession."

"Tell it to the Marines, squid."

"Jarhead."

"You are all related?" asked Assumpta.

"Distantly," Chiun said. "The blood is very diluted."

"And what is your name, old one?"

"I am called Chiun. More than that I will not say."

"You are maya?"

"Pah!"

"There is a word in our language. *Chuen.*"

Chiun looked interested. "Yes?"

"It means *monkey.*"

"Pah," said the Master of Sinanju.

"You ask me—" Winston Smith laughed "—you looked kinda like a *chuen* when you were up in that tree."

That was enough for Remo and Chiun. They decided right then and there that Winston Smith needed an emergency bath. Smith was apprised of their decision when they picked him up bodily and tossed him into a scummy jungle pond, rucksack and all.

When he emerged, Smith stood trembling and dripping while he bestowed several colorful but uncomplimentary new titles upon their persons.

The Master of Sinanju decided he wasn't as thoroughly clean as they thought and took it upon himself to wash Smith's Mouth out with a bar of Lava soap taken from the rucksack.

After that, Winston Smith became a much more agreeable traveling companion.

42

En route to Oaxaca, Comandante Efrain Zaragoza encountered a sight that filled his patriotic soul with rage and fear.

Refugees. Mexican refugees. They were a mix of city *chilangos* like him and rural *mestizos*.

"The monster!" they cried, weeping. "He has taken Oaxaca."

"Then the monster is doomèd to die," Zaragoza returned.

The refugees dribbled down in *colectivos*, mopeds and taxis. The thin trickle became a river and soon a flood. The road became impassable.

Zaragoza rode in the turret of a light armored vehicle. It ran on six huge tires like an APC but sported a formidable 25 mm Bushmaster autocannon. It was very nimble.

"Leave the road to the refugees. Take to the ground," he radioed to the column at his back.

The column left the road and moved on.

The ground was open, growing increasingly hilly, then mountainous. But they would make it. They would retake Oaxaca and end the madness that had been unleashed on a perfectly civilized nation.

Farther along they encountered the straggling remains of Montezuma Barracks.

They limped down in blistered Humvees and APCs.

Linking up with his counterpart, Zaragoza demanded, "Why do you flee?"

From out of his turret the commander of Montezuma Barracks lifted a portable television set. It was on, and on the screen was the incredible sight of the demon Coatlicue herself, surrounded by circle upon circle of *indio* warriors and adherents.

"We were outnumbered," the commander said.

"You have modern guns. I see only sticks in the *indios'* hands."

"I am not speaking of the accursed *indios. La Ponderosa* herself outnumbers us in her sheer *enormidad*. She crushes tanks under her stone tread. She smites helicopters from the very sky, after first shrugging off their rockets. There was no stopping her."

"I have orders to vanquish her."

"Prepare to be vanquished. *Adios.*"

The APC's engine roared anew. It lurched forward.

"Where do you go?" Zaragoza demanded.

"Chiapas. Perhaps Yucatán. It may be safe in Yucatán."

"This is desertion, Commander."

"The capital is a shambles, and Oaxaca is ruled by demons and *indios*. There is nothing to desert unless a miracle also springs out of the wounded earth."

As he watched the armored column with its demoralized crewmen rumble south to the relative safety of guerrilla-held Chiapas, Comandante Zaragoza gave fleeting thought to joining the parade of survivors.

But he was a soldier true and loyal to his nation, and he had visions of making general one day.

"Onward!" he cried. "We drive on Oaxaca."

The column moved on, trembling because the aftershocks continued at irregular intervals.

It seemed as if the whole world had gone mad with fear and panic. It was no wonder that the old gods walked again.

43

In a village whose name Remo couldn't begin to pronounce, they were told in no uncertain terms that Subcomandante Verapaz was marching on the city of Oaxaca.

"What's in Oaxaca?" asked Remo after Assumpta had translated the words for them.

Assumpta answered the question in Spanish. *"La Monstruosa."*

"What monster?" Chiun asked sharply.

"The monster that has escaped the capital. It is being said the upheaval has opened a pit and unleashed her from the fires below."

"Her?" said Remo.

"Sí. The monster is female."

Remo looked at Chiun, and the Master of Sinanju looked back.

"You don't think..." Remo started to say.

"It cannot be."

"What's the monster's name?" Remo asked Assumpta.

Back came the response, which needed no translation. "Coatlicue."

"Why would Verapaz go to fight a monster?" said Remo because he didn't want to follow the conversation to its logical conclusion.

"Because he is believed to be Lord Kukulcan and Lord Kukulcan is the mortal enemy of Coatlicue."

From a *cantina,* a frightened voice called out.

"He is saying that the monster has conquered Oaxaca itself," Assumpta explained. "The army has fled before her."

More rapid words came.

"But the monster has remained stopped for several hours now. She is not leaving. Chiapas may be safe."

"How does he know this?" asked Chiun.

"He watches it in the television, as does all of Mexico."

Remo said, "Come on, Little Father. Let's check this out."

They entered the *cantina*.

It was just like the restaurant in the last town they had visited, down to the semicircle of men in white Texas hats huddled around a flickering TV set. Except this set was in color.

On the screen stood the Coatlicue monster, immobile, armored like a steely beetle, as all around Indians danced and feasted.

"What are they eating?" Remo asked, noticing all the blood.

"Men. They are eating men," said Chiun.

"How long has this been going on?" Remo asked no one in particular.

"Since last afternoon," Assumpta told him.

Remo drew Chiun aside and lowered his voice. "This is either the longest monster movie ever made or we've got a serious problem here, Little Father."

Chiun's eyes squeezed down to glittering slits.

"It is Gordons."

"Who?" asked Winston Smith.

"Stay out of this!" snapped Remo.

"Up yours. Who do you think you are, my father?"

Remo opened his mouth to shoot back a retort. A flicker of strangeness crossed his face. He shut it.

"If that's Gordons, how'd he get so big?" Remo wondered.

"I will ask," said Assumpta.

Before Remo could say *Don't waste your time,* she did and received a short reply from a TV watcher.

"I am told the Coatlicue monster has been eating people since it marched from the capital to Oaxaca. As she ate, she grew."

"Can Gordons do that?" Remo asked.

Chiun regarded the screen, stony of face. "He has. That is plain to see."

"There is a phone around here?" Remo asked.

Someone pointed to an old wooden booth like the one Clark Kent favored very early in his career. It said TELEPHONO in faded black letters.

Remo tried getting a connection to the States and was told the cost would be four thousand dollars.

"Mexican or American?" he asked.

"American. Dollars are American. Mexican dollars are pesos, *señor.*"

"That's highway robbery!" he exploded.

And the operator hung up.

Wearily Remo got a new operator and, when told the price had gone up to five thousand dollars American, read off his Discover card account number without complaint.

Once he had the connection to the States, he dialed Harold Smith by sticking his finger in the 1 hole and spinning the old-fashioned rotary dial over and over, hoping it would work.

It did. Harold Smith's lemony voice came on the line.

"Smith, what are you hearing out of Mexico?"

"It is a catastrophe."

"More than you think. What do you hear about a monster running amok in Oaxaca?"

"Nothing."

"Well, it's all over Mexican TV down here. And it looks like Mr. Gordons."

"What!"

"He's thirty feet tall this time, Smith. You really screwed up, you know that?"

"Gordons was deactivated. You assured me of that."

"Yeah. But we wanted to crush him to powder just to make sure."

"That was not practicable. The Coatlicue idol had been restored to the museum, inert and harmless. It was a Mexican national treasure. And your mission was accomplished."

"You could have let us finish the damn job."

"*You* said it was finished," Smith said hotly.

"Enough!" cried Chiun, slapping his long-nailed hands together.

Taking the phone from a startled Remo, the Master of Sinanju spoke into the receiver. "O Emperor, let us not revisit past errors. Instruct us. The rebel Verapaz has thus far eluded us, but we persevere. This new problem also calls our name. What is your wish?"

"Destroy them both. I want this mission completed by sundown, if possible."

"It shall be as you wish."

"Do what you have to," Smith said testily.

And Chiun hung up.

"Who were you talking to?" Winston asked when they rejoined them. Assumpta was at the door watching for soldiers.

"Never mind," said Remo.

"It wasn't my Uncle Harold, was it? Did he ask about me?"

"Your name didn't come up, and it was a private conversation."

"Fine. Take a hike. Assumpta and I will handle ourselves from here on. You don't need me. I won't need you."

"We're going to Oaxaca," said Remo.

"And I'm going to hook up with Subcomandante Verapaz."

"I mean all of us."

Winston whipped up his Hellfire supermachine pistol and pointed it in Remo's face. "This baby here says I go my way."

Remo looked at the weapon that seemed to point in every direction except back at its owner. "That thing still voice activated?"

"Get real. I took all that crap out."

"So if I take it away from you, I can shoot you with it if I want to?"

"Nice try. But I can still disable it with a voice command."

"That right?"

"Yeah. That's right. You make a play for it and all I have to say is 'Disengage.'"

"Disengage," the gun said in a mechanical voice, going dead.

"Damn you!" Winston snapped, reaching for a side-mounted button. The barrel lit up, and he trained it on Remo's face.

"Too slow," Winston said.

"Guess so," said Remo.

And while Winston Smith was grinning, Remo coolly said, "Disengage."

"Disengage," the gun repeated obligingly, and then shut down.

"But it wasn't supposed to do that!" Smith complained, a dumbfounded expression crossing his face.

He was still wearing it when Remo pried the weapon from his unresisting fingers.

"We're a team till this is done," Remo said.

"Give me back my piece."

"Behave yourself and maybe I will."

They left the *cantina*. Assumpta started off ahead of them, looking for transportation.

"The CIA designed that gun," Winston said after a long silence.

Remo eyed him. "So?"

"It's programmed to recognize my voice. Only my voice."

"Maybe it needs a new chip."

"But it recognized your voice. It did that last time, too."

Remo said nothing. He didn't like the way this conversation was going, either.

"You know what I think?"

"You do not think!" Chiun said unkindly.

"I think there's a logical explanation. And it means one thing."

"I'm not your father," Remo said hastily.

"It means you're CIA. Come on. Admit it."

"If you had a brain, you'd know a CIA agent doesn't admit anything."

"Gotcha! You just proved my point."

"Congratulations, but it's not true," Remo said dryly.

"But you are warm," Chiun said.

"Chiun!" Remo warned.

"Four letters. It begins with a *C* and ends with an *E.*"

"Damn! I know all the intelligence agencies by heart. Let's see. CANE? CORE?"

"You are getting warmer," Chiun prompted.

"Try CARE," said Remo. "If you're going to pester it out of us, it's CARE."

Winston frowned. "Isn't that a relief program?"

"That's the cover story," Remo said dryly.

Up ahead Assumpta was haggling with a fat man wearing a baseball cap that said *"Frente Juarezista de Liberacion Nacional."* She was out of earshot. They kept their voices low.

"We're never going to catch up to Verapaz hoofing it," Winston hissed.

"You got a better idea?" Remo asked.

"We need a helicopter."

"We need a helicopter pilot unless you're thinking of the kind that eats quarters and doesn't go anywhere."

"I'm rated for choppers."

Remo favored him with a skeptical eye. "That the truth?"

"Would I lie?"

Chiun sniffed. "Yes, repeatedly."

"Look, if we can find a chopper, I'll get us out of this jungle."

"There was a helicopter at the army post," Chiun said.

"Let's see if it's still there," said Remo.

44

When the dawn of the first full day after the Great Mexico City Earthquake broke, it failed to break over a hundred-mile swatch from the Valley of Mexico to Oaxaca State.

The brown pall emanating from the unquiet volcano called Smoking Mountain since the days of the Aztecs extended far to the south, blotting out the rays of the rising sun.

The deep black of the night abated somewhat, but no bright blessings fell from Tonituah, the Sun God. The lowering sky refused to permit even the merest ray of sunshine to penetrate.

In the Zocalo of Oaxaca, the adherents of Coatlicue stirred to this phenomenon. They had fallen asleep around the splashing fountain. Now their eyes blinked at the ominous atmosphere.

"There is no sun!"

"The sun has gone out!"

"Call back the sun, Coatlicue. Make him shine."

But Coatlicue stood unhearing.

It fell to High Priest Rodrigo Lujan to bring meaning to the evil portent of a dawn without light. He disentangled himself from a knot of freshly deflowered Zapotec maidens.

"It is the will of Coatlicue that you do not see the sun on the first day of the new Zapotec empire," he shouted.

"What can we do? What must we do? Tell us!"

"Our Mother desires hearts. We must sacrifice fresh hearts to Coatlicue. That will call back the retreating sun."

The logical next question came. "Whose hearts?"

"I will choose the hearts that Coatlicue whispers are needed. Make lines."

They formed ranks, disorderly and uneasy, but no one ran as Rodrigo Lujan moved through them.

Scrutinizing the faces that shifted with downcast eyes as he came to them each in turn, he tapped the chosen ones on the tops of their heads with a heavy walnut scepter.

Jaguar soldiers seized each one, dragging them after the high priest whose long, rabbit-trimmed feather cloak swept the Zocalo flags in his wake.

When he had ten, these were thrown at Coatlicue's feet, and the obsidian blade came out, glittering dully in the weird postdawn twilight.

"Coatlicue, Mighty Mother. In your name I consecrate these hearts as an offering to your indifferent love."

Coatlicue looked down with her flat eyes. Her steel-plated serpent heads were at rest, blunt snouts touching.

The blade slashed and split flesh and rib bone as the victims were opened up. Quick, sure strokes severed the aorta and other arteries.

The first extraction was very bloody, but as he moved along, Lujan learned where and how to slice so that the blood spurted away from his eager face.

Not that he minded blood. But the warm stuff in his eyes soon turned sticky and made vision difficult.

By the tenth and last victim, the blood was a fountain that washed Coatlicue's clawed feet and touched her high priest not at all.

Cheers went up. Only a few faces frowned. All Mixtec faces.

They had good reason to frown, Rodrigo knew. All ten offerings wore Mixtec faces. Mixtec hearts now lay at the feet of Coatlicue the uncaring.

And at a gesture, the dead Mixtec husks were thrown against Coatlicue's obdurate feet, only to be absorbed like liquid into two rude sponges. Even the blood flowed toward her, strengthening her power.

When the ceremony was concluded, all eyes turned to the heavens in anticipation of the returning sun. Instead, there came a distant rumble that was not echoed in the ground at their feet.

Thunder. Not an aftershock. Then it began to rain.

And the hearts of the followers of Coatlicue grew fearful, for the rain pelting from the very black heavens was itself black as the ink of an octopus.

Even Rodrigo Lujan, ruler priest of Oaxaca, felt a distinct chill as he watched the octopus ink rain streak his bare arms, his pristine finery and most terribly, his implacable Mother.

45

Chiapas Barracks was deserted when they reached it less than an hour later. They piled out of the rented rust-bucket Impala that had cost Remo his Discover card. Let Smith worry about the bill.

The helicopter was still there. It was a utility chopper, crudely converted into a makeshift gunship by rocket pods and Gatling guns bolted to the body.

The bad news was that it seated two people—three if someone were willing to squeeze into the storage area behind the seats.

That option was rendered moot when the Master of Sinanju took his steamer trunk from Remo and carefully stowed it there.

"In case you haven't noticed, we don't have room for everybody," Winston Smith said, stowing his gear inside.

"The girl will stay behind," Chiun said.

"I'm not leaving Assumpta."

"Then you both may stay behind."

"Then who'll fly the chopper?" Remo and Smith said at the same time.

"I will," said Chiun.

No one thought that was a survivable option, and it showed on their faces.

"Let's see if she flies first," said Winston, climbing into the cockpit. Once seated, he laid his feet on the pedals and took hold of the collective stick. He snapped switches, and the rotor blades whined slowly to a whirling silvery disk. The chopper vibrated like an eager steed.

Winston called out, "Gas gauge says low. We're going to need a full tank and some spare cans."

Remo looked around. There was a Quonset hut nearby and it smelled vaguely of gasoline. Handing the Hellfire pistol to Assumpta, he started for it. Remo got halfway there.

Behind him the helicopter reared upward. Remo whirled. Assumpta clung half in and half out of the cockpit. Winston leaned over to haul her in.

Chiun was shrieking over the rotor scream. And winning.

Remo went from zero to sixty from a standing start, but even as he closed with the lifting whirlybird, he knew his chances were slim.

Through the swirling dust and the Plexiglas of the cockpit, Winston Smith's grinning mouth formed a single word.

"Sucker!"

46

"What is happening?" asked Coatlicue.

Lujan looked skyward. The skies were still brown, but a darker brown, as if thunderclouds loomed over the haze unseen.

"We have a saying in these times," he said. "Perhaps it is very old. I do not know. It goes, 'Crazy February, crazier March.'"

"Clarify meaning."

"We have our worst weather in the month of February, except for March."

"You have your worst weather in March, then."

"Precisely."

"Then why do you not say March?"

"That would not be very Mexican," laughed High Priest Rodrigo Lujan. "You must know this, Coatlicue. You should know this, for you are more Mexican than any of us."

Coatlicue said nothing to that. Why should she? Lujan had just stated the obvious.

It was raining furiously, a downpour. The Zocalo was drenched. The ground seemed to dance in a million places. It danced like angry obsidian imps, for the splashing rain was very, very black.

The skies opened up in one of the wild elemental electrical storms that are famous from Mexico City to

Acapulco. The rain was a wrath from above, presaging the threat of thunderbolts. There came a rumble of ominous thunder. It was quite distant. It might have been an aftershock, but the earth did not jump. Nor was it Mount Popo, which was too far away for his sound to carry.

A second rumble came.

"Hear the drums of our ancestors!" Rodrigo exulted. "They beat in the far distance! See the rain that falls—are they not like cleansing tears? Rejoice in the tears from above! Revel in the cleansing rain of this new age."

Like a cannonade, a peal of thunder rumbled through the valley to end in a crash of sound like a bowling ball coursing to a nine-pin strike.

The revels ceased. Fear touched every black-streaked face.

"Come, come! Why do you cower? You are masters of this valley once more. Dance! Sing! Make love in the rain! All is permitted. Your Mother on earth permits you to do as you will."

"There is danger," Coatlicue said from above.

"What do you say, Mother?"

"Danger approaches."

Another long rumble ended in a crack of violent sound.

To the southwest, where the ancient Zapotec capital of Monte Alban brooded atop a mountain, a jagged line of electrical blue showed in sharp relief against the lowering sky.

The rain was drumming on the Zocalo, drowning the stone fountain's splashing.

"What danger?" Lujan asked his god.

"The electrical storm approaches."

"So? It is but lightning."

"Lightning is dangerous. My systems are not immune to a lightning strike."

"Systems?"

"I am electrical in nature, as are meat machines. If lightning should strike my present form, it could melt my circuits."

"Circuits?"

"I cannot remain here where I am the tallest object for miles around."

"Circuits?" Lujan repeated. "But jou are a god."

"I am a survival android."

"Jou are Coatlicue."

"I am in danger," Coatlicue said as all around them the adherents of High Priest Rodrigo Lujan and his Mother Goddess Coatlicue scattered for cover.

For the thunder was drawing closer, and bolts of lightning lashed the horizon in all directions. It was as if a storm had surrounded Oaxaca and was pressing in for the kill.

And deep in the pit of his stomach, Rodrigo Lujan knew a dim and growing fear.

The rumbles of thunder came more often. As he listened, Lujan noticed the intervals between the peals of thunder and the crash of the striking bolts came closer together. The echoes would no sooner finish bouncing off the mountain than lightning forked and more thunder crashed angrily.

Coatlicue herself gave voice to the fear rising in his mind. *"The lightning approaches this place."*

"Send it away, Coatlicue."

"I have no such ability."

"But you are a god."

"I am a survival android whose assimilation program is damaged. I cannot assume a more mobile shape. In my attempt to perpetuate my existence, I have taken on a greater and greater mass of surrounding matter, so as to protect my central processor from damage."

"Central processor?" Lujan said dully. The rain sounds filled his ears. Bitter black rain ran down into his eyes, half blinding him. The cloudburst drummed against his skin like cold awakening fingers.

"I am the tallest form for miles around," Coatlicue was saying. *"I will attract the lightning bolts and I am not grounded against lightning."*

"Lightning cannot harm you."

"Lightning is capable of disrupting my damaged circuits. I could be annihilated."

"Annihilated? It is impossible."

"I have never faced this situation before. Instruct me. I must survive."

"Yes, I will instruct you. Let me think. Yes, what has my mother told me? When there is a lightning system, one lies down flat upon the ground."

"I am unable to perform that function. My present form is not equipped with knees or other folding joints. If I become prone, I will be unable to rise again."

"Then jou must seek cover."

"I am sixty meters in height. There is no cover."

"When I was small, I would hide under a tree when it rained this fiercely," Lujan said.

"I see no tree taller that my present form."

"El árbol del Tule!"

"Explain."

"There is a magnificent tree only a mile or three from here. A cypress, heavy with age, for it is said to be two thousand years old. The tourists flock to see it always. Go there. Stand beneath its Zapotec branches. It will protect you, if protection is necessary."

Picking up one gargantuan foot, Coatlicue slowly and ponderously reoriented herself toward the southeast as black rain sluiced down her armored hide. She was slow and deliberate, and her slowness suddenly filled Rodrigo Lujan with a cold dread.

For if Coatlicue feared the lightning, then it was truly something to be feared. And the circle of the horizon was ablaze with devilish pitchforks of electricity.

"I will lead the way, Coatlicue," said Lujan, who dared not voice the selfish thought rising in the back of his mind.

If he remained in the shadow of his Mother, any angry bolt that sought him would be drawn to Coatlicue herself. If by some black fate she should succumb, it would be a terrible tragedy, of course. But Rodrigo Lujan would carry on.

For what was a god without priests to guide the faithful?

47

The Mexican army utility chopper was sluggish. Winston Smith had to skim just above treetop level to make the flight to Oaxaca. But that was good, too. Too high made him subject to a sudden shoot-down.

The green hills and valleys of Mexico rushed beneath them. The Plexiglas bubble swam with a streaky dark rain.

"Hope we can recognize Verapaz from the air," he muttered.

"He moves with a mighty army. How can we not?"

"Good point."

Assumpta looked over pensively. "Why did you leave those two behind? I still do not understand."

Smith frowned. He had dodged the question once already. "Okay, you deserve to know the absolute truth."

"Yes?"

"They were CIA killer agents."

Assumpta's mouth became an oval. "Even the old one?"

"He was the deadliest of them all. Knows super kung fu."

"They did behave strangely at times."

"You saw how they treated me. Like a kid. Me, the wild-haired warrior. Nobody treats the Extinguisher like a chump."

"If they are CIA killers, why did you vouch for them to me?"

"I couldn't be sure. But I got them to sorta admit it back when we were humping along the trail."

"Homping?"

"Military slang. Forget it."

"I like this word *homping*. I would homp with you anywhere, Blaize."

"Call me Winner. It's my real name. Short for Winston."

"Would you homp with me anywhere, Weener?"

Smith winced. Her pronunciation sounded too much like *weiner*. "Yeah. But first we have to hook up with Verapaz."

"Did I tell you that *Juarezista* women are allowed to take whatever man they choose, without asking permission of anyone?"

"No, you didn't."

She inhaled sharply. "I would take you."

Smith swallowed. "You would?"

"*Sí*. And I am not ashamed to admit that if I were to make love to you it would be my first time."

His hands trembling on the collective stick, Winston Smith muttered under his breath, "Mine, too."

And deep in the pit of his stomach, he got a very ugly feeling; he didn't know what to do with it.

48

Comandante Efrain Zaragoza kept one eye on the TV as his unit rolled toward Oaxaca. The evil rain came down, making reception difficult. If it wasn't the rain, it was the interference from the mountains. It didn't help that he was hunkered down in the back of a jouncing armored vehicle.

Through the rain that was black, and the white snow on the screen, he could see his objective lumber on through the very strange rain. Coatlicue the animate.

Lightning blazed. It cracked and crashed.

"¡Santa Madre de Dios!" he cursed. "Why does the lightning not strike the demon and save us all from the terror of confronting her?"

"Perhaps if we pray," a *sargento* suggested.

"To whom?" Zaragoza spit. "To whom do we pray?"

"Let half our number pray to the old gods and the other half to the saints. And let the most powerful gods prevail."

It seemed reasonable, and so straws were drawn and, with the hammering of the rain from hell against the hulls of their APCs and LAVs, the unit prayed silently, nervous eyes on the horizon. Zaragoza monitored the screen.

The monster Coatlicue made her painstaking way onward. She seemed like an unstoppable juggernaut of steel, her torso bearing the haphazard military markings of the armor she had absorbed. The very same insignia marked their own machines. It made one think terrible thoughts about the fate of their crews.

Abruptly the screen exploded in a flash of fire.

"Our prayers are answered!" Zaragoza cried.

When the screen cleared, they saw Coatlicue standing stock-still, electricity running up and down her metallic skin. It evaporated with a spiteful snap and crackle.

Then ponderously she continued her march.

"No," said the *sargento* unhappily. "Ours were."

The order was given to pray to saints, not the ancient ones whose loyalties were in question, and as their lips moved silently, all eyes were fixed on the monster they sought to fight but hoped never to behold through their very own eyes.

49

It had been too easy, Alirio Antonio Arcila felt.

His *Juarezistas* had filtered up from Chiapas to Oaxaca without hindrance. It was as if the army was allowing this.

After some thought he realized this must be so.

"They wish us to fight the monster Coatlicue," he told Kix as they paused to rest.

A rain was falling. It was filled with black particles that made their brown uniforms clammy and gritty at once.

"And we will. For are we not Maya?"

The portable TV was brought out of its waterproof carrying case and turned on.

The monster, now plated and scaled like an armadillo, lumbered toward an unknown destination. They fixed its position on their plastic recon maps.

"We are less than thirty minutes' march from the demon, and it is moving steadily our way," he decided.

"We will defeat it," Kix said. He sounded very sure of himself, so right then and there Antonio decided Kix would be the first to attack the monster.

"But where does it go?" Antonio wondered aloud.

"There can be but one destination," Kix muttered, tapping a point on the map. "The cypress of Tule."

Antonio frowned. "Why would it go there? It is but a tree."

"To get out of the fierce rain?"

No better explanation presented itself.

"We will move out now," Antonio announced, standing up. The moment of truth approached. If he defeated the stone mother, his image would be unshatterable. *El Presidente* himself would doubtless plead to join the *Juarezista* cause after that.

50

High Priest Rodrigo Lujan tramped through the black rain along Highway 190 to Santa Maria del Tule.

They were passing through hills luxuriant with vegetation that was turning an ominous black under a pelting rain. But he had no eyes for their ruined splendor.

For one, he could hardly see. Two, he was having to lead the way through the rain, for Coatlicue did not know the route.

But most difficult of all, he walked without his sheltering cloak and headdress. He had been forced to leave them by the side of the road when the black rain made them too heavy to bear.

It was fortunate that he had discarded them, because the only warning he had of the impending lightning strike was the faint ozone tang and the rising of the hairs on his bare arms.

The knowledge that an electrical connection had been made between earth and sky galvanized him. Panic took him. In his alarm he leaped between the legs of his great stone Mother.

The bolt detonated. That was the exact sound. A ripping explosion, not a crack of lightning. Awesome to hear.

Coatlicue stopped dead in her tracks, and her entire body rippled with blue-and-green sparks and splinters of light.

When his ears cleared enough that he could hear again, Rodrigo heard the creak of her metal carapace as she resumed her untiring gait.

"You live, Coatlicue!" he called out.

"I survive. I must survive."

"We will both survive," he cried, following.

Not two hundred yards farther along, the second bolt struck.

Again the hairs lifted along his arms. Again there was the bitter ozone in his nostrils, and again Lujan sought refuge under the skirts of his mighty Mother.

This time he knew enough to plug his precious eardrums with his fingers.

Still the boom threw him off his feet.

This time Coatlicue crackled and sizzled like hamburger frying, her armadillo armor alive with violent electrical activity.

When it abated, she did not move.

Lujan crawled out to take in the fearsome sight. "Coatlicue! Mother! Do you still live?"

The only answer was the driving rain pattering and spitting off Coatlicue's steel skin. It seemed to spit in the face of High Priest Rodrigo Lujan, telling him his dreams of empire had been dashed by a vengeful bolt from the angry heavens.

Then the soldiers came.

COMANDANTE Efrain Zaragoza saw the second bolt explode and heard silent aftermath of its elemental fury.

He counted a full circle of sixty seconds by his watch. Two. Three.

"Our prayers have been answered," he breathed.

In a corner of the APC, a soldier cursed under his breath and Zaragoza knew the man had prayed for the other side. No matter. The saints had preserved Mexico, if not their lives.

It left only the mopping up and the harvesting of glory.

"Faster! Faster! Victory is ours!"

THEY SURROUNDED the inert golem with their vehicles, leaving no route of escape. It would look very bold on the TV, Zaragoza knew. For the helicopters still patrolled the skies broadcasting all to a cowering nation in need of a savior. Himself, he hoped.

Zaragoza was the first out. He approached the monster with only his H&K submachine gun.

A half-naked man cowered at the feet of the demon that was as tall as a house.

"You are who?" Zaragoza demanded.

"I am abandoned," the man sobbed.

"You are *indio*."

"I am abandoned by my Mother," he repeated.

The man looked so pitiful that Zaragoza decided to ignore him. Glancing over his shoulder, he fixed the orbiting helicopter camera ships and positioned himself so they would pick up his good side. Then, elevating his H&K, he opened fire on the monstrosity of baroque segmented steel plates.

The bullets spanged and dented the armor. But they might as well have been but hard candy. Nothing happened. The monster did not fall over. Zaragoza had hoped the monster would fall over. The sight would appear spectacular on TV Azteca.

"*¡Soldados!* Come! We must fire in unison if we are to topple this behemoth," Zaragoza cried, giving up on the hope of going down in history as Zaragoza the Giant Killer.

His *soldados* were not eager to leave the safety of their armored vehicles, but they did so. They stood around in awe of the silent golem.

"We will spray her breast with bullets so that she topples on her back, forever defeated," Zaragoza told them.

They formed a firing squad and began firing. It was haphazard fire, but it had an effect.

A section of armor cracked and dropped away. It struck sparks when it hit the road.

"*¡Viva Zaragoza!*" Zaragoza yelled, hoping his men would pick up the cry and it would carry to the helicopter microphones.

Whether that happened or not, was not to be known by Efrain Zaragoza. Or anyone else.

As if they had fractured a weak spot, the armor began cracking and falling away in large, dangerous pieces.

The pieces fell thudding, and it was all they could do to retreat before being crushed by the clanging plates.

They backed up sufficiently that the truth of their situation at once became clear. The armor was not breaking under the stress of so many bullet strikes.

It was breaking because the monster Coatlicue was shedding her hide as a snake sheds its skin.

She was casting off the heavy confining shell as she resumed her lumbering walk toward her unknown destination.

"*¡Disparen!*" Zaragoza ordered.

And his men emptied their weapons into the newly exposed brown stone that chipped and gave off puffs of rock dust in some places and actually bled in soft spots, but otherwise showed no sign of flinching or surrender.

Men made the sign of the cross as they backed away in mute awe.

"She is Coatlicue," Zaragoza muttered.

That was when sanity reasserted itself. They piled into their APCs and sent them scurrying south to Yucatán.

Perhaps the cameras had picked up nothing through the drumming black rain after all. It no longer mattered. Efrain Zaragoza had learned an important lesson. Glory was nothing. Life was all. And he was not being paid to fight walking stones that bled like men.

51

"I was just thinking," Winston Smith said over the combined noise of rotor wash and rain.

"*¿Sí?*"

"We lead dangerous lives. Danger is our beans and rice. We could be snuffed out at any moment."

"Yes, this is very true," Assumpta admitted.

"Once we join up with Verapaz, nothing is guaranteed. Not tomorrow. Not even tonight. Surviving the next hour is strictly fifty-fifty."

"This is so, *chilito mio.*"

Winston blinked. "What's that mean?"

"My little chili pepper." Assumpta smiled shyly.

"Look, why don't we just land this eggbeater and do it now? That way, if we're killed or separated or anything bad happens, at least we can say we knew true love before the end came."

"The gas *is* low...."

"Yeah, I was gonna mention it, but I didn't want it to sound like a line."

"We will refuel and make passionate love as *guerrilleros* do."

"Great," said Winston. "That clearing up ahead looks soft."

The chopper skimmed lower and angled toward a landing.

At the last possible moment the ship seemed to lighten, as if dropping a load of fuel. Maybe the engine needed an overhaul, Winston thought.

After he shut it down, Winston Smith turned to Assumpta. "Well, here we are."

Her face was a cameo against the backdrop of the rain-washed Plexiglas bubble beyond which the rain-distorted green landscape seemed to waver and run.

He leaned in to kiss her. Their arms bumped the controls. Assumpta laughed. Then her lips were pressed against his, and Winston wondered if he should stick his tongue in her mouth or wait until later. First kisses were logistical nightmares....

Somewhere the sound of knocking intruded on their silent interlude. He ignored it.

It came again. Very loud this time.

Assumpta drew away in fear. "What is that?"

"Search me."

He saw the shape behind her. A face. It swam behind the swimming Plexiglas.

"Get down!" he cried, reaching for his Hellfire.

Before he could reach his weapon, the cockpit door at his back opened, letting in driving rain and an irresistible hand.

Smith was yanked out and dropped on his back. A foot stamped his gun into the mud. He looked up, his face furious.

The face of his alleged father looked down. It was not a happy face.

"Where the hell did you come from!" Winston raged.

"A magician never tells," Remo told him.

"Nice move. Your timing is fucking excellent."

"Forget it, *chilito*. It's curfew time. We heard every word."

"How's that possible?"

Remo pulled him to his feet. Winston noticed the old Korean standing behind him, also unhappy.

Assumpta shouted, "Let him go, jou-jou CIA *yanquis!* He has told me all about you. You will never defeat Lord Verapaz!"

"Right now we have a bigger problem."

"What's that?" Winston growled.

"The monster. I need you to fly us to him."

"Monster? Don't be stupid. The Extinguisher doesn't fight monsters. Try Raymond Burr."

"He's dead, so you're elected." And Winston found himself placed in the chopper pilot seat like a baby dropped into his high chair.

The old Korean climbed into the cockpit and, crossing his legs, sat on his steamer trunk.

Winston looked to Remo standing in the rain. "What about you?"

"Just take off. I'll hitch a ride on the skid."

"*That's* how you did it!"

"And people say you're slow on the draw."

"I resent that!"

But he took off anyway.

Behind him the old Korean named Chiun prodded him on the right course with a pointing fingernail that Winston sometimes felt in the small of his back. It felt like a white-hot needle.

WHEN HE SAW the monster, Winston Smith changed his mind.

"Holy shit! Look at the size of that mother. Let's blow it up!"

"No," said Chiun. "I forbid it."

"But we've got antitank rockets and a Gatling gun. We can pulverize it in its tracks."

"No," Chiun repeated.

"Give me one reason why not."

"I will give you two."

"Yeah?"

"The first reason is that the monster cannot be defeated unless his brain is discovered and destroyed. Otherwise, the part of him that can assume other forms will take a new form. We must find the brain first."

"What's the other reason?"

"The other reason is that the lightning may do the work we cannot."

And as they flew closer, a sizzling bolt of eye-searing light slammed the monster in his tracks. It wavered, started to take a step, and a second bolt transfixed it. Green and gold sparks jumped.

When the noise dissipated, the monster was immobile.

"Now what?" Winston asked.

"Land this contraption near the monster," Chiun said. "At Once! Our time may be short."

"Sure you don't want me to strafe it first?"

As if in answer, a thick-wristed hand reached up from under the cockpit, grasped the side-mounted Gatling gun and, expending no obvious effort, twisted it off its mount, then flung it away.

52

It was like marching into the face of cannon fire.

The detonations came again and again. They split the dull morning, making it bright. They rattled the sky. Their fury was very great. Fear showed on the faces of the *Juarezistas* who marched behind Alirio Antonio Arcila, their AKs and AR-15s trembling in their rain-wet hands.

Each time they quailed, he called back encouragement.

"See!" Alirio Antonio Arcila cried, holding up the TV so all could see. "Behold the monster! She is attracting the lightning. It strikes only at Coatlicue."

"The gods are just," a man murmured. But there was no enthusiasm. The relentless elements had beaten their courage down.

Antonio swallowed his sharp corrective words. He believed in no gods. Was he not believed to be god-like by these simple ones? He, the son of a coffee grower?

Soon the television was no longer necessary.

The cypress of Tule came into view.

Antonio had only heard of it. It was said to be some two thousand years old. From a distance it resembled the greatest weeping willow imaginable, its drooping branches weighed down with the imposing freight of its years. Its leaves trembled nervously under the unceasing rain. It was older than the Cross, and even though Antonio did not believe in the Cross, still the obvious age of the oldest living thing on the face of the earth took his breath.

A bolt forked down and blotted out the impressive sight.

In the afterimage imprinted on his retina, Antonio saw the tree as a negative film image, stark and threatening.

And when his blinded eyes cleared once more, he saw for the first time the Coatlicue monster in the flesh.

She was making for the cypress. The great tree dwarfed her, made her seem less formidable. From this distance, she might have been a clay figure beside an ordinary oak.

But she was not. She stood wider than three men, taller than five tall men.

And miracle of miracles, the lightning strikes continually sought her. But still she strove onward, ever onward, seeking the cypress that should have drawn the terrible bolts from the sky but did not.

Glancing back, Antonio caught his remaining Maya making the sign of the Cross. There were far fewer of them now. In his heart he forgave them. Coatlicue was an unnatural sight, but the way the lightning spurned the mighty tree for the smaller giant was more unnatural still. It suggested greater forces at work.

"Perhaps our work will be done for us," he told them. All thought of glory and gain fled his reeling brain. This was incredible. Impossible. Unbelievable.

And still the monster trudged on, the bolts slamming, breaking off the last remaining plates of her gleaming armor, knocking them away, until rude stone and a flexible marbled matter lay exposed.

Then came a bolt that ripped downward, exploded and blotted out the universe. The thunder sound was great. The resulting shock wave was greater still.

Antonio and his *guerrilleros* were thrown off their feet.

When their sight cleared, Coatlicue stood still. She did not move again.

"Come," Antonio said, climbing to his feet. "It is time to face this Azteca usurper."

They advanced cautiously. Now Antonio led a meager handful of men. The others had retreated. No matter. When the cause was won, they would return to the fold. Willingly or not.

RODRIGO LUJAN STARED UP at the ominous heavens that had assaulted his Mother again and again. He saw a greenish white light, but no clouds no sky. When he closed his eyes, the light was still there.

He heard nothing. His ears were still full of booming thunder. His brain shook with reverberating shock.

"Mother. Can you hear me?"

But his Mother Coatlicue responded not.

Lying helpless beneath her, Lujan wept bitterly, his salty tears mingling with the rain that fell and fell and fell upon him without understanding or mercy.

ANTONIO APPROACHED ahead of the others. His head pounded. He felt fear yes, but he pushed it back. It was not that he was so brave but that there was no turning back. His future depended upon what transpired here in this place far from the Lacandón jungle.

Coatlicue, he saw, had almost made the shelter of the great cypress, whose bole was over one hundred feet in circumference. It seemed less like the trunk of a tree than some ancient petrified eruption from deep within the earth. The trunk was horny and rugose with age.

"Coatlicue," he said. "Greetings, creature of imagination. You almost made it to safety. But you did not. And now you are dead."

Coatlicue said nothing and moved not. Her ophidian eyes were looking at the tree.

Antonio walked around her still feet. One was poised in the act of taking a step forward. It seemed gargantuan beside him, but the cypress dwarfed it to insignificance.

Between the legs lay a nearly nude man.

Antonio knelt. "Who are you?"

The man looked in all directions with uncomprehending eyes. "I am blind. The lightning has taken my sight."

"You are fortunate. For you lie in the path of the monster. Her foot is lifted to take a step. If completed, she would have crushed you like a locust."

"I would gladly be crushed under the feet of my mother if only I could behold her one last time," the man said dully.

"Then sadness will be your eternal destiny, because that will never come to pass. Coatlicue has succumbed."

Weeping, the man crawled under the shelter of the half-lifted foot. On his back, he struggled up to kiss her heel but lacked all strength to complete the absurd action.

Antonio let him be. He was not important. As he scanned the skies, he saw that helicopters circled above, braving the rain. Strangely the lightning had ceased its dramatic striking, as if considering its job accomplished. The choppers drew closer.

They were even now broadcasting this sight to all Mexico. Well, Antonio would give them a sight to remember the rest of their days. He faced his loyal cohorts.

"My *Juarezistas,* approach with me. The Azteca revolution is over. Their idol walks no more. We are in command now. Let us demonstrate this to a fearful Mexico."

The Maya approached, walking as if on eggshells.

"We must topple this usurper so that she breaks into many pieces," Antonio explained. "It will be a political statement that will prove for all time the righteousness of our cause."

"How?" asked Kix. "It is so big."

"See how the monster balances on one foot? Let us push her in one direction, all of us, so that she loses her imperfect balance."

The Maya shrank from the fearful task. "Show us, Lord Verapaz. Guide our hands that we may do this."

Laying down his AK, Antonio placed both hands on the lifted elephantine foot of the Coatlicue monster. Why not? Was it not dead?

The foot was not cold as he expected. Nor was it hard. In fact, it felt weirdly fleshy to the touch. Instantly his hands recoiled.

His Maya recoiled, too.

"What is wrong?" Kix hissed.

Antonio rubbed his fingers together. They felt wet and clammy, as if they had come in contact with the cold clay of a great dead corpse. "You do it. For as a true *indio,* it is your honor to topple the rival god."

"But you are Kukulcan."

"And as Kukulcan, I offer the honor to you."

Kix looked doubtful but, urged on by the others, he approached the inert thing. He laid hands upon the upraised foot. To judge by the expression that came over his face, the sensation of moist, dead flesh was very distasteful. But nothing happened to him.

Emboldened, Kix said, "Help me, O brothers."

Others gathered around. They got behind the fat ankle and attempted to push this way or that way. But the bulk of the creature was too vast, too obdurate to move. Her eyes regarded the Maya as if they were but ants at her feet.

While they considered the situation, an army utility helicopter dropped out of the sky to land at the roadside. As it drew closer, a man dangling off one skid released his grip so as not to be crushed.

REMO CALCULATED THE DROP, let go of the skid and rolled out of the way of the landing chopper.

When it settled, he opened the door. Winston Smith, Assumpta and Chiun started to get out. Remo pushed Winston back in.

"Look, let me handle this. Okay?"

Winston eyed the monster dubiously. "What's to handle? Looks like the party ended before we got here."

"You don't know what's going on."

"I can see what's going on. Nothing. That hulk is just standing there, collecting raindrops."

"Just leave this to the experts, okay? Chiun, watch them. I don't want any more problems with these two. If something goes wrong, take off."

Chiun nodded. "Be careful, my son. Take no chances."

Winston blinked. "He's your son?"

"In spirit."

And the Master of Sinanju put his face to the cockpit bubble, the better to watch his pupil.

REMO APPROACHED. The rain was still coming down. There was an adobe church beside the drooping cypress. Its white facade was streaked blackish gray with precipitated volcano ash.

From inside, a priest emerged. He carried a cross of gold. He, too, approached the monster.

Remo intercepted him. "You'd better stay clear, Padre. This isn't over."

"God has struck the monster blind and dumb, but it falls to his children to exorcise the demon that motivated it."

"Just the same, leave this to the professional monster slayers."

The priest fell in behind Remo. Considering the circumstances, he didn't seem very frightened.

A handful of *Juarezistas* blocked the way. Remo knew they were *Juarezistas* because in their brown polyester uniforms and black ski masks, they looked like the Serbian Olympic ski team.

"Come no closer," one of them commanded in good English. "We are about to blow up the demon Coatlicue for all the world to see."

"Over my dead body. He's mine."

"This is our monster. We have vanquished him. And it is a she, by the way."

The speaker was taller than the others. A short-stemmed pipe was clenched in his teeth. He also had green eyes.

"You Verapaz?" asked Remo.

"I am Subcomandante Verapaz. Who are you?"

"Monster extinguisher," Remo said.

"What nonsense is this?"

"This is my monster. I saw him first. Just step away and let me handle it."

Verapaz snapped impatient fingers. "Over my dead body."

"Thanks for the invitation," said Remo, who began disarming *Juarezistas* in a novel fashion.

Two opened fire on him. Remo moved in as if to meet the bullets halfway. That was how it seemed to the men behind the triggers and the priest who dropped to the ground and covered his head with his hands.

In fact, Remo's blurred hands pushed the rifles straight up so the bullets discharged harmlessly into the lowering sky. Then he stepped back, folded his lean arms and waited.

While the guerrillas were bringing their weapons back in line for follow-up bursts, the bullets reached the apex of their climb, where they seemed poised momentarily. Gravity brought them back down.

They perforated the tops of several skulls, and when the bodies crumpled, other *Juarezistas* moved in to replace them.

"Can you say 'blunt trauma'?" Remo said.

Remo moved in on them. He didn't have a lot of time, so he just grabbed two by the hair, masks and all, and spun in place.

Whirling combat boots collided with the incoming troops, knocking them down. Remo released the hapless pair whose scalps were inexorably separating from sagittal crests. They skidded some five hundred feet in opposite directions before coming to rest in the form of brown polyester sacks filled with bones.

Subcomandante Verapaz had his AK up to his shoulder and was looking down the barrel at Remo.

"Come no closer, *yanqui.*"

Remo kept walking.

"I mean business!"

Remo watched the middle knuckle of Subcomandante Verapaz's trigger finger until it went white. He stepped out of the path of the bullet stream. One burst. Then two. He didn't have to count the bullets. So many AKs had been fired at him over the years he could instinctively gauge when the clip had run dry.

Knowing that, Remo was able to walk right up to the smoking barrel without fear and twist the muzzle out of shape.

Verapaz stepped back, his green eyes widening in his mask. His pipe dropped from his mouth.

"What manner of man are you?"

"Can you say 'out-of-body experience'?" Remo asked.

"Yes. But why would I?"

Remo looked over his shoulder. In the resting helicopter Winston Smith and Assumpta sat placidly, their faces unreadable through the falling rain. His orders were to make Subcomandante Verapaz's death look like natural causes. For that story to wash, there had to be no witnesses.

"Never mind," Remo said. "Just hang around until I figure out what to do with you."

Verapaz jammed his pipe back into his mouth. "You cannot order me about. I am a Mexican revolutionary hero. Men fear me. Women adore me. I am in all the magazines. I am the future of Mexico. Politically I cannot be killed, so I will never die."

Remo was about to deactivate the *subcomandante's* nervous system when he heard low muttering in what sounded like Latin behind him.

Turning, Remo saw the priest hovering by the foot of Coatlicue. He held his gold cross high and was intoning some kind of prayer. It sounded to Remo like an exorcism was in progress.

"Padre, I asked you to stay back."

At that moment the priest laid the gold cross against the thick ankle. It clinked against the stone.

All at once the crucifix was taken into the stone as if dropped into a placid brown puddle.

And with a low groan Coatlicue lurched forward.

53

The behemoth of stone and flesh took one halting step, and during that jerky movement Remo had faded back three hundred yards. He had the priest tucked under his arm. Now he let him go.

The priest ran for his church.

Remo stood his ground, ready to retreat or attack as the situation warranted. Having fought various man-size versions of Mr. Gordons through the years, he had a healthy respect for its inhuman destructive power.

Nothing in his Sinanju training covered thirty-foot-high giants. But as he watched, he sized up the possibilities. Gordons had started off balance. The poised foot came down, making contact with the earth. A distinct mushy crackle Remo recognized as a human body being crushed floated over the monotonous drum of falling rain.

Remo looked around. Verapaz was hanging back. It wasn't him. He looked back.

At that moment the landing foot lost its traction. Whatever—or whoever—it had crushed must have made a slippery smear because, like a man stepping on a banana peel, Gordons froze, throwing up his stiff, blunt arms.

It was too late. The foot slid forward, tilting the stone giant backward. Compensating, Gordons tried to lunge forward, toward his objective. The sheltering cypress of Tule.

He almost made it. But the gap was too great. The flat, square head fell into the hanging mass of branches. A few broke into kindling. The rest sprang back into place, dripping water.

When Gordons crashed facedown on the ground, he made a thud that felt like a huge aftershock and lay still.

The black rain beat down on him relentlessly.

Remo noticed a distinct blob at the bottom of the foot that had stumbled. It looked like a giant wad of chewing gum, except it was the color of strawberries.

Gordons showed no sign of moving again, so Remo approached.

"Damn," Remo said. "Wonder who that was."

"No one important," said Subcomandante Verapaz, who was sneaking up on the inert hulk, too.

Looking over the situation, Remo saw that Gordons had cracked apart in falling. The head was no longer attached. That was a good sign. Last time the brain was in the head.

"Uh-oh," he said, noticing one stony shoulder had gouged a gnarled, exposed tree root when it fell.

"What is wrong?" Verapaz asked. "It has fallen, therefore it is dead again."

"It's touching a tree root."

"So?"

"Whatever it touches, it assimilates."

"So?"

"So it might be the tree now."

"How can it be a tree when it is still there?" Verapaz wondered aloud.

Remo studied the way the stone shoulder and the tree root were meshed.

"Damn, damn, damn. Now we're going to have to cut down the whole tree to make sure."

"Hah! You can no more cut down the cypress of Tule than you can break the moon with your naked fist."

A squeaky voice from behind them said, "We will do what we must to defeat the monster, Gordons."

"Coatlicue," Verapaz corrected. "Her name is Coatlicue."

Remo turned. "Chiun, I thought I told you to stay with the chopper."

"I did. Now I am here. For my skills are more needed here than elsewhere." And shaking back his kimono sleeves, the Master of Sinanju bared pipestem arms that ended in ten long nails of fierce strength and wickedness.

Chiun floated up to the prostrate idol of stone.

He examined it critically.

"Hello is all right?" Chiun said.

Nothing happened except the spit of raindrops off stone.

Chiun knocked on the stone tentatively.

"Hello is all right," he said again. It was Gordons's mechanical greeting. Somewhere he had been told that was a typical greeting, and never learned to leave off the last three words.

"Could be playing possum," Remo said guardedly.

Setting himself, Chiun brought the edge of his palm against a corner of the hard stone shoulder. It broke off. The Master of Sinanju looked at the separated piece, saw that it seemed solid and stamped it once with his sandaled foot.

It powdered under the force of his stroke. There was nothing metallic in the gritty pile, his sandaled toe determined.

Attacking again, Chiun dislodged another chunk. It fell, came under the heel of his sandals and a larger pile of rock dust was made.

Having created a line of attack, Chiun next closed his fist until only the index finger stuck out.

Then, with swift, sure strokes he began sectioning the shoulder by slicing off wedges of stone. They piled up swiftly.

"Need help?" Remo asked.

Chiun did not look back. "Why is the green-eyed one still breathing?"

"Because."

"That is no answer."

"Look, it's supposed to look like natural causes, and we have witnesses."

"The Thunder Dragon blow was meant for situations such as this."

"Are you speaking of me?" asked Subcomandante Verapaz.

"No," Remo and Chiun said together.

And under Remo's watchful eyes, the Master of Sinanju continued sectioning the great stone idol, exposing the gashed tree root until it was no longer in contact with any part of Mr. Gordons.

"This is too easy," Remo said. "Sure you don't want my help?"

"What I do not want is for you to hog the credit for the man-machine's defeat."

"I didn't defeat him. He slipped on a Mexican or something. Before that, all those lightning strikes must have fried his circuits."

"Pah. Mere incidentals. It will be written in the Book of Sinanju that Chiun the Great finally defeated the Colossus of Mexico."

"You can't write that!"

"I am Reigning Master," Chiun said, going to work on the torso. "The truth is whatever my goose quill inscribes."

"I still say this is too easy," Remo said, deciding the job would go more quickly if he started in on the legs.

ALIRIO ANTONIO ARCILA, being no fool, began backing away. He did not know who these two were, but they obviously possessed fearsome powers and an utter disregard for his cause. And the way they regarded him filled him with a chilly unease.

Their helicopter idled nearby. He could not pilot a helicopter himself, but through the rain he seemed to see a pilot just sitting there with nothing to do. Perhaps he was a fan. In fact, given that it was a Mexican army helicopter, the odds of this were very great.

On the way to the helicopter, his heel struck a thick tree root. Stumbling, he threw one arm back to catch himself.

And to his everlasting astonishment, the root snaked up and caught Antonio instead. It whipped around his chest, pinning him to the ground and, like a python, began squeezing the air from his lungs. Antonio discovered a terrible fact then. With all the air out and none coming in, screaming for help was impossible. He barked once weakly, and that ineffectual Chihuahua sound took away the last of his lung power.

As he lay there, his jungle green eyes growing wide with horror, the thick root insinuated itself into his open and gasping mouth and dropped something down his gullet.

Going down, it felt cold and metallic. It was very much like a steel baseball as it slid down a throat painfully not large enough to handle it, making his inability to inhale utterly moot.

By the time it dropped heavily into his belly, Antonio no longer cared about his lack of oxygen or anything else in the universe. He was brain-dead.

REMO PAUSED in his labors.

"This is going to take all day," he complained.

"Not if you cease interrupting me," Chiun snapped as he stamped a loose stone heart to grit.

Chiun was working furiously. The thick slices of Coatlicue were coming off the knees now—or where the knees should be. They were piling up like home fries.

Not all of it was stone, either. Some was distinctly organic. A few times actual blood flowed.

It was grisly work, but Chiun refused to let it faze him. Each time a section came away, they checked it for any sign of Gordons's electronic brain. It was the small, irreducible heart of the assimilator. Every time they had crushed a Gordons form, the assimilator always found a way to another host, animal, vegetable or mineral, and rebuilt itself. Only by obliterating the brain could they ever be sure he would never return to haunt them again.

The trouble was, they had no idea what it looked like. Only that it was very small.

Remo was hacking away at the other leg now. The first lay shattered and unrecognizable now. His technique was different. He felt along the rough outer skin until his sensitive fingers found a weak spot. Making a fist, he hammered away.

Cracks formed. Rock dust squirted. Liquid squirted, too. The stone fell into large sections that in turn crumbled because they had been disrupted on the molecular level.

"It's not fighting back or reacting," Remo said hopefully.

"Therefore, it is dead," said Chiun.

"So where is the brain?"

"Talk will not find it," said Chiun, face tight, not looking away from his task. "Only force."

It took a while, but in the end the Coatlicue statue lay in heaps like a rock pile after the chain gang had finished. They stamped these into grit and mush.

"No brain," said Remo, looking around.

"No brain, no gain," said Chiun, eyeing the heavy-branched cypress tree with wary concern.

Remo frowned. "This is bigger than the both of us."

"No tree can defeat a Master of Sinanju, much less two."

"No argument there, but I think we have better ways to pass the next year." Remo looked around.

He was wondering how many antitank rockets it would take to blow apart a two-thousand-year-old tree when his gaze fell on the helicopter where Winston Smith and Assumpta waited for them with remarkable patience.

Subcomandante Verapaz was calmly walking toward it. He walked with very jerky steps and was taking great care how he placed his feet on the rain-slick ground.

"Damn," Remo said. "Verapaz is trying to escape."

"Do not worry. I disabled the craft so it cannot fly."

"How?"

"By disabling the pilot's ability to fly."

WINSTON SMITH WAS FUMING. His feet were on the chopper's pedals and he couldn't work them. His hands hung limp at his side, like spaghetti.

In the passenger seat, Assumpta was just as helpless. Her eyes kept looking toward him. Every time their gazes met, he had to look away. They were like a knife in his gut. It was a sickening feeling. He wanted to fly her away. He wanted to find some place where they could just live. Screw Verapaz. Screw the UN. Screw everyone. It wasn't worth it. Assumpta was worth it. He saw that clearly now.

The rain beat down on the cockpit bubble, obscuring his view of his surroundings. All he could do was wait.

A figure approached. He wore a black ski mask from which a pipe jutted.

Then abruptly the door opened and a strange voice said, "Hello is all right."

It was a crazy thing to say. Then Winston remembered what the old Korean, Chuin, had told him just before he squeezed their spines, rendering them helpless in their seats: *I go now. But I will return. Re-*

member this. Trust no one who may greet you with
the words 'Hello is all right.'

It had made no sense, but now someone was saying exactly that. Smith said nothing. His jaw was locked up tight by whatever had stolen his motor control.

"Do you understand English? Are you deaf?" the unaccented voice asked.

When Smith failed to reply, a cool hand began feeling about his neck. With a sudden chiropractic crack of vertebrae, feeling flowed back into his limbs.

"Thanks," Winston said, grabbing the controls.

"I require transportation."

"You got it. Just help my friend the way you helped me."

"Certainly."

The masked man went around to the other side and relieved Assumpta of her paralysis, too. Winston saw then that his eyes were a very distinct green.

Assumpta squealed with joy, "Lord Verapaz! I greet you in the name of the people of Escuintla."

"It is imperative that I escape this area."

"Hop in," Winston said. "There's room in the back."

Assumpta crawled back, saying, "You may have my seat."

Subcomandante Verapaz got in. The chopper settled heavily when he did. He obviously weighed more than his size suggested.

Snapping switches, Winston got the rotor spinning and the ship into the air. The chopper was even more sluggish than before. It rose ponderously, spun once as the lift fought against whatever was weighing it down.

"Damn. We're too heavy!"

"Fire the rockets," Verapaz said.

"What?"

"My enemies approach. We are too heavy, and they will be upon us in under sixty seconds. Fire the rockets at them. This will solve both problems simultaneously."

Winston peered through the rain. Remo and Chiun were closing fast. He hesitated. Once they got within reach, that was it. He could kiss escape goodbye. Assumpta, too.

The words that came out of his mouth surprised even him. "Nothing doing."

"It is our only chance."

At his ear he could feel Assumpta's hot breath. 'Do this, Weener."

"No."

"You are *El Extinguirador*. You yourself have said those two are CIA killers. You must destroy them to save us."

Winston set his teeth. "I can't."

"Then I will do it for you," said Subcomandante Verapaz in his strangely uninflected voice.

Grasping the collective, he jockeyed the ship around. His strength was incredible. Even with both hands, Winston couldn't get it away from him. The chopper began spinning.

With his free hand Verapaz armed the rocket pod.

"Let go, damn it!"

"Weener, do not fight him. He is our Lord Verapaz."

"I said let go, damn it!"

The helicopter stopped its lazy spin.

Through the swimming Plexiglas, Winston Smith saw the fleet figures moving in on them. They seemed to be floating, almost in slow motion. But they were covering the distance to the chopper with breathtaking speed.

A hand arrowed for the firing button, and Winston Smith reached down for his supermachine pistol. Thumbing the safety, he brought it up.

A projecting clip hung up on something. He yanked it free, and in the back Assumpta let out a shrill shriek.

"Weener—no!"

Smith whipped the barrel in line, placing it against Subcomandante Verapaz's masked forehead.

"Don't make me do this," he begged.

"You cannot hurt me with that," Verapaz said.

"This is the machine pistol to end all machine pistols. It will empty every drum and clip in one continuous bullet stream. All 250 rounds. Hollowpoints, Black Talons, Hydra-Shoks, everything. Your head will completely disappear."

"That will not matter."

"Yeah. Why not?"

"My brain is not in my head."

The words were surreal in their casualness. Winston Smith had his eye on the finger hovering over the rocket launcher. If it moved, he would fire. Every sense was concentrated on that finger.

And so he failed to see two tapered hands come up from behind him to grab for his gun wrist.

In that instant three things happened.

He squeezed the Hellfire trigger. The finger hit the rocket switch.

And the two hands pulled the Hellfire away from the *Subcomandante's* head. Pulled back. Back so the muzzle pointed into the rear of the ship. Where Assumpta sat.

The gun made an earsplitting noise in the tiny cockpit. Its sound lifted over the blade scream. Powder smoke filled the air.

As the rain beat down on the outside of the Plexiglas bubble, the inside was spattered with a livid red.

"Noooo!"

Winston Smith didn't hear the *whoosh* of rockets over his own scream of pain and rage. He didn't realize the weapon in his hands was still discharging. He could only see the blood. And it kept raining inside the cockpit and out.

When the clutching hands released his wrist, the gun was empty and the masked face of Subcomandante Verapaz regarded him with emotionless green eyes.

"I will remove the body now," he said. "It will resolve our lifting problem."

The flat words hung like a cold mist in the cockpit.

"You bastard!" With that, Winston went for the *subcomandante's* throat.

All his strength poured through his arms and into his fingers. He found the Adam's apple and tried to crush it with his thumb. It felt like a hard piece of horn.

And the soulful green eyes were looking at him with absolutely no fear or anger whatsoever.

The hand reaching up to his throat was also hard. It squeezed once, and the blood seemed to fill his eyeballs. Smith saw red. Everywhere was red. His mind's eye was even red. And the red was the exact color of Assumpta Kaax's bright blood.

Winston Smith never felt the rain on the back of his head as the door opened behind him. Something pried the hand off his throat and pulled him out into the rain. He landed on his back.

After that, he lost it. Consciousness, hope, everything.

REMO WILLIAMS PRIED the steely hand off Winston Smith's throat and yanked Smith out of the cockpit. The chopper had settled on its skids. The rotor still spun, but it wasn't going anywhere.

Now it wouldn't have time.

In his seat Gordons, still inhabiting the body of Verapaz, looked at him coolly. "Hello is all right. I am a friend."

"Can you say 'sudden catastrophic failure'?" Remo said.

"Why would I say that?" asked Mr. Gordons without blinking.

"Because that's your destiny," Remo told him.

Remo's fist lashed out. Gordons blocked it with a forearm. The forearm, being made of flesh and blood strengthened with assimilated materials like crude wood and metal, simply snapped and hung loosely. Gordons looked at it as if not yet comprehending.

"Where is it this time?" Remo asked savagely. "In your nose?" And he flatted the nose with the heel of his hand. "In your knees?" And he pulled the knee-cap off like taking the cap off a gas tank. "In your eyes?" He speared two forked fingers into the green eyes that became empty sockets.

In the close confines, Mr. Gordons had no maneuvering room. He obviously wasn't up to his full potential, either. His reflexes were fast for a human but slow for an android. Remo removed the jutting pipe. Bridgework came out with it. Then he pulled him out bodily.

Gordons found his feet and dug in his heels. Remo let go.

"You missed," he told the android.

"What is your survival secret?" Gordons asked mushily.

"Never say die."

Gordons's surviving arm threw a blind punch. Remo caught the fist, and the hand came off at the wrist, trailing a vein-and-wire mixture. He threw it over his shoulder.

"Can you say 'undescended testicles'?" Remo spat.

And his foot kicked up and shattered Gordons's groin. The caricature of a man jumped up in place, reeling upon landing.

"How about 'spinal dislocation'?" And he spun the bewildered android around, reached in and removed the spine whole.

The spinal column thrashed in his hand like an articulated snake. Remo began taking it apart, looking for the brain.

Not finding it, he dropped the loose bones and sent the head flying off the shoulder with a sudden swipe.

The head jumped, bounced and Remo stamped it flat.

That left the trunk weaving on two wobbly legs. The neck ended in a raw stump in which the bronchial tubes pulsed spasmodically.

Behind him the Master of Sinanju offered a suggestion. "My ancestors believed that the soul resides in the stomach."

Remo hadn't tried the stomach yet, so he gave it a shot. "Can you say 'esophageal reflux'?"

And taking Gordons by his shoulders, he drove one hard knee into the pit of the creature's stomach.

The result was better than Remo expected. The exposed windpipe in the neck stump went *whoof,* and up popped something that resembled a ball bearing except it was the size of a baseball.

It shot a dozen feet into the air and hung there for a horrible moment. Gordons's central processor. No question.

In that moment a thousand possibilities raced through Remo's mind. If he touched it, anything could happen. It might insinuate itself into his own body, taking it over. If it struck the ground, it could burrow like a gopher until it found something new to assimilate.

In that pause in eternity, Remo decided to bring his two palms together in midair, flattening the brain housing so fast it had no time to think, react or assimilate again. Remo hoped.

He never got the chance.

The Master of Sinanju stepped in, index finger leading, and as the shiny ball fell to the level of his wizened, expectant face, he sliced it back and forth so many times Remo lost count.

When the pieces hit the ground, they landed like a steel apple that had been run through a chopper. They sat formless, still holding some of the shape of a sphere but with the sections slipping every which way.

They watched it as the black rain discolored it.

"It's not moving," Remo said.

Then the Master of Sinanju stepped up and drove a heel into the pile of sliced metal.

They made a satisfying *crunk* as they were mashed into a lump.

His deadly nails retreating into the sleeves of his kimono, the Master of Sinanju turned to address his pupil. "Your way would not have worked. He would have taken you as his next form."

"How do you know what my way was going to be?"

Chiun smiled tightly. "Persons of correct fingernail length know all."

Remo knelt by the mash of metal. It was not moving. It didn't look like anything so much as sliced and mashed slag.

"I think he's down for the count."

"Of course. Nothing can withstand the Knives of Eternity."

"But I won't be satisfied until nothing is left. There's gotta be a way to make sure." And while they were thinking it through, a groan sounded behind them.

Winston Smith lay on the rain-soaked ground, his face buried in one arm. He pounded the ground again and again and again with his fist, and he only stopped when Remo came over and knelt down.

"This is the way the business goes sometimes," Remo told him in a quiet voice.

They stood over him until he had cried himself out and was ready to pick up the shattered remnants of his life.

The rain stopped before he did.

WOODENLY Winston Smith set his feet on the pedals and took the blood-sticky collective in his hands. They had wiped the inside of the cockpit with rags until the red was only pink. He could see enough to fly. That was sufficient. Nothing else mattered.

They flew north. Remo sat in the passenger seat, his face grim. In his lap he held a mass of metal.

In the back the Master of Sinanju sat on his steamer trunk, legs folded modestly under the flowing skirts of his kimono.

Beside him, wrapped in a shroud made of parachute silk, was a long red bundle. Winston didn't look at it. He couldn't. He just looked ahead, where a plume of smoke hung on the mountainous horizon.

Mount Popocatepetl still smoked. The smoke was grayish now. The crater smoldered red and angry as the chopper neared.

"Make a pass over it," said Remo.

Winston nodded. He had the bird near its operating ceiling.

Remo opened the cockpit door and held the metallic lump out. As they crossed over the crater, he let go.

The lump dropped straight down, and through the thin gray haze there came a distinct flare as it splashed into the simmering bowl of lava.

"Go around again," said Remo.

Winston brought the clattering ship around while the Master of Sinanju tenderly passed the silk-wrapped bundle to Remo. He refused to look at it.

The cockpit door was still open. Remo held the bundle in his lap until it was time. The blistering heat of the crater came up to fill the cockpit interior, drying everything that was wet.

Then Remo dropped it down.

Tumbling, it fluttered like a bird. At the last second before it struck, the silk pulled away, showing the only recognizable part of what was left of Assumpta Kaax of the Benito Juarez Liberation Front. Her long, lustrous black hair.

Winston gripped the controls tightly and closed his eyes.

"Sorry, kid," Remo said. "Sometimes the book ends this way."

Winston nodded stiffly. "One last thing."

"What's that?"

Winston tossed his Hellfire pistol into Remo's lap. Around it was wrapped the black ski mask of the Extinguisher.

"Get rid of that stupid thing."

"Whatever you say," said Remo, giving the ungainly weapon a casual toss. It zoomed out, then down, landing with striking precision into the crater.

Winston choked back a sob. "Let's get the hell out of here."

"Make for the border," said Remo.

"What's up there that I should care about?"

"Your future—if you want one."

Winston pushed on the collective, and the chopper put Smoking Mountain and Mexico behind it forever.

54

Sunny Joe Roam heard the helicopter in the distance. He came out of his hogan, his windburned face tense.

He called out to his Sun On Jo braves, who were pitching pennies against a giant saguaro cactus.

"Anybody expecting company?"

No one did. So he set his white Stetson on his head and loped up to the settling chopper on his long, denim-clad legs.

A man stepped out of the cockpit. He was young and blond, and there was something familiar about his eyes, but Sunny Joe couldn't place him.

On the other hand, the two other figures were very familiar. A warmth broke over the sandstone lines of his face.

He raised his booming voice. "Remo! Chief! What brings you two back to the reservation?"

Remo waved without much spirit. Their smiles did not light in return. Frowning, Sunny Joe quickened his pace.

"What's wrong?" he asked as the rotor finished winding down.

Remo shook his hand. "It's a long story. I have a favor to ask."

"Ask away."

Remo set a hand on the shoulder of the young blond man. "This is Winston Smith."

"Howdy."

The boy frowned with all of his face. "Don't call me Smith. It's not my real name."

"This is my son," said Remo.

The boy looked uncomfortable. "I won't fight it if you won't," he muttered to Remo.

"No one's exactly in a hurry to match up DNA, so we're operating on pure rumor," Remo explained.

Sunny Joe's sunsquint eyes blinked several times. "Damned if you don't have your grandmother's eyes."

Winston asked, "Who?"

"My wife. Long gone now."

"Who are you?"

Sunny Joe eyed Remo. "You didn't tell him, Remo?"

"Tell me what?" Winston demanded.

"If you're his son, I'm your grandfather," said Sunny Joe Roam.

"You? You're an Indian!"

"Got news for you," said Remo. "So are you. Get used to it."

"I can't be an Indian."

"Let me talk to you alone for a minute," Remo told Sunny Joe. They walked off together.

As they did, Winston Smith looked at the Master of Sinanju. "That big guy looks kinda familiar."

"He is a very famous actor."

"He is?"

"Yes."

"Looks like a big Indian to me."

"He is that, too," Chiun said.

REMO FINISHED TELLING his story. "I have no right to ask this, but the kid's been through a rough time. He was raised to think his parents were dead. He's only starting to get an idea who he really is. He's confused, needs a home and someone to steer him along until he figures out where his life is going."

"You want me to take him off your hands, is that it?"

"I know this is kinda sudden," Remo said sheepishly.

"That's a rabbity way to put it."

"All he's ever known is military schools and the navy, war and violence. I won't want him to take the path I did. Teach him the ways of peace, Sunny Joe. He needs a lot of peace right about now."

"Think he'll go for it?"

Remo looked back at the Master of Sinanju and Winston silhouetted against the Gila Mountains of the Sonoran Desert. They were talking animatedly.

"I don't see he has much choice."

"Well, the way I see it, Remo, I never did exactly right by you. I guess I kinda owe you an upbringing. Since it's a mite late for that where you're concerned, I guess I can pay the debt to the next generation."

"Thanks, Sunny Joe."

"Don't mention it, son."

They walked back.

REMO PUT THE OPTION to Winston Smith.

"No one will find you here. You won't have to worry about the navy or Harold Smith or any of it."

Winston scratched his head. "I don't know.... This is sort of weird. What kind of Indian am I supposed to be?"

"A Korean one," said Chiun.

"Sun On Jo," said Sunny Joe.

"Never heard of them. I was hoping I was a Cheyenne or at least a Sioux."

"We're not warriors," Sunny Joe explained. "Fighting isn't our way."

"I've seen my share of fighting. I want to do something different." Winston's ice blue eyes scoured the vast, arid expanse of the Sun On Jo Reservation. "Where's the chief?"

"Dead. I'm the Sunny Joe of the tribe. It's sort of a protector. The name's Bill Roam."

"Roam. Roam. I know that name...."

Sunny Joe grunted. "I did a little acting in my time."

"Hey, I know you now! You're Muck Man! I saw every one of those pictures."

"That's right. But my Muck Man days are behind me now."

Remo spoke up. "So what it's going to be?"

Winston Smith looked around. "I could give it a shot, I guess. You got horses here?"

"Can you ride?" asked Sunny Joe.

"No. But I can learn."

"I'll teach you, then."

"Not so fast. Got TV?"

"All you want. But I have to warn you in advance—no squaws. You start hankering to take a wife, you'll have to look beyond these parts."

"I'm in no rush in that department," Winston said quietly.

"Good. It's settled." Sunny Joe put a big arm around Winston's shoulder. "So what do I call you?"

"Big Chief Pain in the Butt, if you ask me," said Remo.

Winston gave a thumb's-up sign. "Call me Winner. I'll come up with a last name later."

"Well, come on, Winner. Let's get you settled in." Sunny Joe looked to Remo and Chiun. "What about you two? Planning on staying a spell?"

"Can't," said Remo. "Gotta get back."

"We will stay long enough to pay our respects," inserted Chiun. "Important work calls us. But we will not be rude."

"We'll catch up," said Remo. "I left something in the chopper."

"Suit yourself. Come on, Winner, let me tell you some tall tales of my wild and wooly days in Hollywood."

Winston held back. His eyes met Remo's. They were full of pain and questioning. Deep behind these stormy emotions was a shine of gratitude.

"Thanks. I can't thank you enough," he said awkwardly.

"Don't mention it," said Remo.

They started walking away. Then Sunny Joe remembered something. "Hey, Remo."

Remo turned. "Yeah?"

"Got any more offspring I should know about?"

Eyeing Winston, Remo said, "Tell you about that some other time."

Winston looked startled. "What's that supposed to mean? Don't tell me I have a brother! Do I have a brother? What's his name. Does he look like me?"

"Later," said Remo. To Sunny Joe, he said, "Swap you a used helicopter for a lift into town?"

"I might see my way clear to that."

THAT EVENING, Remo was loading Chiun's lacquered trunk with the lapis lazuli phoenixes into the back of a Mazda Navajo jeep. The moon rose over the sandstone hump called Red Ghost Butte, washing the Sonoran Desert in a silvery wash of light.

"Well, that's that. Gordons will never bother us again, Verapaz is a bad memory and, according to the news, Mexico is picking up the pieces. And the kid has a good home. There's only one last thing."

Chiun lifted a thin eyebrow. "And that is?"

"What's in this freaking trunk?"

Chiun lifted his bearded chin resolutely. "That is for me to know and you to find out."

"In other words, I'm doomed to lug this thing around for you until I break down and shit-can my nail clippers?"

Chiun smiled. "Yes."

"Never happen."

"When the suspense becomes unendurable, we speak of this matter again."

"Until then, do me a favor?"

"What is that, my son?"

"Next Father's Day, remind me to send Sunny Joe a card."

"If you fail to send one to me, who is your father in spirit, great will be your shame."

"Count on it." They climbed into the jeep. "Hey!" Remo said. "I wonder if I'll get one, too."

"You should live so long," sniffed the Master of Sinanju.

A global war is about to begin. There is
one chance for peace...

STONY MAN™ 21
SATAN'S THRUST

atan missiles, the world's most powerful nuclear warheads,
e being sold on the Moscow black market. The Stony Man
arriors must act with swift and deadly force if they're going
keep the missiles from reaching terrorist launching pads.

ook for it in March, wherever Gold Eagle books are sold.

Don't miss out on the action in these titles featuring
THE EXECUTIONER®, ABLE TEAM® and PHOENIX FORCE®!

e Arms Trilogy

e Executioner #61195	SELECT FIRE	$3.50 U.S.	☐
		$3.99 CAN.	☐
e Executioner #61196	TRIBURST	$3.50 U.S.	☐
		$3.99 CAN.	☐
e Executioner #61197	ARMED FORCE	$3.50 U.S.	☐
		$3.99 CAN.	☐

e Executioner®

1188	WAR PAINT	$3.50 U.S.	☐
		$3.99 CAN.	☐
1189	WELLFIRE	$3.50 U.S.	☐
		$3.99 CAN.	☐
1190	KILLING RANGE	$3.50 U.S.	☐
		$3.99 CAN.	☐
1191	EXTREME FORCE	$3.50 U.S.	☐
		$3.99 CAN.	☐
1193	HOSTILE ACTION	$3.50 U.S.	☐
		$3.99 CAN.	☐
1194	DEADLY CONTEST	$3.50 U.S.	☐
		$3.99 CAN.	☐

(limited quantities available on certain titles)

TOTAL AMOUNT	$	
POSTAGE & HANDLING	$	
($1.00 for one book, 50¢ for each additional)		
APPLICABLE TAXES*	$	_____
TOTAL PAYABLE	$	_____
(check or money order—please do not send cash)		

order, complete this form and send it, along with a check or money order for
e total above, payable to Gold Eagle Books, to: **In the U.S.:** 3010 Walden Avenue,
). Box 9077, Buffalo, NY 14269-9077; **In Canada:** P.O. Box 636, Fort Erie, Ontario,
A 5X3.

me:_____

dress:_____ City:_____

ate/Prov.:_____ Zip/Postal Code: _____

lew York residents remit applicable sales taxes.
:anadian residents remit applicable GST and provincial taxes.

GEBACK11

Deathlands, past and future clash with frightening force

JAMES AXLER

DEATH LANDS®

Keepers of the Sun

The gateways are secret installations from the predark days, which Ryan Cawdor and his band of warrior survivalists use as escape routes. In KEEPERS OF THE SUN, Ryan and his group emerge into a world ruled by the samurai code. Here Ryan faces a new threat that could destroy the only home he knows.

A new dark age has dawned with the hope of a promised land. But in the Deathlands, hope is not enough.

Don't miss out on the action in these titles featuring
THE EXECUTIONER®, ABLE TEAM® and PHOENIX FORCE®

SuperBolan

#61438	AMBUSH	$4.99 U.S.	[
		$5.50 CAN.	[
#61439	BLOOD STRIKE	$4.99 U.S.	[
		$5.50 CAN.	[
#61440	KILLPOINT	$4.99 U.S.	[
		$5.50 CAN.	[
#61441	VENDETTA	$4.99 U.S.	[
		$5.50 CAN.	[

Stony Man™

#61896	BLIND EAGLE	$4.99 U.S.	[
		$5.50 CAN.	[
#61897	WARHEAD	$4.99 U.S.	[
		$5.50 CAN.	[
#61898	DEADLY AGENT	$4.99 U.S.	[
		$5.50 CAN.	[
#61899	BLOOD DEBT	$4.99 U.S.	[
		$5.50 CAN.	[

(limited quantities available on certain titles)

TOTAL AMOUNT	$
POSTAGE & HANDLING	$
($1.00 for one book, 50¢ for each additional)	
APPLICABLE TAXES*	$_____
TOTAL PAYABLE	$_____
(check or money order—please do not send cash)	

To order, complete this form and send it, along with a check or money order for
the total above, payable to Gold Eagle Books, to: **In the U.S.:** 3010 Walden Avenue,
P.O. Box 9077, Buffalo, NY 14269-9077; **In Canada:** P.O. Box 636, Fort Erie, Ontario,
L2A 5X3.

Name:_____

Address:_____ City:_____

State/Prov.:_____ Zip/Postal Code: _____

*New York residents remit applicable sales taxes.
 Canadian residents remit applicable GST and provincial taxes.